THE DARK OF SUMMER

To Valmai and
Robert Bruce of Sumburgh in Shetland

Eric Linklater (1899–1974), was born in Wales and educated in Aberdeen. His family came from the Orkney Islands (his father was a master mariner), and the boy spent much of his childhood there.

Linklater served as a private in the Black Watch at the close of the First World War, surviving a nearly fatal head wound to return to Aberdeen to take a degree in English. A spell in Bombay with the *Times of India* was followed by some university teaching at Aberdeen again, and then a Commonwealth Fellowship which allowed him to travel in America from 1928 to 1930.

Linklater's memories of Orkney and student life informed his first novel, *White Maa's Saga* (1929), while the success of *Poet's Pub* in the same year led him to take up writing as a full-time career. A hilarious satirical novel, *Juan in America* (1931), followed his American trip, while the equally irreverent *Magnus Merriman* (1934) was based on his experiences as Nationalist candidate for a by-election in East Fife.

Linklater joined the army again in the Second World War, to serve in fortress Orkney, and later as a War Office correspondent reporting the Italian campaign, for which he wrote the official history. The compassionate comedy of *Private Angelo* (1946) was drawn from this Italian experience.

With these and many other books, stories and plays to his name, Linklater enjoyed a long and popular career as a writer. His early creative years were described in *The Man on My Back* (1941), while a fuller autobiography, *Fanfare for a Tin Hat*, appeared in 1970.

ERIC LINKLATER
The Dark of Summer

INTRODUCED BY
ALLAN MASSIE

CANONGATE
CLASSICS
91

This edition first published as a Canongate Classic in 1999 by Canongate Books Ltd, 14 High Street, Edinburgh EH1 1TE. Copyright © Eric Linklater 1956. Introduction © 1999 Alan Massie. All rights reserved.

The publishers gratefully acknowledge general subsidy from the Scottish Arts Council towards the Canongate Classics series and a specific grant towards the publication of this volume.

Set in 10 point Plantin by Hewer Text Ltd, Edinburgh. Printed and bound by Caledonian Book Manufacturing, Bishopbriggs, Glasgow.

British Library Cataloguing-in-Publication Data
A catalogue record for this book is available
on request from the British Library.

ISBN 0 86241 894 1

AUTHOR'S NOTE

To my neighbour, Brigadier the Hon. William Fraser, D.S.O., M.C., I am much indebted for the loan of a transcript of the evidence heard at a Scottish *cause célèbre* of the early nineteenth century. The story of the Wisharts and their inheritance – as they are here called – is based on this.

To my friend Mr. Humphrey Hare I am most grateful for permission to quote a passage from *The Military Necessity*, his admirable translation of Alfred de Vigny's *Servitude et Grandeur Militaires*.

Introduction

A novelist is rarely well-advised to write his masterpiece in his fifties, unless his position at the top of the tree is secure. His themes and style are no longer likely to be in fashion. A younger generation of writers is occupying the attention of reviewers and speaking with greater apparent immediacy to the reading public.

This was very much the case when Eric Linklater came to write *The Dark of Summer*. He had had a vogue more than twenty years previously with the two *Juan* books and *Magnus Merriman*. After the war he achieved popular and critical success with *Private Angelo*, a comic study of Italian resilience, in which the wit masked a sense of the futility of public action.

But the Fifties saw the emergence of the post-war generation of novelists, and the middle of the decade was the season of the Angry Young Men. The label was fairly meaningless, and time would show that they were in no sense a coherent group, that some were considerable artists and others not, but for a few years they seemed to have something in common. They spoke of, and for the Britain, or at least the England, which was disengaging itself from Empire. They were mostly insular, hostile to, and contemptuous of, the traditional Establishment. They represented the generation that had voted Labour in 1945 and was enthusiastic about the Welfare State.

Linklater had nothing in common with them, and those who were interested in them found nothing interesting in his work. So *The Dark of Summer* attracted little attention when it was published in 1957. It was well enough reviewed, and become a Book Club choice. But few remarked on its exceptional quality. Nor has it since had much attention from literary critics or historians even here in Scotland.

The novel may be undervalued for another reason. It is a work of exquisite craftsmanship, and some are ready to dismiss craftsmanship as mere professional dexterity. It is a sad truth that books which are well put together are often, for that very reason, less highly regarded than others whose author lacks either the ability or the desire to give the work shape. Strangely, at one point in the writing, Linklater himself had doubts about the construction, telling his friend and sometimes publisher Rupert Hart-Davis that he felt 'a horrid discomfiture', and thought that he had been 'misled by the lure of the rounded shape', so that all the excitement was in the first part. This odd judgement was the product of a moment of uncertainty, such as writers often experience at some point in the making of a novel. In fact, the second half is incomparably moving.

The novel begins in Shetland, at midsummer, when there is 'no darkness at midnight'. 'The landscape becomes an image of the world in which we live. It is not dark but nothing can be seen as plainly as the light of noon pretends – noon flatters and deludes us . . .' Moral questions may provoke answers, clear and delusive as noon.

The narrator, Tony Chisholm, declares that, on the night when he chooses to begin his story, he was happy, and had been so for a year, 'fulfilled'. This beginning is therefore also the end; the quest has reached its destination. He is a man who has been mutilated. We soon learn that he has only one arm, but it is now round the waist of his lovely young wife, Gudron.

Then, protesting that he is not a professional writer, and

does not know how a story should be told, he says he has
one worth telling, 'and that for two reasons'.

The first is that he is 'very much a man of his own time'.
This is not a boast; he does not think much of his time. He
grew up in the knowledge that 'we had come down in the
world', and by that "we" I mean, quite simply, all of us
who are British'. He was born on the first day of the Battle
of the Somme – the most terrible single day in the long
history of the British Army – and throughout his boyhood
and youth, heard of 'the vanity of that sacrifice'. His
father, 'Copper' Chisholm, was a hero, one who, as his
novelist mother says, 'remains to let you see the sort of
man whom our politicians threw away'. So Tony
Chisholm grew up with a sense of inferiority. Neither
he nor his brother Peter was the equal of their father or of
the men who had died. He came to adult station in a world
in which 'the small enjoyable emotion', that was all that
remained of British patriotism, was threatened by the
'messianic politics of the dictators'.

His second reason is to tell how he 'became involved in
the affairs and death of a man called Mungo Wishart, a
landed proprietor in Shetland, whose mind, to a singular
degree, had been shaped, or mis-shaped, by a family
history of long unhappiness', and of how this wretched
history had led to 'no better end than the deformity of a
man's reason and a new project of sedition.'

So, in a couple of pages of rare and economical audacity,
Linklater displays the bones of his novel, a novel which
will deal with the recurring themes of fear, family history
shame, war, betrayal and above all, memory.

The obsessive and distorting power of memories that
cannot be let go and the nature and consequences of
'betrayal', are themes big enough and demanding enough
for any novel. Linklater handles them in masterly fashion,
and is bold enough to incorporate another, even more
demanding theme. This is a novel set in war, and Link-

later, fully aware of war's horrors, yet dares to ask himself and the reader how it is that war may also inspire acts of the most heroic self-sacrifice. 'How,' Tony asks after receiving an account of a battle 'on the shell-torn bank of the Garigliano', 'was I to reconcile my conception of him as . . . the jumped-up drill sergeant to whom a human life was of no moment when weighed against discipline and military propriety, with this self-sacrificing man who, in his final revelation, was moved by a compassion so extreme that sympathy grew hot as wrath and he died in a wrath of love?' That question too runs through the novel, to return at the last of the novel's deaths in battle in the 'blazing, gun-shooting, frozen nightmare' of Korea. It is with that death which, from a selfish point of view, makes no sense, and yet which makes every sense, being the consequence of a moral necessity, that all the threads of the narrative are drawn together.

The Dark of Summer is a novel of an extraordinary range. It moves back and forward in time, as far back as the interpolated section which recounts a squalid sequel to the Jacobite Rising of 1745. The setting is equally various: Shetland, London, the North Sea, the Faroes, the Western Desert, the Italian campaign and the grim battle for Monte Cassino, Korea and its now almost forgotten war, Paris. It begins and ends in Shetland, and that is where its heart is.

This is a lot of travelling for quite a short novel. It sounds as if Linklater is cramming an awful lot in, as if the novel should be a mess. Yet it is curiously leisurely, and there is never any suggestion of haste; there are moments of reflection when the narrative stands still. And yet its impetus never dies. Perhaps the novel's most ironical sentence is Tony Chisholm's disclaimer: 'I cannot tell my story as neatly as, I daresay, a professional author would tell it'.

Towards the end of the novel, the narrator has a dream.

(Dreams were always important to Linklater; his last novel, *A Terrible Freedom*, was about dream worlds.) He is swimming up a stream, and, when he wakes, he reflects on the concept of time, which he has always thought of, as I suppose most of us do, as a stream.

But I no longer think of it as a stream flowing from the past. In my dream it ran the other way, and the more I ponder my dream, the more I am convinced of its essential truth. Now I see time as a river rising in the future, and like – but contrary to – the lordly fish that swim from the lightness of the sea to the darkness of their spawning-grounds, we may swim up-stream from darkness towards the light of its undiscovered source. No compulsion leads us by the nose, but free will permits the choice. In a progress upstream, moreover, memory is not inseparable. Memories gather about us, but against the current memory can be let go; and the stream will carry it away. Mungo Wishart – of whose unhappiness I often thought – was right when he said there was no contentment for a man who remembered everything, for a nation that could forget nothing; and the obvious reason is that such a man, and such a nation, have no faith in the future. They go with the stream and their memories cling to them; they swim in a jelly of unhappiness. But the up-stream swimmer and the spawning fish can shed their yesterdays.

Linklater was an artist, not a writer with a message. But that passage is worth pondering – for individuals and for nations. The past imposes a burden of unhappiness and causes for discontent. The up-stream swimmer can let the past go.

The Dark of Summer is a novel that invites quotation. There are sentences meriting debate on almost every page. But it is first of all a story, and an incomparably moving one. Read it first for that, and then again to allow yourself to grasp its deeper significance. No Scottish novel of this century more completely justifies Ford Madox Ford's claim that the importance of literature is to be found in its ability to make you think and feel at the same time.

Allan Massie

WHERE I SHALL live when I retire – where I am living now, on leave from the great watershed – there is, at the top of summer, no darkness at midnight. The day puts on a veil, the light is screened, and a landscape that, in fine weather, appears at noon to be almost infinite – in which long roads and little houses are luminously drawn – becomes small and circumscribed, and the hills and the shore, the sheep in the fields and the glinting sea, are visible, as it were, through a pane of slightly obscuring glass. The landscape becomes an image of the world in which we live. It is not dark, but nothing can be seen as plainly and decisively as the light of noon pretends – noon flatters and deludes us – yet all that can be seen is solid, solid enough for faith, and if one's heart is whole one can enjoy the beauty inherent in our mystery – a beauty that is, paradoxically, more visible in half-light.

That night – the night of our discovery – my heart was whole, as for nearly a twelvemonth it had been whole, in spite of my duty that made me a sort of tightrope-walker, treading a narrow crest in history. In spite, also, of my previous waste of life, much of which I had spent in a cold mechanism of existence. For almost a year I had been happy. Within the limits of my own imagination, within the scope of my consciousness, I had been fulfilled. I was skin-tight with love, God's grace perhaps, and animal joy. My arm – my only arm – was round my lovely wife's young body, my fingers, the only set I had, were outspread beneath her breast, and as we walked, and looked towards the sea, I recognized the long tentacles of land, reaching round a silver-dappled firth, as a symbol of communion; as my remnant arm was with her bright candour and her beauty.

I could see, and not see. What I saw was transmuted by the diminished light of the sun that lay an inch or two below the horizon; and what I could not see was made real by an expansion of my faith in the solid substance of the nearer view. I had no complaint against a distant invisibility. Is it an insufferable boast, in our world, to say I was content? Though it be intolerable, it was true then, and still is. And partly the blame (if blame is necessary) must lie on the quality of light that in these northern islands is called 'the summer dim' – the dimness, or twilight, at midnight, that is – in which can be seen beauty enough for happiness. Not enough, nor nearly enough, for comprehension; yet enough to make comprehension unnecessary. But most of the blame, and none of the twilight, falls on Gudrun. Gudrun has her own illumination, and it was she who had given me faith in the realities of the foreground and distance too.

We had been married for less than a year, and to touch was still a flicker of fire that could blaze and consume us. We stopped on the road, and kissed, and if I had had my way we would have gone no farther. There was a patch of gorse there, smelling of honey and coconut, and the roadside turf was warm and dry. 'But no,' she said, 'you mustn't be foolish,' and her soft Shetland voice in its nonsensical rhythm went up and down, up and down, like the little clapping waves that strike a green-fringed jetty in the sea when a quick motor boat passes. 'Be sensible,' she said, 'and wait till we get home. I want to see the new road.'

So we walked on to the cart-track that turns abruptly to the right, and the brand-new, black continuation of the road that would presently go down to the beach. With a bulldozer hired from the County Council I had begun, that morning, to cut a path through a belt of peat, a long tongue of peat and dingy heather, that lay athwart the hard foundation of the hill between the house and the narrow, green, serpentine firth a hundred feet below it. Most of our work on the property had had a good economic motive, but the new road was designed for pleasure: it would take us down from the garden gate to a little sandy cove bounded on either side by black rocks, through which, to the north, a narrow stream tumbled, with yellow irises on its banks, and on the other side rose low cliffs where we had found a wren nesting not far from the white-splashed untidiness of a cormorant's roost. . . .

So much for the setting: for the scene which is the end (so far as I can see) of my story, and in one respect was where it began. I am not a professional writer, and I cannot be sure of telling the story as it should be told: there may be devices and tricks of the trade by which a man of letters could magnify certain episodes and give to the whole more 'effect' – but even without these additions (or, perhaps, subtractions) the story is, I think, worth telling, and that for two reasons.

I am, in the first place, very much a man of my own times; and this, God knows, is not boastfully said, though a conclusion shot through with gratitude may to some look too much like boasting – I grew up in the knowledge that 'we had come down in the world'; and by 'we' I mean, quite simply, all of us who by birth are British. I was born on July 1st, 1916, when the battle of the Somme began, that cost us sixty thousand casualties in a single day and destroyed the great army of volunteers with which we began that war; and in the years of my boyhood and my youth I read and was told, again and again, of the vanity of that sacrifice. The Britain to which I was born was in every way shabbier and poorer – materially, spiritually, in political influence – than the Britain my parents had known; and what I found particularly depressing was my mother's repeated assertion that the very best, the cream and the pride, of a generation had been lost. She herself, it appeared, had known a vast number of young men distinguished by the brilliance of their intellect, their personal courage, or their beauty – and all, all had gone. 'All but your father,' she would say, 'and he, thank God, remains to let you see the sort of men whom our politicians threw away!'

To an early appreciation of my mental and physical inferiority was added, therefore, a deep distrust of the politicians whose authority, it seemed, we must still acknowledge. Many of my contemporaries grew up under a like influence, and very few of us were unaffected by the endemic fears and anxieties of our time. We heard – at second or third hand for the most part, because we did not live with intellectuals – of the chaos that Marx had made of history, Freud of the human mind – and, perhaps, Einstein of the universe. We saw for ourselves the chaos in our economy that a money famine in America had made. And we in Britain, who had long since reduced patriotism to a small, enjoyable emotion, and never had any faith in messianic politics, watched with bewilderment and increasing fear the dreadful, the inexplicable growth of mass emotion, regimented nationalism, and apocalyptic leadership in Russia, Italy, and Germany.

That was the world in which my generation grew to something like manhood, and then, for six years, our scrap of manhood was tested in another war. To have survived so much is, I think, something of an achievement, and I admit a persistent sense of wonder about the why and the how of survival. But my own small part in so large a miracle would not, of itself, justify my attempt to write of it; nor, by itself, would it make a story.

The story I am trying to tell springs from my connection – I being so much the product of my time – with a succession or string of events that began more than two hundred years ago. My connection was in part accidental, in part deliberate; and my life was entangled in the string. I became involved in the affairs and death of a man called Mungo Wishart, a landed proprietor in Shetland, whose mind, to a singular degree, had been shaped, or mis-shaped, by a family history of long unhappiness: a history that started from sedition, murder, and dark uncertainties, and was continued through purposeless and wasteful litigation to no better end than the deformity of a man's reason and a new project of sedition.

If I was a product of my own time and a world in chaos, Mungo Wishart was the offspring of a remembered time when human weakness, enormity of human greed, and extreme of passion had convulsed a little, evil-er society of rather stupid, often drunken lairds in one of the remotest parishes of Britain – and time past had done worse for him than time present for me. . . .

I have admitted that I cannot tell my story as neatly as, I daresay, a professional author would tell it; but I have begun it where I mean to end it – and so, if I am lucky, I may draw a full circle – and I have said as clearly, I think, as is necessary, that it springs from my involvement with the affairs of Mungo Wishart. I have admitted also that the story's end will leave me happy – clean-contrary, I suppose, to what is expected of a story nowadays – and to that I shall add a claim to have laid, at long last, the ghost that bedevilled the poor tormented mind of Mungo. It is for that purpose I have begun my narrative with the tale of our evening walk – Gudrun and I, enlaced in love, walking to see the new road – for the ghost of an old injustice had had a corporal essence, and we discovered it. We found, in the peat, the body of a dead man.

The bulldozer was in the blind alley of the new road. An eight-foot-high rampart of peat stood in front of it, and shining black walls confined it. We scrambled up the lower side to admire the view, to consider the descending line of the road, and on the ledge of the cutting a table-top of heather was dislodged by our weight, and slid down. We had time to step on to firmer ground, but when the great clod had fallen away it left a break in the peat, and in the break there was a little surface of something different. The surface of something that had a different texture.

We went down again, Gudrun helping me, and stood beside it. The surrounding peat was smooth and damp, a yielding solidity, but the foreign surface had the slimy hardness of an old rope left and lost in the sea. It was strangely but certainly something made by human hands and, as though the vegetable peat had resisted total marriage with the human body inside the coat, there was a little cleft about its head and shoulders. We had no doubt as to what it was, and leaping conjecture told us who.

I remember Gudrun breathing, as it seemed, through a congested whistle, and though I had less cause for emotion I felt, under the quickness of astonishment, a sudden need to protect her against whatever might emerge from this uncovering of an old mystery – of old rascality, perhaps – and I would not let her look closely at the body. I told her we must wait for the morning to make a proper examination, and I took her back to the house. She came readily enough, and said nothing till we stood at the front door, when she asked, 'Do you think it's Old Dandy? It must be, mustn't it?'

'Not necessarily. I don't suppose Dandy was the only old scamp in Shetland to die of exposure – of drink and exposure—'

'Or to be murdered,' she said.

'Yes, perhaps he was murdered. But it was a long time ago – it was two hundred years ago – and even murder doesn't mean much after a couple of centuries.'

'It does,' she said. 'You can't forgive murder.'

'Wait till the morning, and then perhaps we'll find out more about it.'

'But I'm sure it's Dandy! So near the house, and for you and me to find him at last! Oh, I'm sure of it.'

We went to bed and she lay beside me, holding my hand, but almost as separate as some thin, carved effigy on a medieval tomb of man and wife. I knew what thoughts possessed her – I had seen the havoc they made of her father's mind – but I knew also that she was not haunted, that her mind was not deformed, as his had been, by an old twisted tale of a family so united in hatred that its two bitter branches had clung together in costly dispute that impoverished both of them, and left in both a brooding resentment because the one side still maintained, the other privily suspected, that the lawyers' judgment had been wrong.

But Gudrun had inherited neither their bitterness nor shame. She could not forget the story, but it had not darkened her mind nor disabled her judgment. Her father had prevented that. She had turned in revulsion from his bitter spirit, and gone wilfully into exile from all his people and their history. Her mother came of a different stock – a stronger, simpler stock of crofters and fishermen – and because her mother's character had a placid strength, an untroubled sweetness, and Gudrun had inherited enough of her mother for contentment, her exile from the better blood of her spear-side was untouched by regret. She remembered, with a strong dislike for him, her angry father; but if the old story still teased her, it was only because she had the quick, gossiping curiosity of a country girl and wanted to know what had happened. I had no fear that her excitement and distress would last more than a day or two. Perhaps the night would cure it; for it was not the distress of someone born to unhappiness, but only the shock of dark discovery and a girl's excitement, ordinary and natural enough.

If we could find proof, moreover, that it was Dandy who lay in the peat – the drunken, dispossessed old Jacobite whose death was still a mystery – then the unsolved and teasing parts of the story might show more clearly. Supposition might be strengthened. It depended on the state of the body, and I began, with Gudrun still awake beside me, to try and remember the effect of peat on human tissues. Did it preserve or dissolve them? – But I fell asleep before I could remember, and when I woke Gudrun was sleeping like a child in summer, exhausted under a haycock, so I got up quietly, and dressed and went out.

The men were late as usual, and it was half past eight before they came down to the cutting in the peat. The driver of the bulldozer, who was employed by the County Council, knew nothing of Old Dandy, but my own two men (we shared a fishing-boat and they worked my small farm for me) jumped to identification as quickly as Gudrun, and for twenty minutes or so, while they rehearsed the story, and argued about its details and gave their own explanations of it, no one laid a finger on him. But then, with care and respect in their hands, they began to remove the peat that was so curiously moulded about his body.

I am no expert on costume of the eighteenth century, but his coat and breeches – hard and well-preserved and a little slimy – were certainly the carefully made dress of a gentleman, not the haphazard clothing of a peasant. 'Old Dandy!' said my men. 'No doubt of that!' But when we tried to lift him from his grave, we were disconcerted by the lack of substance within his coat. His body, it seemed, had collapsed. He was lying on his face, and the men did not know what to do and were reluctant to handle him, and grew a little shamefaced about their reluctance.

I knelt and put my solitary arm under his chest, and felt

for a solid hold, and like the others admitted a sensation of nausea at the yielding emptiness of the coat. But I tried to raise him, and then, with a little cry of pain, quickly drew back my hand; and that was foolish. For whatever had pierced my finger – my middle finger, at the base – scored a deep cut to the tip of it, and my hand, when I pulled it out, was a mess of blood oozing on black peat.

I am a little ashamed of my behaviour after that, though I had some excuse for it. It was, after all, my only hand, and in the circumstances it was not unnatural to think of sepsis, of septicaemia, and the total loss of my hand. But I need not have been so precipitate. It was my old habit of fear – long buried, but buried alive, I suppose – that made me exclaim, in too high a voice, 'O God, look at that! I must see a doctor.'

'It is deep,' said one of my men.

'It will be poisonous,' said the other.

'That's what I'm frightened of. Don't touch him, or be very careful. There's something in his chest, it may be a dagger. I'm going to Lerwick to have my hand dressed.'

'You will be needing a driver,' said the younger man.

'My wife will take me. And don't touch him till I come back – or be careful if you do.'

I left them, and in a nervous hurry went back to the house and put my hand under the kitchen tap, and saw the cut finger open pinkly and show pale edges. There Gudrun found me, and I told her what had happened.

'He was murdered,' she said. 'I always knew it! And you must go straight to the surgeon.'

Gudrun was calm and swiftly efficient. It was her turn now to be sensible, as I had been the night before; and I still found common sense miraculous in her, who seemed too young and soft and wild to have any hardness in her mind. She bandaged my finger, she made breakfast for us, and because she was so lovely I thought it a marvel of womanhood that she could do these simple things.

We drove to Lerwick, down the twisted spine of the island – the long road running from tip to tip of the Mainland of Shetland, that is sixty miles long and no broader than a lizard – and because my fear had gone, leaving only a nervous excitement, I felt, not for the first time, that we were riding on a sort of aery bridge – on a parallel of longitude flying above the natural earth – and indeed the view, now on this side, now on the other, of cliffs dropping suddenly to the white crumbling of a bright blue sea, gave to hallucination a shred of reality. I remembered, in my excitement that was darkened by only a small foreboding, my first coming to the islands, and how I had hated them; and when I looked back at the angry years it seemed that my happiness had been trodden out of me by their iron-shod feet as wines of great quality used to be trodden out by the horny feet of lean, sour-smelling, hungry peasants. It was in the year of touch-and-go, the year of the great alliance, that I first saw the islands that lie in three groups in the Atlantic north of Britain.

The nearest are the Orkneys, squat and prosperous, divided from Scotland only by the swollen tides of the Pentland Firth; then the Shetlands, long, dark and narrow, poor and picturesque, bearing good sailors and small brown sheep; and lastly, far out to the north-west, the wild, abruptly rising, cloud-hung Faeroes, breeding also sheep and sailors, as if in her extremity nature could rear only what was born with a good coat or a bold heart – and to two of these archipelagos I went, for the first time, in 1941 – twice in the same year, in spring and winter – and hated them all for their wind-swept nakedness. But now, because time had had its way with me, I took delight in their nakedness, having eyes to see how comely and how gentle it was.

I thought too – and when I looked at my bandaged finger a little *frisson* of superstition sharpened my pleasure – that time had shown its purpose very clearly by using Old Dandy to wound me. I, married with such contentment to the daughter of the man whose life had been deformed by a hatred that sprang, in part, from the death of Dandy, was now related to her more closely than by arms in bed and the conjunctive light of minds in love. I had become a member of her story, and my marriage was dignified by a purpose bred of time. There was in it so much of joy that I looked for, and longed to find, a deeper reason for its happiness than the satisfaction of mortal bodies; and on our flying parallel of longitude, high above common earth, I saw my wounded finger as proof of time's ordination and my relevance to its purpose.

Intent on driving, and the turning road, Gudrun was silent. She has the gift of companionable silence, and drives well. She does not withdraw into silence, but spreads it like a rug, and in the safety of her comfort I was free to traverse memory and play with fancy. I left responsibility to her, and when we reached the hospital she took me, without question or hesitation, to the surgeon's private room, where we found him, having done half his morning's work, drinking a cup of coffee and signing letters that a quiet, primly dressed secretary put before him. We knew him – we were friends in the second degree of friendship – and when Gudrun described what we had found, and what had happened to me, he grew interested at once, not so much in my mishap, as in the possible *éclaircissement* of a story that, in his five years' service in Shetland, he had heard more than once. He told us that we must let the police know of our discovery, and promised to come out in the afternoon, as soon as he had finished his work, to see the body for himself. Then, still talking of Old Dandy, he looked at my finger and, summoning his theatre sister to bring dressings, cleaned and rebandaged the wound.

'And to give you full insurance,' he said, 'I'll pump some penicillin into you. You haven't had an injection lately, have you? That's good. Now come in here' – he led me behind a blue-curtained screen, and because, with only one set of fingers, I am a little clumsy with buttons and so forth, he helped me unfasten and take down my trousers – 'and that, though you'll be uncomfortable for the next hour or two when you sit down, will put your mind at rest,' he said. 'You can stop thinking about septicaemia.'

I dressed again, with a slight feeling of numbness in my right buttock, and we rejoined my wife. The surgeon – a lively, sturdy, interested man – demanded more details of our discovery, and then, turning to the theatre sister, inquired, 'I've plenty of time, haven't I? There's Mrs. Johnson's kidney, and that boy's appendix: nothing else before lunch, is there? – All right, come and see my new theatre equipment. I'm very proud of it.'

I had no wish to look at surgical apparatus, but to refuse would have been churlish, and we followed him along a brown-footed corridor to a room of staring and expert simplicity – a room of white enamel, chromium steel, and brilliant weapons against the indiscipline of nature – and with a naïve pleasure in the forces at his command, he exclaimed, 'But put on the light, Sister. The overhead light.'

The light went on – a pure, dry, anatomical light – and I who, for the past hour and more, had been exploring memory as well as fancy, was suddenly and fully reminded of the very beginning – not of the story, indeed, for that lay with the dead man in the peat – but of my association with it: my involvement with life and death in Shetland. That began in very different surroundings, in London – under a London pavement – and so vivid was the recollection that I had no ear for what the surgeon said, but in the staring light in which we stood I remembered the wound I had suffered, under a light that in memory seemed comparable, a dozen years before. . . .

More than a dozen years; but years dissolve in their own flux, and little remains of them but the scars they leave, or sometimes, but not often, the beatitudes they bring.

CHAPTER TWO

IT WAS LIGHT that dominated my memory: the frightening sensation of the light in that other room – an operating theatre where no anaesthetic was given me – for I had felt on myself the effect I could see on Pelly – Major Pelly! – in whom it laid bare the ridge of a cheekbone and the twitching, greedy nerves behind his pretence of sympathy. But my memory cannot be quite true, for perhaps no light ever shone so fiercely, without killing its victim, as in retrospect my mind pretends . . . My nerves, more deeply than Pelly's, were exposed by the shock of what he told me, and they in their nakedness shrank and were shrivelled under the radiance of those long glass tubes in the ceiling.

We were underground, somewhere beneath Whitehall, in a brilliantly illuminated dungeon of the War Office where innumerable little rooms like cells for political prisoners opened off a long corridor, at either end of which a sentry stood. I had been, for forty minutes, in a room at the far end of the corridor, where I had listened without any pleasure to an obscure and, as I thought, improbable story of mischief in the North Atlantic – it might be treason, but, knowing the men, I suggested a drunken holiday as the likelier explanation – and glumly I had received instructions for a winter journey. I got up and put on my cap, and, in the armour of discipline to which already I owed my life, saluted.

Then, in the corridor outside, I met Pelly, with whom I had been at school; where, though he was a year older than I, and cleverer, I had spoiled him of two cherished ambitions. I won the English essay prize, that he had confidently expected, and, what was more important in the estimation of us both, I beat him at rackets in successive years, and by getting my colours deprived him of his. But in the flensing light under Whitehall he had his revenge.

He was, at first sight, glad to see me. In those days, at the end of 1941, people were always glad to meet old acquaintances, for it seemed a personal triumph over fate that you and your friend should both have survived the commonness of disaster; and cordially, in his loud and hollow voice, he said, 'You've ten minutes to spare, haven't you? Come in and tell me what you've been doing.'

I followed him into his room, his pale cell walled with plaster-board on which large maps were pinned and a graph I could not understand; in which two tables and two chairs stood at opposing corners, and in the corner opposite the door was a green steel cabinet; and where, at the farther table, sat a very young and pink-cheeked captain. Pelly was already a major.

He invented an errand for the young captain – it was manifestly invented – and when we were alone he asked me, perfunctorily but not too obviously so, about my health. He knew that I had been wounded on the way back to Dunkirk, and he told me a plausible little story of his own efforts, and failure, to go to France with the first expeditionary force. He had had his commission in the Special Reserve, but in spite of being mobilized as soon as war was declared he had so far been denied the opportunity of active service. 'Planning,' he said, 'that's the bugbear. But we've got to plan, we've got to think ahead, and those of us who seem to have a little more grey matter than the majority, well, we're tied to our desks. We're the leather-bottoms. And it seems damned unfair to me that you should be one of the adventurers while I'm chairborne. You took the essay prize at school, and you ought to be here drafting Army instructions or rewriting the drill-books. But instead of that – well, where are you going now?'

Without saying what it was, I told him I had a dull and comfortless job in prospect, and he, showing little interest in a subject I had no intention of discussing, interrupted me to say, 'I was so very sorry to hear about your brother. I never knew him well, of course; he was – what, two years younger than you?'

'Just two years,' I said.

'But I remember him perfectly. That absurd gaiety, and so handsome. Now, looking back, it does seem that he was too good to be true. Certainly too good to survive this – oh, we have to admit it – this filthy muddle of a world, and this damned unnecessary war. I was bloody sorry, Tony.'

'It was a blow,' I said, 'and, by the feel of it, below the belt.'

He went to a map on the wall, and pointing a thin, precise finger, said, 'That's where it happened. But why, oh why, did he ever think he could be a soldier?'

'I tried to dissuade him,' I said, 'but nothing would stop him. And in the upshot, I suppose, he did as well as the rest of his half-trained, shoddily equipped, and badly led battalion.'

'You can't say it was badly led,' said Pelly. 'After the colonel was killed, Cromar took command.'

'An exalted drill-sergeant. A man of perverse stupidity.'

'A very brave man,' said Pelly.

'With no manners, no sense of decency. He never wrote to my mother.'

'You could hardly expect him to do that. Not in the circumstances. . . .'

It was then that I became aware of the light, of the unfastening of my defences. The light, I felt, had already begun to reveal my fear and my instinctive, unadmitted knowledge of what had happened. Half a dozen times, in half a dozen directions, I had tried and failed to discover exactly how Peter had been killed, and though I knew, from my own experience, the gross confusion that covered, with a thicker pall than the dust of summer roads, so many tributaries of the river of escape to Dunkirk, I was still, when I thought about it, perturbed by my failure to find anyone who could, or would, tell me the circumstances of his death. Knowing Peter as I did – knowing him from infancy – I had been afraid from the moment in which I heard he had been given a Territorial commission; but, of course, I had subdued my fear, put it away in some boxroom of my mind, and now, in punishment for that failure to act, that lethargy of spirit, I had to listen to Pelly while he told me how intolerably my fear had been realized.

The light of those implacable tubes on the ceiling – it was faintly blue, and in its rays there seemed to be an infinitesimal stammer – so magnified Pelly's cheek-bones that they threw a shadow, and his lips, under his little clipped moustache, looked indecently damp and loose. But in his eyes, in their nacreous shimmer and the pin-point elusiveness of the pupils, I could see his duplicity: he pretended reluctance, he made play with sympathy and sorrow, but all the time he was watching, avidly, for my distress and my defeat. And under that light I could scarcely disguise it. I felt the blood ebbing from my brain. I felt my face grow white and corpse-like, transparent to the stupor of my mind.

I heard my thin voice say, 'And Cromar – it was Cromar who did it?'

'He really had no choice,' said Pelly, turning away – having got what he wanted – and fluttering his hands in a clumsy imitation of some theatrical gesture he once had seen. 'He was responsible, you see, and you know how quickly panic can spread. There were three or four hundred men on the other side of the embankment, and if

Peter – oh, God knows I don't blame him! I can't. I haven't been put to the test myself. – But if they had been infected by his example, well, you can see for yourself what would have happened.'

I went again to the map on which he had shown me where Peter died, and could see nothing but a blur of pale colours, a spider's web of shallow contours, and a fly-blown print of indecipherable names. I wondered why he kept it there, for its significance had long since dissolved and vanished; but Pelly himself had had brothers, and what their luck had been I neither knew nor wanted to. With a trembling finger I traced a red line that had been drawn on the map and said, 'Yes, I see what you mean.'

'It's better you should know,' he said. 'It really is. Otherwise you might hear it, accidentally perhaps, from some half-stranger. Someone who had no cause to spare your feelings, and show his sympathy. You do realize how sorry I am, don't you?'

I put on my cap again and said dully, as if I were a bolster that had been thumped into shape, 'It has been a great blow, of course, but probably it's a blow I couldn't have avoided for ever. And now I had better go.'

I looked up, and for a moment was almost sorry for him. Under that light, I think, I had exposed the utter desolation of my soul too nakedly, and he was shocked by what he had done to me. Shocked and anxious, like an amateur boxer who sees his opponent fall too heavily, and belch a little blood. He made a move towards me, and began some disordered exculpation that I did not stay to hear.

Instinctively I composed myself to pass the sentry at the end of the corridor, but in the astonishing kindness of the natural light in Whitehall – the diminished light of a late winter afternoon – I began to cry, quietly and miserably, and had the utmost difficulty in maintaining the upright carriage and determined movement proper to an officer in war-time. But at the corner of Horse Guards Avenue my

self-pity was abruptly dammed, my self-concern brutally
diverted, by two small and shabby women, the plump and
rosy one weeping beyond restraint, the thin and white one
standing in a ghost's perplexity. – 'What do we do now?'
asked the weeping sister, and 'What does it matter?' said
the other.

I asked if I could help them, and at first had difficulty in
understanding their plight. They had come from the
Inquiry Room at the War Office, that place of tears,
and were so distraught by what they had learnt that they
hardly knew where they were. It was the thin, silent
woman, with cheeks like wrinkled ivory, who had lost
her son – the third and last of her sons – and it was she, not
her tear-drenched sister, who told me where they lived.

She spoke in the voice I had heard from the lips of dying
men – a voice too tired for life's remaining problems – and
paid no attention to the sniffling, gulping misery of her
sister, who told me, in a sort of continuous moan, 'Three
of them, all gone, and you never saw better boys! They
were lovely boys, and all she had. Oh, what's to become of
her now?' – But the stricken mother, though wounded
mortally by the loss of all her poor, work-shrivelled body
had brought forth, still kept her wits and a scrap of dignity
in the field. She thanked me for my interest, she told me
her address, and at last I managed to stop a cab. I gave the
driver a pound, and told him to take them home.

That cured me, for a little while, and I crossed Trafalgar
Square without seeing the traffic, without feeling my hurt;
and from Haymarket I turned down Jermyn Street, then
into Piccadilly. I had not joined my father's club, though
several of his friends had offered to put me up for it,
because my mother had persuaded me that Button's would
be better for me. – 'Those military clubs are so restricted,
really so parochial,' she had said – and her old admirer,
Charles Aytoun, who reviewed popular biography for the
Sunday papers, had proposed me for membership in 1938,

when Button's, in financial difficulties, was willing to accept a newly hatched subaltern.

I had, at first, made little use of it, and taken no advantage from the 'cultural influence', 'the association with writers and artists and the better sort of critics', which my mother, optimistically, had intended for my escape from the narrowness of regimental life; but I was fond of old Charles, his friends were kindly and tolerant people, and since my return from Dunkirk I had, on several occasions, been very grateful for membership. In the strident pressure of war-time London Button's was still a sort of tribal reserve of comfort and good humour; and I crossed Piccadilly to its white paint and bow windows (a small, tidy, domestic building in that long, anarchic façade) with a sense, if not of coming home, at least of reaching friendly shelter.

I went up to my room, and had a tepid bath; and then, at the bar, fell into conversation with a young American whom I had first met some eight or nine months before. Then, in February or March of 1941, he was in plain clothes, but now he wore the uniform of a lieutenant in the American navy; and to him I related my encounter with the two sorrow-stricken women at the corner of Horse Guards Avenue. I was holding their story firmly in the forecourt of my mind, to exclude any picture of my brother's death, and he, in the frankness of American emotion, at once responded with sympathy, with indignation, with a proposal to discover from the War Office who the women were, and do what we could to comfort them; and by his unwitting help I kept my private grief in the backward parts of consciousness, and went up to dinner in apparent composure.

We sat at the long table, and he said, 'It was noisier than this, the last time you were here.' I remembered, then, that we had once sat together when London, night after night, was battered and harassed by German bombers; and to complete my memory, and round off a small coincidence, an old and distinguished member took the chair on my left. He, too, had been my neighbour on that rough, earth-shaken night, but unlike the American lieutenant he had no recollection of it, nor of me. But in the manner of the club we talked together, and gradually, as sentence followed sentence of the tale he was telling me, I realized that I had heard it all before. He had told me the same story when the bombs were falling.

I, on that occasion, had been less accustomed than my fellow-diners to suffering shake and clamour indoors; and with a nervous admiration I had watched the steadiness with which three or four old waitresses – most of our male servants had already left us – put down our plates of soup, and the unperturbed demeanour of the ancient wine waiter. No one spoke of the raid, no one referred to the indecent disturbance of our comfort, but voices were a little higher than normal and our uniting friendship more clearly evident. Presently, through the outer din and inner babble, I heard the thin, protesting voice of my distinguished neighbour. He was complaining of ingratitude and the decline of manners. Or, to be more accurate, inquiring of me, who was young, if lack of good manners and absence of gratitude were indeed characteristic of a generation with which he had lost touch.

He was, to eyes of my age, a figure of remote and almost foreign grandeur. Hawk-nosed and aristocratic, ivory white – the colour of the bereft mother in Whitehall – his eyes were a clouded blue, his hands long and delicately wrinkled. He had been a Liberal Member in Asquith's Government, a good man, not widely known, but married to a generous, flamboyant, and famous wife of whom my mother used to speak with envious, unwilling admiration for her devotion to the arts and to young men in whom she alone had detected, in their chrysalis-phase, a promise of coming brilliance. She had housed and fed, encouraged and subsidized a dozen at least, of whom two or three had found success and grown more famous than she; and two of them had carved the first steps of their ascent to fame by lampooning her.

'Lampooning' was the word the old Liberal used. 'They came to us, those two,' he said, 'when they were hard-up and no one believed in them. No one except my wife. But she took them in – not at the same time, of course – and gave them the run of the house. Fed them and flattered them. Listened to them, and introduced them to influential people. And then they wrote novels and lampooned her. They were very smartly satirical about me, too, but I didn't mind that. I had done nothing for them, or very little, and I never really believed in them. Didn't take to them, as a matter of fact. But my wife was really good to them, and pinned her faith to their quite invisible genius. I don't say she made them, but they'd have found it much more difficult to make themselves if it hadn't been for her. And then, to show how clever they were, they lampooned her! Well, what do you think of that? Do you think that's all right, or do you think, as I do, that there's something odd about it?'

I cannot remember what I said, but I must have suggested that a writer's standards were not necessarily, perhaps, those of a gentleman; for in a brief silence that held the table under the menace of a bomb that was going to fall nearer than the others, his high, thin voice was clearly heard as he replied, 'But Walter Scott was a gentleman, and so was Fielding.' – The bomb exploded, the windows clamoured, and glasses tinkled; and before the curtains had time to calm themselves and hang straight again, he finished his sentence: 'And on the other side of the house, so to speak, I'm sure I'd have been very comfortable with Jane Austen. . . .'

Now, in the quietness of December, when the German bombers were occupied with Russia and London was allowed to dine in peace and sleep without interruption, I was told his sad tale again; and I wondered at the persistence of a grievance that seemed so trifling in comparison with a poor woman's loss of her three sons. Or in comparison with my dark sorrow. But was it trifling? His wife had been dead for several years, and the injury done to her had become, in him, a deepening wound. It had become incurable, because he could not forget it. . . .

The American lieutenant and I went to pay our bills, and found at the desk a woman of pleasant appearance but slow at arithmetic. She was new to the job, and it seemed unlikely that she would hold it for long. I told her that, as well as the club ordinary, I had had a pint of beer, a glass of vintage port, and coffee.

'What a mixture!' she said, and looked at me disapprovingly.

We went downstairs to the bar again and, when the hall-porter came to say that a War Office car was waiting for me, I left Button's with the reluctance of someone called from a warm fireside to face a winter night. For as well as a long, cold journey I knew that now I must face the grief which, for a few hours, I had kept in the hinterland of my mind.

CHAPTER THREE

NO ONE WHO experienced it needs to be reminded of the squalid, multitudinously huddled confusion of railway travel in war-time, and no one who escaped it can realize, in terms of a known emotion, what made it tolerable. Euston and King's Cross, Waverley in Edinburgh and the Central Station in Glasgow – stations in Liverpool and Newcastle, Leeds and Cardiff and a dozen others – were a dark and hustling conflict of innumerable sad or drunken, boisterous or coldly resolute mortal men, horribly encumbered with rifles and kit-bags, sharp-cornered packs and string-tied cheap suitcases – with weeping or tipsy, tight-lipped or studiously gay women come to kiss them goodbye – with a horde of inarticulate slaves of their century who, fortified neither by drink nor the natural vigour of their minds, were strong only in patience and incomprehension. And that seemingly disordered struggle, in the darkness that fear ordained for all, was only the prelude to night-long journeys in over-packed, ill-lighted, airless carriages or littered, sour-smelling corridors: then cold and darkness and more confusion at the other end.

It was a state, a condition of life, that no rational man could have tolerated. But in those years, of course, we were not rational. We had a sense of purpose, a feeling of community, and what was patently unendurable we sustained by sympathy with, and pity for, the uncomplaining, shoulder-rubbing multitude that a common imperative ordered to travel with us. Patriotism was in ill repute – there were few, on the frontier of conscience, who would

have declared patriotism in their baggage – but pity was
evident on every platform. And I do not mean self-pity.
That, for the most part, was deeply hidden or had been
discarded as useless. . . .

On that journey to the north, however, I was lucky,
because I was temporarily working for a branch of the War
Office that had peculiar authority. I was driven to King's
Cross, a soldier carried my kit, and a place had been
reserved for me. I arrived in good time, but the other
seats in my carriage were already occupied. There were
two civilians, a captain of the Royal Navy, a wing-com-
mander, and a red-tabbed colonel: a little, pursy, genial
man, rubicund, with a vulgar but well-tended face, who
looked as if he had been dining well. He stood up to shift a
suitcase on the rack, and make room for mine; and I saw
him reading my name on a label. He sat down again – we
were in opposite seats – and leaned forward to identify my
regiment.

Then he said, 'Chisholm? Is your name Chisholm?'

I admitted it, and he asked, 'A son of Copper
Chisholm?'

'Yes.'

'I thought so, when I saw your regiment. I knew him.
Knew him well! We don't breed 'em like that nowadays,
more's the pity.'

I muttered something to conceal embarrassment, and he
repeated, 'Yes, I knew Copper Chisholm, and I'm very
glad to meet a son of his. I hope you'll be a credit to him.'

He screwed his vulgar, good-natured features into a
look of fierce encouragement, and appeared to be searching memory or imagination for some stimulating anec-
dote of my father, or observation on his character, with
which to fortify me against my journey. But he had dined
too well, the effort was too much for him, and after a few
harmless questions he widely yawned and composed
himself for sleep. With the blessed indifference of the

English, none of the others paid any attention to our exchange, and I settled down to a night's confinement with five strangers and my own thoughts. They were, to begin with, dominated by memories that the plump colonel had evoked.

My father's nickname had a simple origin. Academically and on the playing-field his schooldays were undistinguished, but at some time – in his preparatory school, I think – he took the part of a policeman in a farce produced by the dramatic society, and for a reason that I do not know – perhaps because he played with a schoolboy's sudden talent, perhaps because he was ludicrously inept – he was thereafter known as 'Copper', and kept the name all his life. He is not remembered now, but in the first of our two wars he was one of that small group of officers who, by the exercise, I suppose, of a courage that was combined with a tactical sense akin to genius, were decorated in succession with all the medals for gallantry. It was because he had won the Victoria Cross that I, who was poorly suited for a soldier, became an officer in the Regular Army, and Peter my brother, who had not the smallest capacity for war, joined the Territorials.

My father was a little, lively man of simple mind and cheerful habit. There was nothing martial in his appearance except, perhaps, his upright carriage and alert, decisive movement; and to his family life he brought none of the discipline that he must have exercised in the regiment. He was permanently kind, patient without term, and active in finding occupation for his sons. Too active for Peter who, far more timid than I – and I was never brave – often shrank from the amusements he devised for our holidays. Dinghy-sailing, rock-climbing, and swimming in deep water from an anchored boat all drove Peter, at one time or another, into helpless fear or screaming rebellion. My father, on these occasions, never showed anger, though certainly he was disappointed. 'Give him time,' he would say; 'time and schooling are all he needs.' And quietly but firmly he would pacify the boy as if he were a frightened horse. But I, stubbornly controlling my own fear, was deeply ashamed of him.

Sometimes it seemed that my father was right; for Peter did indeed learn to swim well and strongly, to handle a boat with smart dexterity. He found, eventually, more pleasure in swimming and sailing than I ever did, for beneath a skin of competence I always felt hidden nerves of tension and anxiety, and Peter's enjoyment was easy and relaxed. But he never learnt to climb. He could trust neither rock nor his own strength on it – his own grip and balance – and he had no head for heights. I have seen him, over a drop of no more than forty feet, turn sickly white and tremulous. In extremity his pallor always betrayed him, as though his rebel fear had run up a white flag to cry for mercy.

As we grew up I became a tolerably good climber, and Peter learnt to make bluff excuses for his avoidance of mountains. 'I feel no need to risk my neck and cultivate discomfort,' he would say. 'I'm neither a romantic Teuton nor a frustrated schoolmaster, and I can easily prove my manhood without hanging by my finger-tips from the top of the Coolins.' – At the age of nineteen or so he was keenly aware of his manhood, in a restricted sense of the word, for his beauty was exceptional and among the many young women who were attracted by it, some showed quite clearly the greed that moved them. He had a sufficiency of male friends, whom his gaiety had won, and his gaiety protected him against the greediest of the young women, who found it disconcerting; but 'manhood' occupied much of his thought and time.

We had divided, as if by boundary lines, our physical inheritance, for Peter had taken his mother's height and beauty, and added to her stature the appearance, if not the reality, of his father's easy confidence; while I, copying my father's small and limber figure, was the heir – or so my mother assured me – to the literary talent which, as constantly she boasted, ran in the veins of all her family: an ichor, I suppose, that faith could recognize though analysis failed to detect it. Neither of us, however, had any part of the quality that, for a little while, gave my father his fame: nothing of his brave response to danger – the rise of spirit, the quickening of the mind, in the face of danger – had come down to us. Instead of that we had inherited our mother's nature: I got something of her cleverness and gift of words, which was smaller than she thought, and Peter her undisciplined egotism and shameless emotions. Though Peter was the richer by her beauty and commanding height, I was the better-off with the fragment I had of my father's will-power. He exercised it without effort, as a natural force, and I with spiritual labour and anxiety; but even so, it saved me from such an end as Peter's.

He should have known what would happen! Again and again he had shown himself incapable of facing even the trivial, common accidents of life. He would fly his white flag of fear if he found himself in a railway carriage with a couple of drunken toughs coming home from a race-meeting. He had abandoned a girl with whom he was in love because a rival suitor, smaller but more serious than himself, had warned him to keep clear or take the consequences; and I had seen him as pallid and shaken as when, in boyhood, he had lost his nerve on a little cliff, because a woman, older than himself, told him that her husband was growing suspicious. Her purpose, I imagine, had been to incite him to some warmer or more positive statement of affection; but Peter, so far from speaking boldly up, turned and fled, and she never saw him again. – In spite of all this, however, he joined, and was presently commissioned in a Territorial battalion in the spring of

1939, when war was imminent and inevitable; and his mother's egotism, his father's Victoria Cross, were, I suppose, equally to blame. . . .

With a shuddering, then jolting pressure of brakes the train stopped at some unseen station – Peterborough or Grantham – and in the dark, blinded carriage, lit only by small purple bulbs, two or three of my fellow passengers stirred and woke and, moving resentfully in their over-coated bulk, opened narrow, ill-tempered eyes. They stretched their legs, they moved their ponderous shoulders, and glared with drowsy suspicion at their companions of the gloom as if they were the great beasts of a dangerous forest, discovering unknown neighbours. They were indeed great beasts in the jungle of the world, resentful because their proper right to privacy had been denied, their claim to familiar comfort had been ignored, and they were forced to travel on unwilling duty in the confinement of a padded cage. It was their sort – the buffalo sort, the senior officers, the lions of the forest – who had turned on Peter and killed him; and I, in the confinement of their cage, felt rising in me a wave of panic, a momentarily insane desire to escape.

But escape was impossible. Mentally impossible, because I was a junior member of the hierarchy to which they belonged; physically impossible, because the material way of escape, the corridor beyond the carriage door, was tightly full of soldiers sitting on their packs and kit-bags, sleeping with rifles in their arms, or leaning in heavy, ungainly slumber against the carriage walls. There was no way of escape.

I was imprisoned, in fact as well as in my own order, and for a moment or two I felt my panic struggling for release, kicking to get out. But I could deal with it – I had learnt a discipline to subdue it – and presently it obeyed, and was still. But then remorse came in, for I realized that I had been thinking of Peter only in his ungracious aspects: as a coward who could not control his cowardice, as an egotist of my mother's sort, as a woman-chaser who could too easily be chased away. But he was other things, and better things, as well. He had had a gaiety, a lustre of gaiety, that not only lighted all he said with a singular, untranslatable charm, but lent something of its luminance to the very ordinary friends whom he customarily gathered about him, and disguised their lack of distinction with the overplus of his. In his sensuality, too, there was the excuse of beauty and his youth; for indulgence of the flesh, even flagrant indulgence, is surely forgivable when flesh is so fair and vivid in its strength. Or so it seemed to me, now that he was dead, and I remembered his lithe body, the look in his eyes, and his laughter.

I remembered, too, what had sealed us in love. – It was not until he, too, was a soldier, in the first October of the war, when both of us had short leave from our regiments, that he told me how, ever since our father's death, he had dreamt of him every few weeks. His dreams always began in the same way, with the opening of a door, and through the door came father. Sometimes he was in his dressing-gown, as if, in the early morning, he was looking in to see if we were awake. Sometimes, smiling, he carried a newspaper, and seemed about to ask, 'What do you think of all this nonsense?' And sometimes he wore an overcoat and had, apparently, come home from a journey. Then, when Peter, choking with excitement in his dream, asked where he had been and what he had been doing, he would answer calmly, 'Why, what's the matter? Has anything been worrying you? There's no need to worry.'

It was in Button's, late at night – we had both had rather too much to drink – that Peter told me of his dreams; and I confessed that I too, again and again, had dreamt of father in his dressing-gown, opening a bedroom door (it was through a schoolboy's eyes I saw him) and telling us to get up, get up quickly, for the day was fine. But in my other dream I went to a door and opened it, expecting to find him on the other side; and, when I saw there was no one there, I would fall into such grief that I was wakened by its desolation.

In the two years since his death, neither of us had been able to accept the closing of the door as final; and realizing, for the first time, that Peter had loved him as deeply as I did, I felt for Peter such love and pity – self-pity, too, of course – that all the shame he had caused me, and all my jealousy of him, were washed away in a flood of grateful emotion. For a little while we were wholly brothers, in heart and mind, and I could say nothing more for fear of crying.

But Peter quickly recovered, and said he must go. There was a girl waiting for him. 'A new girl, and I've lost her address. But instinct will guide me, and the old hunter will pick up the trail again. Somewhere near the Brompton Oratory, I imagine. Come and walk with me as far as Hyde Park Corner.'

We walked up Piccadilly, arm in arm, and he talked about Cromar, his company commander. 'A proper swine,' he said, but amiably, as if, in the circumstances of war, such a character must be tolerated.

'He's a good soldier, after a fashion,' I said. 'It's not a fashion I like, but I suppose it's necessary.'

'He complains that I can't stand still on parade, and when I told him that I didn't see why I should, as this was going to be a war of movement, he was bloody rude.'

'You may not like him, but he'll look after you.'

'Unless he gets a bullet in the back of his head first. That does occasionally happen, I'm told, when a too zealous officer leads his ungrateful troops into battle.'

But it wasn't Cromar who was shot in the back of the head. . . .

Under the light in the room beneath Whitehall, Pelly

had shown me the place on the map. It was near Arras, where, on the tenth or eleventh day after the Germans began their offensive, two of our divisions had made a little, abortive counter-attack, and been forced to withdraw as the German armour came round their flank towards Lens . . . It was easy to imagine the scene, and as the train dived shrieking into a tunnel I heard again the screaming roar of dive-bombers. – Tanks nosing down a road, and the field-guns hauling round to face a new front. The taut, thin discipline of a flank as the rearward company withdrew behind it. Fire and movement, noisier, more nervous and more ragged than on Salisbury Plain, but the drill-pattern still recognizable. Then discipline – a single strand of discipline – snapping under strain. Peter hoisting his white flag of fear (God knows how he had controlled himself so long) and a flutter of uneasiness about him as fear began to spread. It had to be stopped, and Cromar was behind him. . . .

I stumbled from the carriage, blundering over kit-bags, and with a brutal disregard for the cramped and drowsy soldiers in the corridor I forced my way past them to the lavatory, where two men were sleeping, one on the floor and one on the seat. I drove them out, and was sick into the pan. I knelt there a long while, I think, too weak to move, and when I went back to my carriage the soldiers uttered no protest, but made themselves thin against the walls of the corridor and looked at me with a grave sympathy. I fell asleep, and did not wake until we reached Edinburgh. It was still dark and very cold, and in the evil-smelling gloom of the station men bowed beneath their warlike loads moved hurriedly past the glare of a fire-box and the hissing of steam with the mindless purpose of elvers in a black night of summer.

I went to the station hotel, and had a bath and shaved. I had breakfast, and read in a newspaper that the great ships *Prince of Wales* and *Repulse* had been sunk by Japanese torpedo-bombers somewhere north of Singapore. The world was dying – or so it seemed, in the mood of that morning – dying in tremendous gouts of destruction and bleeding to death through thousands of invisible and private wounds. But the prospect of death could have no effect on behaviour, nor turn anyone away from a commanded duty. Like the soldiers in the dark station I was merely an elver, fetched from the mystery of the deep Sargasso to swim up some unknown stream in obedience to a purpose preordained . . . The emotion of the night had emptied my mind, drained me of feeling, and I continued my journey without interest or complaint: an elver or automaton, at best an actor who had learnt his dull part in a dreary play.

I crossed the enormous bridge, and on the other side of the Forth reported to the Naval office in Donisbristle. An hour later, with half a dozen other passengers, I was flying in a small biplane over cloudy hills to the north. It was a sullen, windless day, and to the west a mass of impenetrable purple cloud lay over the Grampians. We skirted the mountains, and beyond Inverness flew over a sombre land so pocked and pitted with small lochs that it looked like an old coat full of holes: a land worn out.

I was, at that time, a little nervous of aeroplanes: a consequence, perhaps, of my father's death, who had been killed in a glider. He was only forty-five when he retired from the Army, in 1934: too young, for a man of his sort, to settle down on a small estate in the West Highlands to shooting and fishing and the County Council. So, with a growing enthusiasm, he took up the new sport of gliding, and very quickly showed an aptitude for it. He broke several records, and enthusiasm became a passion. He, who had always been a balanced man, a man whose strength had seemed to float on a natural ease and sweetness of temper, became ardent and greedy in his pursuit of lifting clouds and the heights of the sky. He exhausted English skies, grew impatient with the leisurely air-currents over the Downs, and in the late summer of 1937 went to the Austrian Tyrol in search of thermal streams more lusty and dramatic.

We were all at home – Peter, my mother, and I – when news came of his death. It was early evening, and a few neighbours had come in to meet a cousin of my mother's and his American wife, who were staying with us. Our house stood close above the sea, and the west window of the drawing-room was full of the blue Atlantic and a golden light. We were talking, idly enough and perhaps a little too loudly after the second cocktail, when the telegram was brought in and given to my mother. She read it in a sudden silence, and without a word, but clutching it to her breast, went towards the big window. She stood for a moment, facing the sunlight, and then, her hands still at her breast, fell unconscious, heavy and straight as a falling tree.

In spite of my horror and consternation I remembered, in the fragment of a second while she fell, the week we had spent in Paris in the spring: Peter, mother, and I. We had seen a performance of *La Dame aux Camélias* in which the actress who played the part (I have forgotten her name) stood in a theatrical light to face the imminence of death, and fell as suddenly, and seemingly as stricken as my mother. She was a superb and most moving actress; so, at her best, was mother. She lay in bed for a month, a victim of what she later called 'brain fever'. Then she went on a world cruise, to put, as she said, 'the whole round earth between me and a tragedy I can never face'.

But she never told us that she dreamt of father, and, if she had, I think she would have boasted of it. . . .

I looked down and saw the Pentland Firth and the tide crumbling on a meagre island. A few minutes later we

landed on a small airfield near Kirkwall. I was met and
driven to a little pocket of a harbour where I boarded a
drifter for Lyness: the northernmost centre of Naval
administration, a slum of long huts crouched under a
wet hillside, tucked into a drab corner of Scapa Flow,
and peopled that day with as glum and surly a set of Naval
officers and ratings as ever I encountered. The loss of their
two great ships at Singapore lay upon them like the cloud
of an erupting volcano. They went to and fro in the
echoing corridors of their squalid huts, coughing, as if
they tasted sulphur in the air.

My interview with an Intelligence Officer was brief. He
was tired, and showed no great interest in my task.

'You've been told the whole story – as far as there is a
story – and what we're worrying about? And you know the
people involved?' he asked.

'Yes, both of them.'

'That's why we asked for you, and I'm very glad you
were able to come so promptly. Now if nothing has
happened – and that may be the case – we don't want
to upset them. We're very anxious to avoid anything in the
nature of official inquiry. Get their confidence, and persuade them to talk. And if they've nothing to talk about, as
the I.O. at Tórshavn seems to think, you ought to discover
that by the second bottle. You can drink schnapps, can't
you?'

'Yes, but they prefer whisky.'

'I'll put some aboard for you. Is your cover the same as
before?'

'Just the same. I've got an honest job to do, though it's
of no importance.'

'All right, then. If there's anything else you need, to put
you in the picture, you'll get it from the I.O. there. Now
come along and I'll introduce you to Silver. You're sailing
tonight.'

'In what?'

'A trawler. But she's fairly big and quite new; you'll be comfortable enough.'

It was my second voyage to the Faeroes that year. I had not enjoyed my first, in a troop-ship, and I thought it unlikely that a trawler would be any better.

CHAPTER FOUR

I FORGET WHO said that if he were given the choice of betraying his friend or his country, he hoped he would have the strength of mind to betray his country; but it is not a judgment I admire. It is clever enough for a cocktail party, but on the way home one might reflect that many, perhaps very many, friends and friendly associations would be sacrificed in the betrayal of a country – and if, to simplify the choice, a man has only one friend, he must be a curious fellow, or his country so abominably inhabited that he should have left it as soon as he had money for his ticket.

The result of my journey to the Faerocs might well be the 'betrayal' of two men with whom, a few months before, I had been, for a little while, on friendly terms; but the prospect did not unduly worry me. I was not in love with my task, but I accepted it as a by-blow of my duty as a soldier. If, in some way, the men were collaborating with the Germans, they were enemies of my country and of all my friends, and common sense declared the necessity of disarming them. Sensibility had no standing in comparison with common sense; and common sense, in this instance, was identical with duty.

I had no official, or regular, connection with Military Intelligence, but after I was wounded at Cassel, in the retreat to Dunkirk, I was unfit for a long time for regimental employment, and by the kindness of one of my father's old friends I was given a temporary job under the Director-General of Army Welfare. That brought me to the notice of a cousin of my mother's, a man I hardly knew, who for some years had been in M.I., but cannot, I think, have done much to enhance it. When I was about to visit the northern archipelagos, in the spring of 1941, he sent for me and asked what it was that I had to do there.

He listened patiently to my résumé of the duties of a Welfare Officer, and said, 'I'm not interested in Orkney and Shetland, only in the Faeroes. Will you be visiting any of the smaller islands there?'

'Wherever there's an outlying troop, or coast defences.'

'Will you have any spare time?'

'A lot, I think. The Lovat Scouts are the bigger part of the garrison, and a good Territorial battalion doesn't really need much help. It looks after its own people just as well as we can, or better.'

Then he told me something of the several small political parties in the Faeroes, and suggested I should take an interest in them, and, as a detached observer, write my impressions. – 'Your mother once told me you write very well. Could have gone in for it, if you'd cared to: so she said. And if that's the case, a job like this ought to be right up your street. Oh, and one other thing: there are seven or eight people you're almost sure to meet – Faeroese, I mean – and I'd like a few notes on them. Just say what you think of them, take note of anything that strikes you in conversation, and express your own judgment in your own way. It's not very important, but a little more knowledge of them might come in useful some day.'

I was, of course, flattered by his request: I was young enough to enjoy the prospect of working under cover and alone – even at so innocent a task – and as a regular soldier I was naturally pleased to know there were senior officers who thought me sufficiently intelligent and responsible for confidential employment. I accepted it without hesitation, and in the event did no harm to anyone except myself; for the men on whom I had to report were robust and hardy, enormously convivial, great talkers and deep drinkers, and for two or three weeks I hardly ever woke without an aching head.

There were, in the Faeroes, several political parties or factions – romantic Nationalists, moderate Nationalists or devolutionists, conservative adherents of the Danish throne, advocates of union with Britain, a sprinkling of academic Communists, and so forth – but all seemed at one in their fervent belief in the Allied cause, and the eight men whose names I had had to memorize for special attention were, so far as I could judge, as notable in their common loyalty as they were outspoken on behalf of their own factions or ideals. They were individualists and enthusiasts, and by three o'clock in the morning their enthusiasm was sometimes deafening. I liked them all, and my only difficulty was in give my report a sobriety that our evenings together had conspicuously lacked.

But two of them were now under suspicion: a vague but deepening suspicion. Both are dead – the elder died, unhappily, of cirrhosis of the liver, the younger was killed in a very gallant foray into Norway – and neither, as I discovered, was ever guilty of anything worse than conduct too strongly Faeroese: their individualism was excessive, their enthusiasm indiscreet, and that was all. In the circumstances of the time, however, their behaviour did invite inquiry.

The older man was known as Bömlo. He was a Norwegian by birth, a sailor who had served, and twice been torpedoed, in our merchant navy in the first war. He had married, about 1933, the daughter of a man who kept a little general shop in Tórshavn, and after his death a year or two later Bömlo settled down there, and quickly became a popular figure in the town. Bömlo was the name of his birthplace – an island off the west coast of Norway – and because he never wearied of telling its charm and amenities (though it is, I believe, small and windswept) he acquired, in the fashion of simple humour, a nickname that he enjoyed as much as those who had labelled him with it. He was a big man, lame of one leg, with thickly growing, grizzled hair and a solemn look that melted like ice in the sun after two or three glasses of schnapps.

The younger of the suspects was one of the romantic Nationalists: a poet of sorts, a deep-sea fisherman, part-heir to a little croft on one of the northern islands of the archipelago. He was remarkably handsome, with a bold and lively look – a devil of a fellow, one would say, and not be far wrong – and a dandy as well: when he was at home he usually wore the national costume of dark blue, hard-woven, woollen jacket and knee-breeches, embroidered red waistcoat with silver buttons, buckled shoes and Napoleonic cap. At the *grindadráp*, the whale-hunting which is an island sport, he was a local hero, and in Norway, where he died, a true hero. His Christian name was Tórur.

These were the men whose behaviour I had to investigate: the men whom I would certainly 'betray' if they were in communication with the Germans. I thought it unlikely, but the possibility had to be faced, and in that season of history it was worth no more than a shrug of the shoulders . . . We lay dismasted in a gale of the world – under-manned, ill-found, off a leeshore of utter catastrophe – and our anchors were dragging. Peter was dead, twice dead, for I had mourned his death in battle and now I carried with me the picture of his death in shame, and Cromar standing above his body, shouting to the waverers who had turned to follow the white flag of my brother's fear. In such a season I would have no compunction, or so I thought, in leading a few more cattle to the butcher's yard.

The ship in which I was to sail was a fine-looking, new trawler of about six hundred tons. Her Captain, a lieutenant called Silver, was manifestly pleased with his command, and I had to admit that she was probably big enough for a voyage of less than three hundred miles. But I hoped the sea would be calm.

We sailed soon after midnight in still, cold weather, and went out west from the Flow, through Hoy Sound. There were black clouds in the sky, more sombre than the general dark, that seemed as solid as the round bulk of Hoy, raising its vast shoulder to port; and to starboard a flounce of white water fluttered on sunken rocks. Suddenly, from the low shore, a searchlight stripped an incandescent ribbon in the dark: for a moment it wavered in its aim, then struck us full in the face with blindness, and voices on the bridge replied with loud and blasphemous abuse. – The searchlight went out. Someone nearer to the nervous gunner in his emplacement – somewhere on shore – had also called him a bloody fool.

The Atlantic was almost as calm as the inland water of Scapa Flow, but the air grew colder and before long I went to bed; without undressing, however. The Captain had lent me his cabin – he took what rest he could on a bunk in the chart-room – and, though small, I found it uncommonly well furnished. I had already discovered, from conversation, that Silver was a man of character, and now I learnt something of his taste. His character – and, I suppose, his taste also – are not irrelevant to my story, for within the next few days, when I shrank from making decisions, I took his advice, for good or ill – for good and ill – and I am inclined to believe that by his seamanship he saved my life. Though in regard to that (for I am no seaman) I may exaggerate.

The walls of his cabin were cream-coloured, and screwed to them, in thin gilt frames, were half a dozen coloured prints of ballet design and costume: designs by Léon Bakst and Derain; others, I think, by Natalia Goncharova – and Dufy? I cannot be certain, but all were bright, fantastic, orgulous – and serenely defiant of war and the cold Atlantic. He had a bookcase almost as strangely populated, for all its authors were women: Virginia Woolf, Colette, Rosamund Lehmann, Elizabeth Bowen, and, among others, two of my mother's novels that I was sorry to see there; though I was safe enough from questioning, for she wrote under her maiden name. I took *The Waves*, and read myself to sleep with it.

I was wakened by Silver's entrance. It was full morning, and after a night on the bridge he looked alert and fresh, though his eyes were red with cold. He apologized for waking me and, with perhaps an exaggerated courtesy, asked if he might wash and shave. 'I hate the sensation of the morning's bristles on my chin,' he said. 'I've no objection to dirt and sweat, but I detest the sprouting of my beard. I like to be as smooth as an egg – and how I wish I were as hard.'

He took off a muffler and his duffle coat, a shabby tunic with two tarnished strips of gold braid – he was a lieutenant in the Volunteer Reserve – a fisherman's jersey, a woollen shirt, and a string vest. He kicked his feet out of sea-boots and two pairs of socks and, filling the basin with hot water, dipped his head in and scrubbed it vigorously. 'I'm one of those eccentric people who really like the sea,' he said, 'but need it be so salt? Even in calm weather it coats you with stickiness.'

He was a man of my own age, or a little more, with a narrow, finely moulded head and thick dark hair. He had somewhat Italianate features, and his skin was a ruddy bronze like a ripe apple. His arms and body were well muscled, his hands and feet long and thin; as if bone were reaching out for eloquence. But more impressive than his physical appearance was his whole manner and demeanour of natural assurance, and for a moment I was tempted to break through the brittle, miserable reserve within which I was so desperately living, and tell him all my woe. Peter, in my place, would have had no hesitation. Peter would have told him everything, and got in return Silver's sympathy; but lost his respect. I, perhaps wiser and certainly more unhappy, had sufficient strength of mind to say nothing. But so immediate, so enveloping, was the feeling I had of his strength and competence that I was already prepared, I suppose, to accept him as my leader.

'I'm going to give you a fine, flat sea all the way to Tórshavn,' he said. 'I can't take you the shortest route – for one reason or another we have to make a little detour – but you won't suffer any discomfort except cold. It's going to be very cold, I'm afraid. But you'll be reasonably warm down here, and you've found something to read, have you? Do you like Virginia?'

A little nervous, because of my late impulse to confide in him, I picked up *The Waves* and fumbled with its pages. 'Not this one. It's too laboured, too artificial.'

'I dote on them all,' he said, and waved his shaving-brush towards the bookcase. 'That's what I call my harem.'

'Do you read no authors but women?'

'Not at sea,' he said. 'The sea has two disadvantages: it's salt, as I mentioned before, and there are no women on it. Not in war-time. So female authors are a necessity, as well as a luxury. All those books – and some are a lot better than others – contain a woman who's undressing herself. Oh yes, they do! Some of them only unwrap their sensibility and their intelligence, but even they give you the feeling that there's a bed behind the door. But most of them take you on a beautifully observant, roundabout walk, that might be a little bit boring if you didn't know where it was leading; but it's leading you all the time, with un-faltering purpose. The whole thing – the whole female art of novel-writing – is an exquisitely prolonged strip-tease. Have you read this one?'

He threw a book on to my bed – a book that has been much admired – and said, 'That's one of my favourites.

How wonderfully the disrobing of her sensibilities leads, at long last, to taking off her petticoats! And then what intimacy! Oh, nothing vulgar, but how her mind embraces you. And what good soap she uses. You can smell the steam in her bathroom. In reality, I expect, she would be an infernal nuisance, but in a book, at sea, she's pure enchantment.'

Carrying his duffle coat, he went out, and I more leisurely washed and dressed. A steward in his shirt-sleeves gave me a large breakfast, which I ate and enjoyed, and presently I went on deck.

There was no wind, but neither was there any kindness in the air. Its stillness was the rigor of winter, that arrests a running brook, and under the pressure of our speed it seemed hard as ice. The day was sunless, and the dark sea, a sullen, endless calm, carried no visible tenant but ourselves and menaced imagination with thoughts of utter vacancy and profundity beyond measure. Sometimes a mysterious swell rolled us slowly, far over, as if in the deep an ocean giant had sighed and stretched himself.

But the trawler carried herself with a jaunty assurance. Her bow rose high in a proud sheer, broken but not spoiled by the gun on her fo'c'sle deck; and abaft the bridge, on either side, lay in lethal queues the depth-charges she could drop in submarine explosion should the Asdic find a U-boat in the cold womb of the sea. She carried light automatic guns to fight off aircraft – twin-Vickers mounted at either side of the bridge – and the servitors of all her weapons were, for the most part, very young, and all, as it seemed to me, absurdly cheerful. Our First Lieutenant was nineteen, and the oldest man aboard was the engineer, a chief petty officer of thirty-two who aggravated his years by a gruff solemnity. Conversation, except with the Captain, was almost wholly professional: out of an experience far beyond their years the young men spoke of foul weather in the North Atlantic and the gales that swept their crowded anchorage in Scapa Flow – of lame ducks lost from a convoy and seen, for the last time, when the flames of their burning broke and dazzled a night sky – of German bombers and fierce confusion in Norwegian fjords; for some of them had travelled far. But the Captain preferred general topics.

We stood together on the after deck between the depth-charges and looked at the white stream of our wake; and cheerfully he exclaimed, 'What a horrible country we lived in before the war! Don't you agree? Appeasement abroad and unemployment at home – the dull incompetence of the Right Wing and the shrill absurdity of the Left – and the dim squalor of our amusements: talking nonsense about Spain, drinking too much gin, and making love out of sheer boredom. Do you think we deserve to win?'

'Do you think we shall?'

'It's doubtful isn't it? It's like putting your shirt on an unknown, twelve-year-old, Irish-bred horse that someone bought from a milkman and entered for the Grand National; the odds are still against us, but we've got over the first few fences. And life's more interesting than it used to be. In the last couple of years before the war, life was half a hangover, half waiting for an operation.'

That was before lunch, but after, I think, a mug of Bovril and sherry. We ate lunch in the minute wardroom off a table-cloth so dirty that the Captain said – to the steward who was still in his shirt-sleeves – 'That's a revolting table-cloth, steward! If we haven't another, can't you turn it?'

In the afternoon – as steadily, in the meagreness of northern light, we ploughed towards another dark – he spoke of the war, of books again, of the ballet, and surprisingly, as it seemed to me, of mathematics. He questioned me in a hard, masterful way about the retreat, about what I had seen of the French, and about the behaviour of the troops on the beaches at Dunkirk. He had a brother who had been taken prisoner, and his brother had written to ask for books on the ballet and pure mathematics. They had shared an enthusiasm for the ballet, and now, because of his brother's interest, he had taken to reading about such, to me, incomprehensible matters as Vectors, Calculus, and, I think, something called the Theory of Sets. He found them, he said, 'fascinating but profoundly disquieting'.

'I read constantly,' he said, 'and mathematics is a useful antidote to my female novelists. Too much of the harem isn't good for you. I don't often read the harem when I'm ashore. Then I prefer Stendhal and Smollett and Stevenson and Mark Twain: people who don't exhibit themselves, but go to work and make things. Which, of course, is what a man ought to do. I can't imagine anything attractive in watching an elderly male novelist unrolling yard after yard of shabby bandage from his old shrivelled legs to show, at last, what he stands on. Or in listening to some old egotist talking to his own image for half a century and pretending that he's "realized" himself. . . .'

The table-cloth had been turned for dinner, and we ate an abundant meal of dry hash and pale green cabbage off linen dully stained, from its other side, with brown bottle-sauces and raspberry jam. I listened to more talk of storms, fire and torpedoes, and went early to bed. I read another twenty pages of *The Waves*, but fell asleep thinking of Silver. I needed someone to confide in, to tap for sympathy, and he seemed so wholly the master of his own world that I thought, in my weakness, he might let me in; as a sort of feudatory.

In his ship, it was clear, he was entirely the Captain. He spoke to everyone with the light and easy, natural confidence of one who had never dreamt that his word could be disputed. And in the cold vacancy of the winter sea he had talked to me, his guest, as a host should, in a vein of critical gossip about men and books, about war and the ballet. Whether his criticism had any value I cannot say – I am not competent to judge – but in that setting, in mordant cold, with men alert at the guns and the Asdic alert for hostile echoes in the deep, it was agreeable to listen to; and in the dissolution of my own confidence I was grateful to him for showing so much, for showing it with so cheerful and sometimes profane a spirit, and for being disquieted only by vectors and the calculus.

Before I fell asleep I had decided – or very nearly decided – to tell him about Peter. I was even wondering if I could go farther and ask how I should deal with an adulterous wife whom I had married without my Colonel's permission, and with whom, as I thought, I was still in love. 'She looks at you like a spaniel,' I said to him in my dreams, and in my dream he answered, 'Beat her.'

I was on the bridge next morning when we came in sight of mountain-tops rising, abrupt and savage, from invisible submarine bases. They were clad, imperfectly, with snow; not, like the alps in winter, brilliant peaks of solid snow, but ragged heights that showed the naked rock beneath thin shawls. When I had last seen them, in early summer, there had been a selvedge of bright green below their barren slopes – a braid of grass above the sea – and it was possible to believe they nurtured a human populace. But now they looked like the outposts of a frozen world where men had died; and in the desolation of the scene I thought – for such was my mood – I had found my proper landfall.

We sailed in between Streymoy, largest of the islands, and the lower, hump-backed island of Nólsoy. The sea was ruffled and a bitter wind blew down from the hills. It is said, by guide-books and kindly travellers, that the climate of the Faeroes is mild, and frost in winter rare; but my only experience of them, in winter, was like a story of Arctic explorers. The wind in our faces, though light enough, seemed to shred flesh from bone.

When I went ashore, however, I found almost as lively a stir of humanity as had greeted me in summer. The little houses whose roofs had all been green and gay with flowers and lushly growing grass were now capped in white, but the people on the quay and in the narrow streets were brisk as ever, and again I was surprised, in what seemed a land so sterile, by the multitude of children. Two of them, with whose parents I had been friendly, remembered me and came running to meet me. The Faeroese – so I realized with envy – were sturdily indifferent to their climate.

CHAPTER FIVE

THE INTELLIGENCE OFFICER with whom I had to confer knew as much about the Faeroes and their people, with regard to their political or military importance, as anyone living in the islands. He was a young man with great charm of manner and real, not merely professional, intelligence. (In private life he was a scientist of some sort, but whether physicist or biologist I cannot remember.) He was, however, primarily concerned with the security of the garrison, and he had found nothing in the behaviour of our two suspects, Bömlo and Tórur, that threatened danger to the troops. He was inclined, as I had been when I first heard the story of their unusual – but only mildly unusual – behaviour, to suppose they were relieving the dullness of winter by drinking too much, and, perhaps, a village intrigue.

He had to leave Tórshavn, as soon as he could, to investigate a small disturbance of the peace in Suduroy, most southerly of the islands, where a pro-British sentiment and a too-talkative bombardier had caused some embarrassment to the Danish authorities; but before leaving he gave me his account of the circumstances that had wakened such unhappy doubts of the honesty of two good men. Twice before I had heard the story, or parts of it, but I listened carefully to what he had to say. For he knew it in more detail than my other informants.

The story began with the arrival from Norway of a thirty-foot boat with two dead and three dying men aboard. Since the German occupation of Norway many such boats – some even smaller – had crossed the North

Sea, bringing refugees from Nazi dominion. They were not, however, refugees in the ordinary sense. They were not simple fugitives, but men and women of indomitable minds who, refusing to live under the tyranny of a Teutonic philosophy and German policemen, preferred the dangers of the sea and the risk of machine-gun bullets from a hunting aeroplane. Most of the boats had made for Shetland, which lay nearest to the Norwegian coast, but some had reached Orkney and some the Faeroes. The boat which prompted my journey had made harbour in the northern island where Tórur was heir to a little house and a minute property of land.

He was at home when the boat came in, and instead of notifying the proper authorities he had sent word, privily, to Bömlo. This was not so grave a breach of regulations as it may seem, because for several months Bömlo had regularly been employed, by the military authorities, to interrogate Norwegian refugees. The Germans knew of the west-bound traffic, and several times had planted an agent among the escapers; or tried to plant one. On at least one occasion Bömlo had discovered a Nazi – one of Quisling's followers – among the genuine resisters, and more than once he had been helpful in establishing the *bona fides* of a man who, because of fright or the exhaustion of the voyage, had replied to investigation in a way so evasive as to rouse suspicion.

Bömlo had not only an extensive knowledge of the Norwegian coastline, but a gossiping acquaintance with, as it seemed, innumerable people from Stavanger to the Lofotens. He was a sailor of long experience and a naturally friendly person with a royal memory for names and faces; on both counts he was a valuable interrogator, and quite invaluable if truly loyal.

Neither he nor Tórur could be blamed for any failure to look after the dying Norwegians. The boat had come ashore in darkness, not far from Tórur's house, where

he was living alone; and Tórur had been one of the first –
but not quite the first – to see it stranded, in the pale
morning light, and hurry to give what help he could to its
exhausted crew. The two who were dead were boys of
sixteen or seventeen; they had died of exposure, aggravated by sickness and hunger. There was no remnant of
food in the boat – not a crust of bread nor scrap of salt fish
– and the water-breaker was empty. Of the three men who
were still alive, one was raving mad, another looked quiet
and competent: haggard and half-frozen, but in possession
of his faculties except that he so mumbled his words that
no one could understand what he said. When he was
helped ashore he stood, unaided, and smiled. He shook
his rescuers by the hand, and made a gesture as though to
say, 'Now I am all right!' But when he tried to walk, he
tripped and fell, and had to be carried to the nearest house.
The third man – the biggest and most obviously robust –
lay unconscious with a broken skull. He had, perhaps,
fallen when the boat lurched in a heavy sea, and struck his
head on a coaming or a corner of the deck-house. But it
was possible, of course, that someone had hit him on the
head.

The local doctor had been quickly summoned, and
everything possible was done for the men. They were
taken to hospital in Klakksvík, and there, within the next
three or four days, they died. None of them spoke before
his death except the madman, and he chattered inces-
santly; but there was no meaning in his words. Bömlo
returned without delay to Tórshavn, and gave a good,
detailed account of what he had seen and what had
happened; and, with a mild reproof for Tórur, the episode
might have been buried in the quick oblivion of war, as yet
another tragedy of time and the winter sea – 'Poor devils'
their epitaph, and a shiver for their suffering in the storm-
tossed, hungry boat.

But Tórur had a jealous neighbour, who presently came

to Tórshavn to say that he, at first light of the morning when the Norwegian boat was found, had seen a man come ashore from it and walk towards Tórur's house. There had been six in its crew, not five, he said; and when he was asked why he had waited four days before bringing information, he answered that he had been unwilling to say anything that might discredit so good a friend as Tórur, and while the Norwegians were still alive there was hope that one of them, at least, might recover and not only speak of the missing man, but say who he was. Now, however, they were all dead, and it was his duty – his ungracious, most unpleasant duty – to report what he had seen.

His story was not believed, for it was widely known that, so far from being a friend of Tórur, he had quarrelled violently with him a year before when Tórur, coming home from sea, had paid extravagant attention to his neighbour's wife, and, according to local gossip, seduced her. His story was put down to a brooding jealousy, and disbelief in it was apparently substantiated by the two facts that no one else had noticed a stranger in the district, and the several people who had visited Tórur in his house had seen nothing to suggest that he was hiding someone.

'I went there myself,' the I.O. told me, 'as soon as I heard the man's story, and Tórur laughed at me. His neighbour, he said, was a man so blind that he couldn't even see when his own wife was misbehaving herself, though everyone else in the parish knew it. If there had been a sixth Norwegian in the boat, he would have been the last man in the north isles to spot him. Then he gave me a drink, and asked if I had ever been jealous. "It makes you dream," he said, "but a man shouldn't tell his dreams."

'I like Tórur,' he continued, 'though I wouldn't let him come within a mile of my own wife, if I had one; and I believed him rather than the other fellow. But since then, I admit, he and Bömlo have been behaving a little oddly, and, though I still can't persuade myself they're engaged in dark iniquity, I'm very glad to see you here, and let you carry the ball.'

Bömlo, it appeared, had returned to Tórur's island a day or two after the I.O.'s visit, and someone had noticed that he was carrying a parcel which he handled tenderly and which looked very like two well-wrapped bottles of aquavit or schnapps. Spirits, at that time, were strictly rationed in the Faeroes – or were prohibited? I cannot remember. – But inevitably there was some traffic in them, and everyone had eyes preternaturally sharpened for evidence of their possession. Bömlo, with a shop of his own, with personal privileges and important friends, was known to have sources of supply that his neighbours envied – though his neighbours were often grateful for his generosity – and his movements were well watched.

Then, two days later, Tórur had come to town, stayed twenty-four hours, and when he went north again he had carried a similar parcel.

'How do you know these things?' I asked.

'Children are very observant,' said the I.O. vaguely, 'and we're on good terms with most of the people here. I always join a *krákuting*: a good gossip, that is.'

'Have you searched Tórur's house?'

'Good God, no! We're in the Faeroes as a friendly power, to protect them. The last thing we want to do is to offend anyone. And Tórur's a man of influence. A personality – and a very likable personality. We can't treat him as a criminal, and I don't believe there's any need to. I think he and Bömlo are having a big drunk, and perhaps his neighbour's wife is slipping over to see him again. She's a very pretty woman.'

'I had better go and see Bömlo first,' I said.

'I'm afraid you can't. He was here till yesterday, but I went to his house last night – I didn't mean to tell him you were coming, of course, but I wanted to make sure he was there – and, well, he wasn't. He's off again.'

'With another parcel of aquavit?'

'That I don't know. I haven't had any information yet. But I think you ought to go and see Tórur as soon as you can.'

'I can't go today. I must establish myself as a Welfare Officer first, and I thought I could do that – and do a small but honest job as well – by going to see the gunners at Hoyvík, and that other lot on the other side of the fjord.'

'Yes, that's a good idea. I'll lay on a boat for you, and let them know you're coming. But tomorrow morning . . .'

'I have a date with Tórur.'

'I wish I could come with you, but I must go down to Suduroy. I'll lend you a sergeant who speaks Faeroese as well as I do – and you know Tórur, you know both of them. You'll get on just as well as if I came too.'

He took me into the room that served their Headquarters Mess as an ante-room, where I found a large, benign, and rather elderly major talking to a red-faced young captain who had just walked in from some outlying squadron. – The Lovat Scouts were prodigious walkers, and daily their patrols covered great distances on foot. – We talked for a little while, and drank very good coffee: a Faeroese taste that the Scouts had learnt quickly and gratefully. I looked from the windows at the steel-grey ruffled waters of the sound, and the white hump of Nólsoy beyond, and remembered how, a few months before, in this house, I had been shaving one morning when I heard the noise of an aeroplane, and looking out saw a Dornier turning quickly over the water and machine-gunning a little open fishing-boat. We were not so far from Germany that we could forget the realities of war, though in a room so kindly they were not insistent. I accepted, gladly, an invitation to dine when I returned, and went about my business.

A little model of a viking long-ship – but driven by a petrol engine – carried me to the gunners at Hoyvík and across the fjord. Broad in the beam, double-ended, with a high and lovely sheer and low freeboard, she would have filled the eye with pleasure on a summer day, but the December wind filled my eyes with tears; and when I remember that short voyage I still feel its piercing cold.

The gunners had established themselves in reasonable comfort. They were better off, and more contented, than in June. I had been able to do something to keep them supplied with books and gramophone records, and there were now ladies' guilds, in the Midlands, I think, that sent them socks and mufflers and Balaclava helmets to supplement their army clothing. The young Territorial officers in charge of the detachments were looking after their men, and wanted only carpenters' tools to start classes in boat-building: boredom was their people's most persistent enemy. The men wanted more beer and a quicker delivery of letters. I promised, without much hope of success – except in the matter of tools – to do what I could for them, and on either side of the fjord spent a couple of hours in conversation that ranged from such simple questions as 'Ever been in Huddersfield, sir?' – or Paisley, or Brighton – to the unanswerable demand, 'How much longer's this bloody war going to last?' They were not homesick, they were marvellously patient, but always the flavour of home dwelt lovingly in their minds.

I went back to the trawler, and told Silver where I had to go in the morning. I had decided that I must also tell him why. He knew already that my little task as a Welfare Officer covered some other duty, and I thought it no great breach of confidence to tell him what it was. I needed, moreover, his support. I had hoped for the company of the local I.O. when I went to look for Tórur and Bömlo, and without him I felt a little insecure, a little shy. I had no reason to be afraid, but much cause for shyness. I did not know how to start my interrogation. It would be embarrassing – should I find them both – to ask, 'What have you

been doing lately, and is there any truth in the story that a
sixth man came ashore from the Norwegian boat? If so,
where is he?' – Yet that was what I had to discover, and
with Silver in the background (if not at my side) my task
would be much easier.

Silver listened to my story with a gratifying interest. He
asked some shrewd questions, but his only constructive
suggestion was, 'We must try and see the neighbour's
wife. I like what you tell me of Tórur – I like what you've
told me of both of them – and I do hope Tórur hasn't been
wasting his time with a girl who's not worth his attention.'

He had 'made his number', he said, with the Naval
authorities at Skansin – the little fort which, before the
war, had been a prison – and promised to give them no
trouble. He had borrowed a chart of the northern islands,
and when I showed him where Tórur lived he said, 'I've
always wanted to go there. These ridiculous islands are
merely mountain-tops, and the navigable channels are
mountain-passes. It will be delightful to go hill-walking
in one of His Majesty's trawlers.'

The Sergeant whom the local I.O. had promised me
came aboard soon after seven o'clock next morning and, as
the sluggish remnant of the winter night began to melt and
thin, we set off on our voyage. Sergeant Fergusson was a
small, lean, confident-looking but taciturn man from Fort
William. 'I live and work in the Hielans,' he said, 'but
thank God I'm no a Hielander. I was born in Girvan, and
I'm dependable. I'll do what you tell me and ask no
questions, and that's fair enough, as you'll agree.' I did
agree, and told him how grateful I was for his company.

As an impressionist judgment, Silver's description of
the Faeroes was roughly true. North-east of Streymoy
there are six or seven islands, most of them long, high and
slender, divided by narrow fjords – remarkably like mountain-passes – that run from north-west to south-east. On
either side the hillslopes rise steeply, are often precipitous

to pyramidal crests, and here and there are broken abruptly as though a cheese-scoop had torn out a great round hollow. The hills rise to two thousand feet or more, directly from the sea, and their flanks are lined with braids of basaltic rock, called *hammars*, where in a prehistoric past a flowing lava stopped. Great gullies, or dark chimneys, split their sides, and the snow that covers them in winter is divided by darkly gleaming fissures where the life-defying rock shines through. In such a landscape the smoke that lies above a village, or rises from a lonely farmhouse, is a curiously moving reminder of man's puny but indomitable will.

The smoke above Tórshavn, when we sailed in the ebbing of the dark, was like incense rising from a vulgar but faithful altar – an altar in a wilderness of ocean – and among the northern fjords the blowing peat-reek of a solitary chimney seemed to be the assertion of human hope against geology's excommunication. I did not agree with the assertion – not then – but on either side I was outvoted.

The wind now blew strongly, coming down in black squalls from the hills, and for part of the way a big glaucous gull sailed above us. Silver, on the bridge, found his way through the mountain-passes, and about midday dropped anchor off a newly built concrete jetty that was no more than a couple of miles from Tórur's house: or where, on the chart, I had pinpointed his house. We had a last discussion, and decided that if I needed his help I should send the Sergeant back to the jetty, where his boat would wait. We went ashore, the Sergeant and I, and walked along a rutted road three inches deep in snow.

I was more anxious for the companionship of talk than he, and prodded him into conversation about the Faeroese. 'They're a fine people,' he said, and his voice was gruff; his burly accent seemed to stiffen the reluctance with which – for my benefit only – he delivered so obvious a judgment. 'They're better than we are, in some ways. They're independent, for one thing, and they're clean and tidy, for another. – You're Scotch yourself, are you not?'

'Not only that, but Highland Scotch,' I said.

'Well, if you're born to it,' he said, 'you've just got to make the best of it. But you'll admit, sir, that as a nation we're a dirty, untidy, scruffy lot of bastards! Look at any of our towns and villages, and you can't deny it. We're fully as bad as the English, sir. – You'll have been abroad, I suppose?'

'Once or twice,' I said.

'I've been abroad three times, not counting this,' he said. 'I made good money on civvy street. I'm a fitter by trade, and I shouldna be in the army at all, I ought to be earning twenty pounds a week in munitions, but what the hell! Money's no everything, is it? Well, as I was saying, I've been in Holland and Belgium, in Switzerland, and Denmark and Sweden – twice on bus-tours and once on a cruise – and that was a lesson worth having! All those countries are well swept and sweet and clean: they make you ashamed to be British, they're so clean. But they tell me, sir, that in Switzerland and Sweden the suicide rate is the highest in the world, in spite of cleanliness. And how do you account for that?'

I could not tell him, so asked, 'What's the suicide rate in the Faeroes?'

'It doesn't exist,' he said. 'They live too hard a life to have time for luxuries.'

He made one more observation when, as we passed a ruined cottage, a wren flitted on to a broken wall. 'They call that bird a *músabródir*, which means the brother of a mouse,' he said. 'They're a whimsical lot of people, sir.'

Tórur's house stood at the butt-end of a little rocky peninsula, of which, with a strip of hill-land, he would be the owner when his father died. His father was an *ódals-bóndi*, that is to say a proprietor in his own right, though of small extent; and under *odal* law he had to divide his property among his several children. Tórur had already been given possession of his share, remote from the rest of the little estate, and he made small use of it except to live in the simple house that commanded it, where, when he came ashore from his voyages, he entertained his friends and wrote a simple sort of poetry that was published in the Tórshavn newspaper.

Under its thatch of snow the house, with red-painted walls, had two storeys and a loft. The lower storey was little more than a shed, where, if he owned them, Tórur could shelter a cow or two, and mend his nets, and store farm implements. The main floor was approached by a flight of steps and contained two rooms, the equivalent of a but and ben in Scotland, and above them was a loft where, in time past, there may have been a handloom or a couple of spinning-wheels. There was no stir or sight or mutter of human activity as we approached.

I climbed the steps and knocked at the door. I had to wait a few minutes and then, cautiously, it was opened a little way and I saw the sullen, drink-reddened and sleep-crumpled face of Bömlo. I spoke to him, but he did not recognize me. Then slowly remembrance came, his expression changed from suspicion to a reluctant friendliness, and in a slurred and heavy voice he said, 'Captain Chisholm! Tony, it's Tony! *Vael afturkomin!*'

With a violent gesture he opened wide the door, and in the main room of the house, beyond the kitchen and the little porch where you kicked off your boots, I saw Tórur sitting on an uncomfortable, wooden-ended and wooden-backed sofa. The sofa, a round table with a green velveteen cloth on it, and a big ornamental stove in a corner were the principal pieces of furniture in the room. Against the walls were four or five straight-backed chairs of Victorian appearance, and on the walls a few romantic water-colours, of a Victorian sort; a couple of brilliantly dyed, well-woven rugs lay on the floor. Tórur, dissolutely handsome, was only half awake. He and Bömlo both wore heavy grey fishermen's jerseys, with nondescript trousers, and neither had shaved for a day or two. On the table were glasses and an empty bottle.

Tórur took longer to recognize me. Then he rose, stumbling a little, and in a thick voice said, 'Tony! *Vael afturkomin!* But why do you come here?'

Sergeant Fergusson sat down on one of the straight-backed chairs, and with deliberate ostentation I put on the table the haversack I carried. 'I'm still a Welfare Officer,' I said. 'I spend my time going from place to place, asking the soldiers what they want and telling them they can't have it. That's how we keep them happy. I've been to see the gunners on the Tangafjørdur, and I'm going on to . . .' I told them the names of several places in the north isles, where we had small detachments of artillery and signallers.

'But why do you come here?' said Tórur.

'Just to see you and Bömlo.'

'How did you know he was here?'

'I guessed it. He wasn't in Tórshavn—'

'You are a clever man.'

'When I said goodbye to you, in June, you said we were friends. You told me to come and see you again.'

'Tony,' said Bömlo. 'Captain Chisholm, I mean. I called you Tony last time, because we got drunk together, but now you look like Captain Chisholm. I want to know why you have come here.'

'Take a look in that haversack,' I said. 'In Scotland, about this time of the year, we've an old custom of sitting down to drink with old friends. Open the haversack.'

In the haversack that I had put on the table were three bottles of whisky, wrapt in towels, that the I.O. in Lyness had given me. When Bömlo undid the straps, and took off the towels and saw them, he stood back and looked at them

with the instant glee of a child, given its present from a
Christmas tree. But that simple pleasure deepened, and
became an expression of beatitude that was almost mys-
tical: a saint's expression, confronted by a vision of the
ineffable.

'And we had finished the *brennivín*,' he said. 'We had
drunk it all, not a drop was left. And now – Tórur, Tórur!
Stand up and look.'

Tórur stood, swaying a little, and having bent a poet's
gaze on the bottles – Wordsworth, feeling in his soul a
sense of possible sublimity, could hardly have shown
himself more entranced – said 'Tony! Captain Chisholm!
We called you Tony before, I call you Tony now. We are
brothers, are we not? Why did you not come sooner, much
sooner? – Oh, for God's sake, Bömlo, go and get glasses,
clean glasses, quick!'

He thrust half a dozen clods of peat into the big round
stove, that soon gave out more heat and filled the room
with a moorland scent. We drank our first round ceremo-
niously, standing stiffly and bowing slightly to each other.
I filled their glasses again, and said, 'Help yourselves the
next time. There's plenty of it.' They drank nervously at
first, as if reaching for comfort but doubting it; then
relaxed, grew plumper (as it seemed) and more like themselves. We chatted of island topics, we spoke lightly about
the nonsensical behaviour of the Army and the Royal
Navy. Bömlo with his majestical great face under its thatch
of grizzled hair seemed to become larger and larger as the
room grew hot and, when he rose to fill my glass again, his
limping stride, with its reminder of the first war, stirred a
draught of affection for this foreign man who had fought
on our side.

A little while later, Tórur, standing in a corner of the
room, full glass on high, said, 'Tony, my jung friend! I will
tell you what I said in my great speech in Klakksvík, when
I spoke about the yust aims of us Nationalists, and the

yobs to be done. I was good, I was very good! I won great applowce from a wowciferous owdience. They jeered and jeered.'

Tórur, who had lately been drunk, was getting drunk again: no doubt of that. He had a fine command of English and it was only when he was drunk that he mispronounced it so badly, maltreated his vowels, and came a cropper with the sounds of 'ch' and 'j' and 'y'. But he was a robust drinker, and for many hours a rising degree of drunkenness would disable neither his legs nor his power of speech. He delivered his oration, in English, with considerable spirit, and made its meaning perfectly clear.

The war, he said, would ruin the greater part of western Europe, extinguish its civilization, and utterly destroy its political influence. Until the last act of the tragedy the Faeroese would loyally support Britain and its allies, but at the same time they must think of the future. For they would survive! They and all the old lands of the Norsemen, on the fringes of Europe, would be left intact, and the old Norse power would come to life again. The future of civilization lay in the hands of the sea-coast peoples and the islanders, from Tromsö to Reykjavík, from Tórshavn to Kirkwall and Thurso, to Stornoway and Wexford! And in their hearts they must carry, joyously, the burden of their coming greatness!

It was an excellent speech he made – spoiled only by Sergeant Fergusson's comment, from time to time, of 'Bullshit! Plain bullshit!' – and Bömlo was an audience almost as appreciative as if all the Nationalists of Klakksvík had been there. He blossomed and grew red with pleasure, he stamped and thumped on the floor with his lame leg, and hoarsely cheered.

But I, with yet another drink in my hand, was so bold as to ask, 'And how will you bring all this about?' – I was not drunk, I was very far from that; but with three or four glasses of neat whisky in my stomach (the Faeroese don't believe in diluting their spirits) I was bolder than my ordinary habit.

'We won't need to bring it about,' said Tórur. 'History will do that.'

'Bullshit,' said Sergeant Fergusson.

I drank my whisky at a gulp, and asked, 'Who has given you the idea that history is on your side? Did the man who came ashore from the Norwegian boat tell you that?'

Their look of half-drunken ease and pleasure was suddenly spoiled as if a black squall had come down from the hills and ruffled smooth water. Their faces grew hard and rough, their eyes narrowed, their hands and arms were tense.

'Who told you a man came ashore?' asked Bömlo.

'It was gossip I heard in Tórshavn. At a *krákuting*, don't you call it? Just gossip.'

'It was Jákup told you,' said Tórur. – Jákup was his neighbour, whose wife he had seduced. – 'Jákup believes in the *huldufólk*, Jákup saw a *grýla* come ashore.'

Both of them, leaning forward in their chairs, stared at me with fierce and hostile eyes. 'What does *grýla* mean?' I asked the Sergeant.

'It's a sort of bogle, sir. Or maybe a bogeyman is what the English would call it. It looks like a sheep with two legs. And commonly it bides in the hills with the other *huldufólk*.'

'Well, if it was a *grýla* that came out of the boat, where did it go? Is it living here now?'

I stood up, and with a fine affectation of ease – but it was whisky that gave me courage – I opened the second bottle and said, 'Another *pisa*, Tórur?'

Both he and Bömlo held out their glasses. For a little while – perhaps a minute, perhaps more – there was silence; and then Bömlo, with as it seemed a more ponderous reliance on his lame leg, stood up and coming

towards me laid a thick, black-nailed forefinger on the
white and purple ribbon on my tunic. 'Tell us,' he said,
'how you won your medal, Tony.'

'I'll be damned if I do,' I answered.

'You have told us once before.'

'When you made me drunk.'

'Tell us again,' said Tórur, 'and perhaps I will tell you
about the *grýla*.'

In the train, on my way north from London to Edinburgh, when I had staggered through the crowded corridor into the lavatory, and been sick, I had considered
for a little while tearing the ribbon of the Military Cross
from my tunic and throwing it into the pan with my
vomit. Nothing but inertia, I think, had stopped me
doing that. I was half a fraud, and I knew it, but I
had not the strength of mind to strip myself of fraudu-
lence and stand before the world, thin, transparent, and
without value. And now, remembering that failure and
being suddenly filled with a weak and foolish anger –
against myself, and against these men who had awakened
an emotion so useless – I exclaimed (and I heard the
shrillness of my voice), 'Very well, if you want to hear an
ugly story, here it is.

'I was given a medal because I was a coward. I'd been
told that I had "permission to retire", and I was so God-
damned frightened that I couldn't move. There were two
German tanks looking down their guns at me as if I were a
flounder in shallow water – a flounder on a sandy shore,
under clear water – and they were going to spear me. I
couldn't move! Then one of them fell into a cutting, arse-
over-tip, and the other panicked, and turned away. So I
found my nerve again, and my half-company held on for
another couple of hours. That was useful, that gave us
valuable time, but I was wounded. Splinter in the chest,
not serious. Then we got to Dunkirk, I can't remember
when. And I didn't go aboard with my own people,

because I was ashamed. I stayed on the beach to try and expiate my bloody cowardice. It was my only chance to regain a scrap of self-respect. And I couldn't even do that, because I collapsed after three or four days and was dumped into a bloody little pleasure-boat as if I was a drunken tripper. And when my M.C. was gazetted I was still too much of a coward to tell the truth and refuse it. – And that's the story of my medal.'

I was, I believe, a little more affected by whisky (and perhaps the heat of the room) than, at the time, I supposed. For now I remember my words with some embarrassment. At the time I thought them true, but I was in too emotional a state to be objective, and now I admit their dishonesty. I was secretly pleased with myself – pleased, that is, with the discipline that had let me recover from a moment of panic which might have earned me, as it earned Peter, a bullet in the back – though in the bitterness of youth I still deplored and abominated my innate tendency to fear; and that measure of self-contempt took control and wagged my disingenuous tongue.

But my tongue, however dishonestly, did its work. Sergeant Fergusson said approvingly, 'A very interesting story!' and Bömlo and Tórur, who had heard it before, listened with close attention, with a sentimental gravity, and drained their glasses.

'You are a good man, Tony,' said Bömlo.

'He is a brave man,' said Tórur. 'To be frightened is natural, but to behave well after you have been fearful, that is brave. And I think he is our friend, Bömlo.'

I report their words, their emotions, only because of their effect on the situation. Tórur stood up and, fetching his breath with a sigh that deepened to a groan, said, 'Let us show him, Bömlo.'

'Yes, I think so,' Bömlo answered. 'Now we do not know what to do, and perhaps he will tell us.'

'Come,' said Tórur, and led us into the porch, where we

put on our boots and then went round to the back of the house. It was still light, but the light had the yellowish, autumn hue that foretold the dark.

Behind or beside the Faeroese farmhouse there usually stands a small building called a *hjallur*, the walls of which consist of narrow wooden planks with gaps between them, so that the wind may blow through. It is used as a curing-house for dried fish and mutton. It was to the *hjallur* that Tórur led us.

The door was locked with the old-fashioned Faeroese wooden lock, and Tórur fumbled with it, and was slow. Then he held the door wide open, and beckoned me to go in. I could not, at first, understand what I saw. For there, in the shadow of the roof but dimly lighted by the yellow glow of early evening, there seemed to be a man waiting to receive me. A man seated in a chair of a Victorian sort, such as I had seen in Tórur's ben-room. But he did not move as I went in and, when I was near enough to see his face clearly, I was appalled by its frozen grimace. A face white as dough, but hard as bone and slightly glistening; and writhen with hate or agony.

Foolishly, and hearing my folly in the tremor of my voice, I said, 'But he's dead.'

'Yes,' said Tórur. 'That is what we found this morning.'

'Who is he?' I asked.

'The *grýla*,' said Bömlo.

Sergeant Fergusson came in and in a business-like way examined the corpse and demanded, 'Who tied him to the chair, and why? And who took his boots off?'

I saw then that his feet, on the cold ground, wore only grey woollen socks, and that his arms and body were bound to the back of the chair. He wore a high-necked, navy-blue jersey, and in his pale, short-cropped hair a little frost reflected the evening light. His eyes were open and appeared to be frozen. His mouth gaped, and the left side of his jaw was bruised and swollen. He was a man in his middle thirties, and had been, when alive, not ill-looking.

'Is this the man who came ashore?' I asked.

'We will tell you all about him,' said Bömlo. 'And then, Tony, you must tell us what to do.'

Tórur locked the door of the *hjallur* again and we went back to the house. Sergeant Fergusson whispered to me, 'Would you like me to fetch Lieutenant Silver, sir? Three heads are better than two, if we're going to escape trouble.'

'Yes,' I said. 'Tell him to come at once – and come alone.'

I followed Tórur and Bömlo up the steps, and Fergusson, quick-stepping, went back to the jetty. Neither Tórur nor Bömlo seemed to notice he had gone – they had paid very little attention to him – and in the warm room Bömlo filled our glasses again as if it were a necessary rite of which he had grown weary.

I felt within me a chill of nausea that the whisky did little to dispel, and Bömlo, on the uncomfortable sofa, looked sad and sober. Both, indeed, now appeared to be quite sober, and Tórur seemed bereft and mournful.

Sadly and gently I asked, 'Did you murder him?'

'No, I do not think so,' said Tórur. 'But he was a bad man. He deceived us! We thought he was a good man at first, and then it turned out that he was bad. Oh, God, how bad! He tried to buy my soul.'

A good deal of the second bottle had been drunk before I disentangled the truth of what had happened; and I, upon oath, had only a single glass after seeing the body. – The dead man, the frozen man, was indeed the sixth man who had come ashore, and he had persuaded Tórur to hide and shelter him with a story that he was the personal emissary of Vidkun Quisling, charged with a mission of high importance. He had sworn that he was no enemy to Britain.

So Tórur said. So Bömlo, nodding heavily, agreed.

'But Quisling,' I said, 'is Hitler's deputy in Norway. How can one of his people say he is no enemy?'

'Tony,' said Tórur, 'you live in the north of Scotland, in the Highlands. You are like one of us. It does not matter what this man said, or what Quisling says. You and I are brothers.'

'What did he want you to do?'

'First of all,' said Bömlo, 'you must hear what he said. About Quisling, about Hitler, about us.'

Put briefly, the man's message was the substance of Tórur's speech about the great destiny of the Atlantic islands and the sea-going races of Norse descent. Quisling, he maintained, had come to the conclusion that neither Hitler nor Germany would survive the war. Quisling was now out of favour with Hitler – it was true, at that time – and the reason was that he had been talking too freely. Germany and Russia would consume each other: so he had said. France was already defeated and could never recover, and Britain, shattered by air attack and rotted from within by moral decay – Törur was apologetic about this – would presently collapse like the wicked civilizations of Mesopotamia. Then the peoples of the seaboard, descendants of the vikings, would come into their own again, and from their dominating shores rule all the western world.

It was the Nordic myth again, but translated from its Teutonic origin to people who, if they thought it worth their while, could more legitimately claim descent from viking stock. I, who call myself a Highland Scot but know how the last three hundred years have mixed my blood, have little faith in claims of racial purity, but considerable respect for small communities, such as those in Iceland and the Faeroes, where belief in it is apparently a source of confidence. I respect their emotions, that is, and I found no difficulty in believing Tórur's assertion that he and Bömlo had been deeply stirred by the Norwegian's eloquence.

He had called himself, very discreetly, Jón Jónsson, and sensibly had stiffened his rhetoric with hard, commercial facts. He reminded them that Norway, with its scanty population, had covered the oceans of the world with its ships: with 5,000,000 tons of merchant shipping. And Quisling, he said, was a very clever man. Cleverer than Hitler. And because he knew he would outlive Hitler he wanted now to establish his agents and his chain of command across the frontiers of the Atlantic.

Jón Jónsson had both inspired and entertained them. He had flattered their aspirations, admired the fertility of their islands: a population growing from six or seven thousand to thirty thousand in a hundred years was a fine example of Norse virility. He had fortified faith in their economic future with well-memorized figures of Norway's natural wealth of forests and fisheries, of molybdenum – what he said about molybdenum had deeply impressed them – and sulphur pyrites. Molybdenum and racial destiny were a heady mixture, and the persuasive Jónsson had insisted, again and again, that collaboration would entail no hostility to Britain.

'We made him drunk,' said Bömlo pathetically, 'and still he told us the same thing. Vidkun, he said, was no enemy of Britain, but Vidkun would like us to give him information, because the more he knew, the better he could play his cards against Hitler. Hitler, he said, was quite an ignorant man. He knew nothing about molybdenum, for one thing, till Vidkun told him what it was. And Hitler, he said, had never been to sea. That made us laugh! For how can anyone be a great man who has never been to sea?'

'Jónsson wanted you to supply information: was that all?' I asked.

'But not information for Hitler. Only for Vidkun Quisling.'

'What did he say about the boat? What happened to them, and why had they no food?'

'The weather was too rough. The engine broke down, and they were driven too far north. They were fourteen days at sea, and the two young men died.'

'There was a man who died of a fractured skull,' I said. 'Did he explain how that happened?'

'It was the man who went mad who killed him. So Jónsson told us. There was a boat-hook, broken in two, and the madman with one piece of it hit him on the head.'

'Do you believe that?'

'I do not know,' said Tórur glumly. 'Now I do not know what to think.'

'But why did you quarrel with Jónsson?'

'God in high heaven!' exclaimed Bömlo. 'Who would not have quarrelled? Tell him, Tórur. Tell him quick.'

'Night after night we listened to him,' said Tórur. 'It was very interesting, what he said, and Bömlo brought much *brennivin*. We liked him, for quite a lot of days, and we understood why we must not tell about him. Why we must be secret that he is here with us. But then he said, "Now I must go to Shetland. There is a man there I have to see. A man of much importance. Quisling said I must see him, he is an old friend of his. So how can you send me to Shetland without any people knowing?"

'Well, we say, that is difficult. Very difficult. And he says it does not matter about money.'

'But it did,' said Bömlo.

'Yes, by God! For when I say it is difficult, he gives me forty pounds in English money, and ask, "Is that enough?" Then I look surprised, and he say sixty. And I am thunder-struck, I look thunder-struck, and he say a hundred. "Send me to Shetland, with no one knowing, and here is a hundred pounds," he say, "and now you are rich man." So then I hit him on the jaw, the dirty bugger! He would bribe me, he would make me a spy! It is only spies who take money, and I am good Faeroe Nationalist. So I smash him on the jaw, and Bömlo is here, and we say, "Let us take him to the *hjallur* so he can cool his mind." We tie him to a chair, and carry him to the *hjallur*, and leave him there. – That was last night. – Then we began to drink, and because Bömlo has brought much *brennivín*, and we are very angry, we drink too long, and become drunk. And so we forget all about Jón Jónsson. And when we go out in the morning, this morning, we find him dead in the *hjallur*, and frozen hard like a sheep who has died in the snow. Like a *grýla*! And now you have seen him, Tony, and what are we to do?'

What I have written here in a few hundred words took, in telling of it, more than an hour; and the latter part of the tale was told to the wild tune of an increasing gale that spilled between the hillsides and howled above the house. I hate the sight of a corpse (I have a squeamish stomach) but I could not deplore Jónsson's death, and I must admit that my heart beat like a drum, when the drums beat a salute, as Tórur told me how he, who had so warmly, if foolishly, responded to an evocation of pride, answered immediately the invitation of bribery with a right-handed punch to the mean man's jaw. – For that was the essential difference, the proper cause of hostility: that one was mean, a buyer of men and their ideals, who thought truth and loyalty worth no more than a hundred pounds, and the other, though not very wise, was starkly honest and generous enough to pay for belief with his life.

I stood up and took Tórur by the shoulders – this I am not ashamed of – and said, 'I have lost my own brother, and I need someone in his place. If you still call yourself my brother, I am very proud.' – And then the normal sobriety of my temper spoiled a momentary enthusiasm, and peevishly I added, 'But it was damned silly of you to let the fellow freeze to death.'

'Yes,' said Bömlo, 'and what are we going to do with him? We cannot go away and leave Jónsson in the *hjallur*, and the ground is so hard we cannot make a grave and put him out of sight.'

Then, through the noise of the wind, we heard loud knocking at the door, and I went across the kitchen and opened it to Silver and Sergeant Fergusson. They threw off their boots and duffle coats, and stocking-footed came into the *daglistova*, where I introduced Silver as my friend, and said he had come to help us in our difficulty. They welcomed him the more readily because he was a sailor, but they were now of a mood to welcome assistance wherever it came from.

I gave Silver a drink, and said, 'I'll tell you the story as briefly as I can.' – I knew that if I left it to Tórur it would last another hour. – So I told him there was a corpse in the *hjallur*, who had been the sixth man in the boat from Norway, and how, after posing as a friend of Faeroe Nationalism, he tried to bribe Tórur to send him secretly to Shetland, where, according to his tale, he had to make contact with someone of importance to his purpose.

Here Tórur interrupted: 'Someone who is a good friend of Vidkun.'

'Who is Vidkun?' asked Silver.

'Vidkun? Why, Vidkun Quisling. Who else?'

'I didn't know that was his name,' said Silver. 'I never heard his Christian name before.' – He turned to me and asked, 'Did you know it?'

'I think so,' I said. 'I've never, until now, heard him referred to, in a familiar way, as Vidkun. But I'm sure – I'm almost sure – that I've seen his name in print.'

'I haven't,' said Silver and, standing up, poured himself another glass of whisky.

'Does it matter?' I asked.

'It does indeed. It means that I know the man your corpse wanted to see in Shetland.'

He had become preternaturally grave. He looked from one to another of us, with impatient inquiry, and then, dismissing a faint hope that we could tell him anything more, he seemed to forget us. Head bent and hands behind his back, he stood in silent thought, reluctant to admit his thought. Then with a little grimace, as of one who wakes with sourness in his mouth, he shrugged his shoulders and said, quietly and bitterly, ' "The ghost of Roger Casement is beating at the door." '

'What does that mean?'

'I think the explanation will have to wait. I want to look at the corpse.'

It was dark now, but Silver had an electric torch, and in its sharp, dry light the body in the chair showed a sinister unreality. A strong unlikeness, I mean, to the humanity it had lately shared with Bömlo and Tórur. It was more sculpture now — the word made frozen dough — but the eyeballs glittered — and shadows played on its immobile face as if the artist had not yet decided his meaning: decided the last expression he meant to leave. — The cold struck through my ribs, the big scarred wound on my right breast began to ache, and a wind from the hills raised a howl from the roof and a flurry of dry snow at our feet.

But Silver was calm and objective, precise and assured. 'He's perfectly preserved,' he said, 'and easily recognizable, if we can find anyone who knew him. Are there any marks on him?'

'Marks?' asked Bömlo, mystified.

'Anything to identify him: old scars, or tattooing.'

'I don't know,' said Bömlo.

'You haven't looked? Well, what about his clothes? What else was he wearing?'

'A coat, and boots, and oilskin.'

'Anything in his pockets? Any documents?'

'How should I know?'

'I would know by now, if I were you. But perhaps it's just as well that you haven't interfered with him. — We'll take him with us, Chisholm. The body, and all his possessions. We'll take him straight to Lyness, and hand him over to the I.O. there. It's quite possible they can find someone to identify him.'

'But we can't do that without permission from Force Headquarters, and your Naval people at Skansin—'

'My dear fellow, the last thing they want is an unknown corpse on their doorstep! Think of the difficulties it would create. Endless signalling, courts of inquiry, interrogation, all their daily drill and routine interrupted while they ask each other, and every authority in the kingdom, what to do with an unknown stiff who used to be an enemy agent and is now melting in their hands. Talk about a whore at a wedding! By God, this corpse would be worse than that if you took it to Tórshavn. But take it to Lyness, and there it's evidence – and they can bring the man from Shetland down to tell them its name.'

He turned to Bömlo and asked, 'You don't want to keep him, do you?'

'No, by God!' said Bömlo.

Silver felt, approvingly, the frozen hardness of the body, and said, 'The weather isn't quite as cold as it was, but it's cold enough. The temperature's still below freezing-point. We'll keep him on deck, and he'll be all right. But first of all I want to hear the story again. I want to hear it in detail.'

We went back to the house, and Sergeant Fergusson said admiringly, 'There's a man who knows his own mind, sir!' – I acknowledged the implied rebuke, and admitted, too, that I was disposed to fall in with Silver's plan. As if I were myself a murderer, I had been embarrassed by the body and the problem of its disposal. My only positive feeling was a resolute desire to save Bömlo and Tórur from punishment. And if the body of Jón Jónsson were taken to Scapa and identified as that of an enemy agent, there was small likelihood that they would have to face any serious charge.

In the over-heated room, with its stiff, uncomfortable furniture, I listened again while Tórur repeated his story, and on the walls the primly framed, little Victorian pictures – paintings of waterfalls, pink roses, and blue hills – appeared to dissociate themselves, with a shrinking disapproval, from a tale so rough and perplexing. The wind, for a little while, fell still, and a half-curtained window let moonlight in, that was like a primrose-glow against the buttercup light of the oil lamp on the table: on the green velveteen cover of the table, where glasses and a bottle of whisky stood.

In the lull of the wind we heard a knock at the door – a light *tocketty tock, tocketty tock* – the victory tune that was popular then – and Tórur, looking embarrassed, got up and went out. We waited for five minutes or so, and when he came back he said gruffly, 'When you go to Scapa, I will come with you, if you please. I am tired of living here, I am a strong man, very strong, and I would like to join commandos. You will take me with you, Mr. Silver, please?'

'Very willingly,' said Silver. 'I was going to ask you to come. You'll be a great help.'

'Was that Ragnhild?' asked Bömlo.

'Yes,' said Tórur. 'Jákup is away tonight, so she comes here. But I told her to go home again. I said young women who go to a man's house late at night will get a bad name in the neighbourhood. She's very nice girl but you can have too much of nice girls.'

'I'm sorry I didn't see her,' said Silver. 'But that can't be helped now – and you were telling us that Jónsson insisted on going to Shetland?'

Tórur finished his story, and Silver said, 'That seems perfectly clear, and I don't think you need worry too much about the consequences. But how are we going to get Jón Jónsson to my ship?'

'There is a sledge,' said Bömlo.

'I will go and pack my clothes,' said Tórur.

We could not, we discovered, remove the body from the chair. The seat of its trousers was frozen fast to the wood, and when we tried to separate them the cloth ripped loudly. So we laid chair and body together on the open sledge – it was no more than a couple of broad planks on runners – and covered them with a piece of canvas; and Tórur's suitcase was stowed behind. Over the rutted, snow-clad road we dragged it for two miles in the darkness, seeing no one, to the new-made, concrete jetty where the trawler's boat obediently waited, its crew tramping up and down or beating their arms to defeat the cold. The wind was howling a lunatic song among the hills again, and the moon had gone.

Still in its chair, and under its canvas hood, we carried the stiff body of Jón Jónsson into the boat, and I said goodbye to Bömlo and Sergeant Fergusson.

'Tell the whole story to Captain X when you get back to Tórshavn,' I said. 'There's nothing to conceal. We are going to Lyness, and we'll tell Naval Headquarters at Skansin when we sail. We're not evading the authorities here, we're only trying to save them trouble. Tell Captain X that I'll write to him, privately, and he'll get a full official account, as soon as possible, from the Naval I.O. at Lyness. Give him my regards, and ask him to apologize to the Mess President for my failure to accept an invitation to dinner. You two will have to go back to Tórur's house and spend the night there. But you'll be comfortable enough, there's plenty of whisky left.'

I shook hands with them, and oddly felt the pain of parting. Bömlo's eyes were wet – I could see his tears in the darkness and smell the whisky on his breath – and hoarsely he exclaimed, 'But you will come again? You have saved our lives, perhaps – and you will come back?'

'Perhaps,' I said, and Sergeant Fergusson walked with me to the boat. He had behaved very well, and with whisky at his elbow had shown his admirable temperance. But he had drunk his share, and now, at the last moment, he betrayed for the first time a little emotion. 'When you write your report, sir,' he said, 'will you be sure and spell my name with a double "s"? You'll have noticed there are two ways of spelling it, and maybe you'll have seen for yourself that some of those who spell it with a single "s" aren't always the clean potato, sir. There's some of them I wouldn't associate with on a desert island. You understand, sir, don't you? It's a matter of family pride.'

I understood, and told him so. I know my fellow Scots, and in some ways they are very like the Faeroese. They are capable of being superbly obsessed by ideas that the rest of the world must always regard as trivial.

'Come along!' cried Silver. 'We can't wait all night for you.'

'Thank you very much for your help, Sergeant,' I said, 'and I shan't forget your double "s".'

'It's been an interesting occasion, sir,' he said, and clapping his heels together, saluted firmly in the iron darkness.

CHAPTER SIX

IN THE LITTLE sitting-room of Tórur's house, the *daglistova* with its gentle water-colours on the papered walls, I had recognized in Silver the natural *régisseur* of the drama and the persons among whom he had been thrown. I had realized why his own cabin, decorated with designs by Bakst and Goncharova, revealed his enthusiasm for the ballet: it was not the obvious, quickly appreciated beauty of the dancers that attracted him, nor elaborate and fantastic scenery, but the workmanship behind the spectacle – the devising, the planning, the choreographer's exquisite and muscular duty to arrange the flux and reflux of lithe and decorated bodies, the moment of sculptured stillness, the tension, the reiterated surge of movement and a solo dancer's arresting, spectacular leap in the air – all this in alliance with the development of a story, the demands of a composer. I, who had begun the present action, had quickly dwindled into the obscurity of a walking gentleman; but Silver, as soon as he perceived the stage, had become the choreographer, or *régisseur*, of a performance far beyond my power to invent or control. He had determined a course of action, the parts we were to play, the *tempo* of the music (loudly the wind was orchestrating his theme), and reorganized the production in obedience to his own dramatic vision. The frozen body of Jón Jónsson stood in the midst, like a concentration of the wilful death of the world, against which we were arrayed.

I did not resent his assumption of authority. I welcomed and was glad of it. I have always wanted a leader – a man to say 'Do this' or an idea to compel my action with the authority of tradition – and when Silver took command he did it with such easy competence that almost immediately I fell into the position where I was told to go. I thought his plan outrageous, and accepted it. I yielded willingly to discipline – formally he, as a lieutenant in the R.N.V.R., was superior to me as a temporary captain in the Army – and as if it were a sunlit morning on the parade-ground at Sandhurst I 'fell in on my marker' and was absurdly pleased to have him on my right hand.

Aboard his trawler he showed an undeviating sense of command. – Of command not only over an acquiescent crew, but of the situation. – The boat was secured amidships on deck, aft of the bridge, and in it he had the corpse of Jón Jónsson, still frozen to its chair, laid on its side, insinuated between the thwarts, made fast and covered with a tightly lashed canvas. 'He'll be all right there,' he said, 'and if he gets a little wet, he won't feel it.'

Then from his chart-room he made signals to Skansin, to Force Headquarters at Tórshavn, and to Lyness. He requested permission to sail, and asked for an approved course. He declared that I had completed my mission and was now in possession of information that demanded my immediate return to Scapa. He was formally deferential, intrinsically exigent. He said nothing of the corpse, secured to the floor of his dinghy – or whaler, or whatever it may have been – but so charged his signals with the sense of a *corpus delicti* that authority was compelled to approve my speedy report on it. He told no more than he wanted to tell, and got his own way. And when his way was made clear, for the action he contemplated, we went below to his cabin – the cabin where I slept – and his steward brought us a cold supper of American ham, and whisky and soda.

'Bless the Faeroese!' he said. 'I love and admire them, but after a while I grow tired of a diet of dried mutton, boiled puffins, and undiluted alcohol. – I like my whisky drowned in half a pint of soda-water – and what have you had to eat all day, except *skerpigkjøt*?'

'A lot to drink,' I said, 'but nothing to eat except *skerpigkjøt*.'

Skerpigkjøt is mutton, dried for a long time in the *hjallur*, and eaten raw. You use your own knife, and cut it from the joint. It is blood-red in colour, it has the consistency of toffee, and undeniably it is sustaining and nutritious. To the Faeroe man it is a delicacy, a delight; but the foreigner eats it under a certain discipline, he must hold his nose against its horrible smell, and grow accustomed to its sticky deliquescence in the mouth. – I could do all that, and I admitted that *skerpigkjøt* was an excellent food. – Tórur had given us a splendidly rose-red and odorous joint of it. – But I didn't really like it. I preferred American ham, and whisky diluted, as Silver said, in half a pint of soda-water.

Soon I felt easier – I could listen to the raving wind unmoved – and I asked him, 'What part does Roger Casement play?'

'How much do you remember about him?'

'The essentials, I think; and I know Yeats's poem. – Casement was hanged in 1916 for running guns from Germany into Ireland. I've always thought it a damned shame.'

'It was,' said Silver. 'Casement was a gentleman, and ought to have been shot.'

'I agree with you,' I said. 'He wasn't a criminal, he was an enemy. And if our moral standards can't show the difference between one and the other, our moral standards need revision.'

'Moral standards have usually been odious,' said Silver. 'The only agreeable standards are the standards of propriety, of fitness. Casement and a bullet would have been congruous; but Casement and a rope were incongruous and horrible. And perhaps, in consequence of that, the ghost of Roger Casement is still a menace.'

'There is a ghost?'

'I have a tolerable command of my emotions,' said Silver, 'but you may have noticed that when Tórur spoke of Vidkun Quisling – when he spoke of him as Vidkun – I showed a flicker of surprise. Even, perhaps, of a startled interest. It took me back, that name, to a day in 1938, the summer before Munich, when I was serving as sailing-master to a friend who had a yacht, of some considerable size, that he was racing against Norwegian yachts in the Oslo fjord. – I have never been rich myself, but I've always been so fortunate as to have rich friends. They give you the privilege of wealth, and save you the responsibility of looking after it. – Well, one day between races we were sitting in an hotel near Oslo – it was raining, I think – and a Norwegian friend said to another Norwegian – they were both of the sort that knew everyone, and treated the Crown Prince (as I thought) with an excessively democratic familiarity – he said, pointing to a nearby table, "There's Vidkun with his English friend." The name Vidkun meant nothing to me, but the Norwegians chattered away about him, and naturally I had a look at the fellow they were talking about. And, of course, at the Englishman he was sitting with. A rather outmoded type of Englishman, I thought. Something like a picture of a hero of the Indian Mutiny. I didn't pay much attention to him, however, because at that moment we were joined by a tall, sunburnt, silver-gilt, long-legged girl with a dreaming eye – blue eyes full of the interminable northern light, and perhaps a little dazed with gin. She occupied my attention, thereafter, to the entire exclusion of Vidkun and his friend from the Indian Mutiny.

'But you mustn't think me frivolous: I really am not. I take my fun where I find it, but I pay my debts. Since the war began I haven't been south of latitude fifty-eight, except for ten days' leave, and that's no life for a hedonist. – Well, three or four months ago I was knocking about the west coast of Shetland. I had been taking up some moorings for the Fleet Air Arm at Sullom Voe, and doing odd jobs here and there. And one day I went in to Scalloway, to buy some eggs. – You've got to keep your people happy, you know that, and a contented belly's the first step to happiness, from mess-deck to Cabinet level. – I hauled in alongside the fishing pier and, while my steward and a couple of volunteers went ashore with baskets, I found a small hotel and asked for tea.

'I was given a dismal little plate of elderly biscuits in a room decorated with stuffed sea-gulls and enlarged photographs of very black cliffs, and I settled down to read a pre-war copy of *The Field*. Then the door was thrown open, and in came a tall, massive old fellow in Edwardian knickerbockers, a deerstalker cap, a rather ragged tweed jacket, and a Fair Isle jersey. He was carrying one of those long Highland walking-sticks, and first he thumped on the floor for attention, and then, when no one came, he walked across a corridor to a door marked Private, and banged on it. "The ghost of Roger Casement is beating on the door!" he shouted; and the door opened, an elderly, untidy woman came out, and said nervously, "Oh, Mr. Wishart! What is it you're wanting?"

' "A lot of toast, two soft-boiled eggs, and a large brandy and soda," said the old boy. "I've walked all the way from Weddergarth, and I've got to walk back."

' "I'll see to it myself, Mr. Wishart," said the woman, "and I'm sorry you've been kept waiting. But you know how difficult things are nowadays . . ." And so on and so forth. But in five minutes' time he got his toast, his brandy and soda – this out of hours, you'll note – and not a glance did he give me, not a word passed between us. I didn't exist, so far as he was concerned; and normally, as you may have noticed, the uniform I wear invites free and easy conversation from one and all.

'Well, I looked at him – I looked at him very closely

when he was too busy with his eggs to be aware of inspection – and all the time I thought I had seen him somewhere before. But I couldn't remember where or when. The sunburnt, silver-gilt girl with the dream in her eyes had come between us when I first saw him, and expelled him from my conscious mind. It wasn't till your friend Tórur spoke of Quisling as Vidkun that I remembered the hotel near Oslo. Vidkun was the word that did it, and Oslo was where I had seen him before. The people I was with, the Norwegians, had said, "Look at Vidkun and his English friend." And there was his friend, though I didn't know it at the time, eating boiled eggs and drinking brandy and soda in Scalloway!'

'Did you learn anything about him?'

'I asked who he was, and discovered where he lived. His name's Mungo Wishart, and he lives in a big house called Weddergarth on the west coast; a rather inaccessible place except from the sea. There's deep water and a good anchorage immediately below the house. He owns several thousand acres, most of them unproductive, and his active life he spent abroad: in, I think, the Consular Service. He's married, and there's something slightly odd about his marriage; but I don't know what. He has a local reputation for eccentricity, bad temper, and a solitary habit. – That's all I know of him, but I had no particular reason to inquire more deeply. If you want the truth of it, it was only because I was piqued by the cold and splendid way in which he ignored me that I took the trouble to find out as much as I did.'

'The pique went under your skin,' I said.

'I carry an overload of humanity. I talk to strangers. I'm interested in perhaps two out of every five people I meet, I know the family circumstances and infidelities of every man aboard. – I should hate to serve in a big ship, where that would be impossible. – And, of course I enjoy managing people.'

'You like to manage events, too. There's no valid reason for connecting the corpse of Jón Jónsson with your man in Scalloway – even if, which isn't certain, you're right in thinking he was the Englishman you saw with Quisling in Oslo.'

'But I'm sure of that. The two pictures, the two scenes, came together like the focusing of a spectroscope when I heard the name Vidkun. – And there's every reason to suppose Wishart is the man our corpse was going to visit. How many friends do you think Quisling has in Shetland?'

'You may be right.'

'They told me he was eccentric – and that's the essential quality in a friend of Quisling's.'

'So we'll go to Lyness, and you'll persuade him to come and submit to questioning?'

'That was my first idea, but it isn't good enough. It isn't strong enough. We'll have to contrive something more positive. Whether you like it or not, we're involved in drama, and drama requires a dénouement appropriate to the action.'

He was deeply and entirely serious, but the plan he proposed was blatantly theatrical. As theatrical as the play-within-a-play that Hamlet devises to unmask his father's murderer. And I rebelled at once; or, at least, protested. I told him it was impossible. To my mind, conventional both by instinct and training, it did indeed appear unthinkable to do what he suggested: to use a ship of the Royal Navy (even a trawler) on a private exercise, and take responsibility into our own hands. I grew a little angry with him, for I was genuinely alarmed; but also I was envious of him. I found it hard to bear the enjoyment he got from a stage where death sat plainly in the middle, and treason, it seemed, was waiting in the wings. We were at war, and war, if one was lucky – patient and very lucky – war could be endured. But no one should take out a licence to enjoy it.

He listened quietly to my argument. He stood, with hardly a movement, leaning against the door of the clear-lighted, small cabin, its walls so brilliantly decorated, and his dark eyes mocked me, his lean cheeks took the light like apples in an old-fashioned orchard. I could almost feel my words dropping, as if they were blobs of wet paper, at his feet. Nothing I said affected him. 'It's monstrous,' I complained, 'to try and make a game of this. To set a trap, and bait it with a dead man. As if it were a play—'

' "The play's the thing," ' he said, 'wherein I'll catch the conscience of – Mungo Wishart.'

'I've already thought of that. But we're not playing *Hamlet*.'

'In a sense, we are always playing *Hamlet*. The native hue of resolution and the pale cast of thought are perpetually at odds – and now, for a little while, let's wear our proper colours.'

'You'll come to grief, and have to strike them.'

'Listen to that!'

As if reinforced by some horrid chorus from the deep Atlantic, the wind came swooping down and yelled in the fury of a hooligan multitude through the fjord. – 'The weather,' said Silver, 'is getting worse, and that will make our plan more plausible. The Shetlands are a good deal nearer than Scapa Flow, and if our Mr. Finch finds some fault or failure in his engines – I shall tell him when to report it – our proper course, in dangerously bad weather, will be to find shelter and effect repairs. There's perfect shelter in the Voe of Hammar, and a good anchorage not far from Mungo Wishart's house; and while we're un-avoidably delayed there, we'll ask him to come aboard and drink a glass of gin or sherry with us.'

'He will probably refuse.'

'Have you no gift of persuasion? Between us, I'm sure we can woo him. Or almost sure. And if we fail, we shall have to take the mountain to Mahomet – and then, "if he but blench, I know my course".'

'If he's innocent, if he's harmless – Wishart, I mean – we'll be in serious trouble. We'll have to face court-martial—'

'Don't be pedantic. Use the language of our time and say, "If we put up a black" we'll "get a rocket". – But what's a departmental rocket in war? Their Lordships can't send me to a more uncomfortable station than this, but you, if you're fit, may get a posting to the Western Desert. Would that worry you?'

'I want to go back to my regiment as soon as I can.'

'Then you're practically invulnerable, and we'll drink another whisky and soda before going to bed. What a horrid noise the wind's making!'

The gale that filled the fjord with its abominable chorus was, however, only a local prelude to the storm that awaited us. The Faeroes breed their own weather – fog in summer, wind in winter – as well as gather about their peaks the clouds and tempests of the open sea. The wind in the fjord fell still before morning, and we sailed in a sombre calm. But before we parted company with the islands the first freshets of a gale from the south-east were blowing.

They tore the snow from the pyramid-steep hills, filling the nearer air with a drifting pallor – through which stark cliffs glared blackly against the wind – and above the driven snow a moving continent of clouds came marching with a terrible weight and purpose. The sea was still calm, but recurrent squalls opened savagely shaken fans on its dark surface, and the shores of the tall islands were hung with a ragged flounce of spray. It was a land of wild and desolate aspect that we were leaving – and with what reluctance I watched it diminish! For ahead of us lay a wilder desolation.

For an hour or so the trawler's movement was easy enough, but gradually its small and playful rolling became a progress in which we rose and fell with ponderous deliberation. Gravely the well-flared bow came up, and with unhurried gravity descended into a trough of the waves. This movement continued for another hour – two hours, perhaps – and by a change of imperceptible growth turned into a worried, even nervous motion. Now waves rose up and smote our ship, and the shudder of their impact was communicated to all her parts. She sank now, not into smooth valleys of the sea, but with a tumble into steep and barbarous glens. Sometimes the waves caught and held her, so that she had to shake herself to get free of them. She would rise with the lift of a balloon, but only to be punched in the side and fall again. Inside the ship there was a constant groaning and creaking.

The wind was on the port bow, and towards it the waves came hurrying in long, thin ridges, leaden-grey, showing white teeth in snarling grimaces. Over wrinkled hollows they impended with implacable ferocity, and here and there shot up in a jaunty white plume of spray. But the general colour of the attacking sea was a very dark, glistening grey.

On the starboard side, from which the waters fled, the sea was grossly patched with white, as though, turning belly-up, the malignant waves revealed a torturing salt leprosy that drove them howling round the world.

On the weather side the wind beat with a continuous shrill bellowing, and over the weather bow rose high arcs of spray. Often the whole bow dipped and flung, not a curtain or a cloud, but a wave itself upon the deck, where it fell with a dull and shuddering roar, then broke to white and swept away as if across a half-tide rock. Under the lee side, bent over the sea, there raced always a thick and hissing spray.

As the motion became more violent, and the waves rose

to more dreadful heights, my simple emotions, of fear or sickness, were banished or grew numb. Fear gave way to primal awe, and sickness yielded to the sheer, moment-to-moment necessity of holding on: of saving oneself (as if in a wrestling match) from being thrown abruptly to the deck.

Now the gale was at its height, but the movement of the sea was still increasing. It was no longer merely very rough. It became a huge and vehement, an abysmal violence, on which roughness supervened. Now the movement came from great depths that had been slow to answer the gale's demand, but now, as it seemed, were rolling in a cosmic tide from whose gigantic billows, rising dark and high above the bridge, the storm tore a continuous spray: and in whose sickening troughs an undertow, or contrary swell, often laid us low upon our side. Into these deep valleys of the sea the trawler sank and shuddered; then, with its bow pointing to the sky and the gun on its forward deck aiming at high clouds, it climbed to mountainous and tattered crests that filled its main deck with white water, and with a roll and a twist rushed down again, out of the wind, but into the rearing menace of the next great wave.

Time lost its ordinary measure. Time was measured only by the black hills we must climb, the monstrous valleys into which we swooped. There was no sun, but for a little while a half-transparent cloud let through a meagre light that silvered the ragged tops of impending waves and scored more deeply the wind-cut runes in the sucking, swirling hollows beneath. Ridge after broken ridge in endless procession, the howling of the gale, the deck vanishing under a cascade of water, and the little ship with its little company of men tumbling madly, groaning and protesting, but holding its course and fighting stubbornly, mile after mile, towards the south. . . .

My body grew as tired as if I had been forced-marching for many hours. My brain went numb as a boxer's brain in the tenth or twelfth round: a boxer fighting against defeat, whose mind, under a hail of punches from a stronger, cleverer opponent, goes singing into a vast inane. – There was a sailor at the wheel who had been a boxer in a travelling circus, a booth-boxer, taking on all comers at country fairs: a yellow-haired, raw-boned welter-weight. I remember him, at the wheel, turning white and sick, and Tórur, who had slept off his drunkenness, taking his place with tough assurance. Silver, in the wheelhouse, rode the plunging deck as if it were a bucking horse he had mastered: he wore a fur cap, stared at the fearful sea with jaunty disdain, and sucked peppermint sweets that gave his conversation – when he turned to shout a word or two – an unlikely flavour. But his First Lieutenant, who was not yet twenty, stood like a boy defying death, with all his courage visible in the resolution of his eyes and delicate young mouth.

I remember trying to drink a cup of soup, and spilling half of it down my neck. I remember deciding, at last, to go below, and falling at the foot of an impossible ladder. Someone – who it was I don't know – came to help me, and guided me to Silver's cabin. I lay on the floor and was sick beneath his bright pictures of the ballet. I clambered into his bunk, and fell out of it. I climbed in again, and with an access of animal cunning found a position of relative safety. I fell asleep, or sank into a coma of exhaustion.

Some hours later I woke in sudden panic, when a movement of great violence turned me face to the wall – to the ship's side – and with a sort of eccentric gravity held me there; or seemed to. I had a sensation of utter helplessness, and then, as the ship righted and abruptly heeled to the other side, I was again thrown to the floor. I got to my knees and was trying to reassure myself when my mind was more horribly daunted by the deep-drowned bellow of a huge explosion. The whole framework of the trawler shuddered with its force – responded, almost gave tongue in agony – and I thought, This is the end, and I must show a proper composure. 'God help me,' I said aloud, 'for I feel none.'

I opened the door, and in the reeling alley saw one of the young sailors – his dissolute white face a pale blur between black oilskin – who said, in a voice strangely unperturbed, 'That shook the ham out of your teeth, didn't it?'

'What happened?'

'We must have lost our depth-charges. Gone overboard. And one of them was cocked. Some silly bastard—'

The young First Lieutenant came down and said, 'Get a move on, Jackson.'

I asked again, 'What happened?'

'We were swept, I'm afraid. And the depth-charges on the starboard side have all gone.'

'One was at full cock?'

'It sounded like that, didn't it?'

'Are we all right?'

'Oh yes, I think so. Don't worry about that.'

I tried not to, and went back to bed.

There was daylight – daylight of a sort – when I woke, and the movement of the ship, though still very violent, had not the wild and perilous, lurch and dive sensation of the previous afternoon, but had changed to a sullen, heavy plunging. I felt a sort of vacancy within me, I was light-headed as though I had lost gravity and my attachment to the earth. But with an effort I conquered my dizziness, pulled on my boots, and put on my duffle coat. Slowly, and with nausea coming up like a wave again, I climbed to the wheelhouse and found Silver in argument, or lively conversation, with Finch the engineer: Finch who, at thirty-two, was the oldest man aboard. The grey light caught his face as he leaned to and fro, and there was a gleam of fiery gold on his unshaven chin: but Silver, with forty-eight hours' growth of beard, had a dark, youngbrigandish look. His eyes were red-rimmed and blood-shot, but his manner was still brisk.

I had not energy enough to pay attention to what they were saying, and Tórur, who was at the wheel again, gave me a thermos-flask of hot tea. 'We had dirty night,' he said. 'We have lost the boat. Did you sleep good?'

I could not quite understand what he was saying, but during the night, I gathered, we had suffered damage of some sort and survived a perilous few minutes in which the trawler, caught by some contrary and errant wave in a trough of the sea, had fallen far over on to her side and failed to rise to the advancing mountain; which, like a landslide, had fallen ponderously over us.

Tórur could not properly tell his story without gestures, nor could he let go the wheel; he was badly handicapped, but with sweeping movements of his head, with eyes eloquent of disaster and a torrent of words, he made me realize that our danger had been extreme, and very shamefully I was grateful for the exhausted sleep that left me unaware of it.

Finch went below again, and Silver with a lurching stride crossed the little wheelhouse and took my arm.

'Whistler, thou shouldst be living at this hour!' he shouted against the wind and a thunderous jolt of the sea. 'It was Whistler, wasn't it, who said nature was always creeping up on art? And now she's caught it – if you can call our steering-gear nature.'

'Were we really in danger last night?'

'No, I don't think so. We turned our face to the pillow and lay down for a minute or two, and took a big lump of sea aboard; but a trawler's built to stand that sort of thing. It's only the steering I'm worried about.'

'What's gone wrong there?'

'You remember my plan? I was going to tell our Mr. Finch to report some minor damage that would make it advisable to look for shelter to effect repairs. But nature didn't wait for Mr. Finch. That bloody depth-charge knocked the rudder out of trim – and we're leaking a bit, too.'

'Is that serious?'

'It might be, but I hope not.'

'What are you going to do?'

'Haven't you noticed any difference in her movement? I've altered course and reduced speed. We're going dead slow and just creeping up to windward. Or thumping up to windward, if you want accuracy.'

'And what lies to windward?'

'Shetland, roughly. Just where we meant to go, though nature jumped the gun and set the course before art could look at the compass.'

'How far away is it?'

'Not much more than a hundred miles in a straight line. But the way we're going – up and down – about six hundred.'

'Will we get there?'

'I'll be damned angry if we don't.'

As though it were everlasting and ubiquitous, the fearful sea presented the same aspect as the day before: grey, liquid mountain-ranges that half-hid the dirty sky when we dipped to meet them, and raised us sickeningly, and frighteningly, to broken, dizzy heights from which we looked down into yet a new tormented valley. – Could there be another world than this? It confined us with such omnipotent and dreadful power that the mere thought of a calm and placid, unshaken earth, seemed remote as the good fortune of a fairy-tale. This was reality – this shuddering and enormous tumult – and life aland, on steady feet, no more than dreaming. – But suddenly a memory of my purpose, of my task and duty, broke into the numbness of my mind, and with belated alarm, with a delayed but overwhelming consternation, I asked, 'When you lost the boat, did he go too? The dead man, the Norwegian?'

'No,' said Silver, 'he's all right. He's still aboard, and for that you've got to thank my Number One. It was about midnight when he lost his blanket – the canvas that we lashed over him split and was blown away – and Number One very sensibly decided that he'd be safer inside. They'd a hell of a job shifting him, and it took them a long time, but they managed it. They got him in, and lashed him to a bulkhead, chair and all, and did it just in time. It was an hour after midnight when we lay down in the valley of the shadow and half the Atlantic fell on us. And when we got up again the boat had gone, all but a few splinters. But he's all right. – Do you feel strong enough to come out and see the damage? You'll have to hold on, if you do.'

I mustered all my strength, and followed him into the outer storm. The gale blew upon us like a solid though invisible element of great malignity, and salted with a fiercely stinging spray. The tumbling of the ship was a deliberate assault, intending to throw us down and hurl us overside. We climbed on tilting, stooping decks, clinging to life-lines like mountaineers in a hurricane. The wind drove tears from our eyes, and filled our mouths, choking us; and the trawler reared and pitched, striking the unyielding sea with deadly blows that echoed throughout her thin, steel-sided shell. I saw the wounds that the great midnight waves had left, the vacancies, the twisted stanchions, the mutilations and great bruises we had suffered; and could not understand how we were still alive. I fell once, and once only, and though I hurt my wounded chest I felt very pleased that I had been able to go where Silver went.

In the wheelhouse again, Silver and Tórur and the First Lieutenant ate sandwiches of thick white bread and bullybeef that the dishevelled steward – white and chattering with cold, but still in his shirt-sleeves – brought them on a napkin'd tray. I could eat nothing, but from a thermos-flask drank tea laced with rum, and felt a little better. The welter-weight boxer – the booth-boxer – relieved Tórur at the wheel, and Silver went to rest for an hour or two in the chart-room. The First Lieutenant, swaying to the movement of the ship, stood in command.

He, who had hardly begun to shave, looked cleaner than Silver with his brigand's chin, and his taut aspect of resolution had, as it were, become naturalized. It was taut by custom now, not by the constant exercise of will. He was a good-looking boy in a rather girlish way: but a girl of Diana's sort, an aquiline girl. He spoke to Finch with apparent confidence when the engineer came up again, and, increasing our speed by a cautious fraction, raised curtain after curtain of spray over our bows.

He was now in such command of himself and his situation as to talk of the disabilities of his ship. 'It's that gun on her fo'c'sle head that spoils her,' he said. 'The weight of the gun, and the reinforcement of the deck, have put a load on the bow she was never meant to take. That's why we fell away in the trough last night, and couldn't get up again: these trawlers can ride out any storm in their own trim, but it's unfair to them to plant a bloody great gun and a steel deck on their nose. You mustn't blame her for what happened – blame us! We gave the poor old girl too big a handicap, and put it too far forward: she hates it, and no wonder. But she stood up to punishment, didn't she?'

'What do you do in civil life?' I asked.

'I haven't done anything yet, and it's rather difficult to make up my mind. The only things I'm really interested in are music and horses. Do you like Schönberg?'

I couldn't, at that moment, remember who or what Schönberg was. I thought it likely that he was a composer, but he might have been a race-horse, a winner of the Grand National perhaps. I couldn't think of anything but my own problem of how to maintain, against recurrent sickness, a decent semblance of dignity. I was a soldier at sea, quite out of my element, but obscurely aware of a necessity to conceal my insufficiency. A necessity to show myself better than I was; for I wanted neither to embarrass my hosts nor to arouse their sympathy. I was extraordinarily unhappy, both physically and mentally, but I managed to conceal my unhappiness – or the worst of it – and remained on the bridge till night fell, and for some hours after that. With Silver, when he came back, and with his Number One, I maintained at least a pretence of conversation.

I watched darkness cover and disguise the sea, and the sense of estrangement that is never separate from that occlusion almost unmanned me. But I stayed with the others till about nine o'clock, and saw a segment of the sky blow clear of clouds, and a star or two incandescent on the sombre calm of outer space. Silver said that Finch was more hopeful than he had been, but the interminable heave and crash of our movement was still so brutal that I could hardly believe in our survival.

I went below, took off my boots, and tumbled into my bunk. For a long time I slept as invalids do: in a dream of unhappiness, on a ragged fringe of unconsciousness, but then dropped so far into untroubled, childish sleep that Silver, to wake me, had to pull and twist my arm.

'Come on deck,' he said, 'and take a look at heaven.'

The ship was still – quiet and still – no throb of engine or warring struggle with the sea – and on deck I looked at a long, lightly rippled firth, and on either side of it the protecting land. It was a land December-dark in hue, rising in gentle slopes to the naked serenity of low, fluent hills. A mild, an unassuming land, with here and there a little white-walled house, with ploughed fields and winter-dun pasture nuzzling the moors. A long pale beach on the one side, a narrow beach on the other. A plain and modest church in the distance, the roof of a bigger house showing

above the bare branches of some meagre, spindly trees. A
white road curved across the opposite hill, and from the
door of a cottage a couple of hundred yards away a woman
came out, and a flock of hens gathered about her in
expectation of corn. – 'Could you ask for more?' said
Silver.

After the wild antagonism of the open sea – its fearful
buffeting and terror – the landlocked firth and these dull
but kindly shores had indeed a heavenly peace, and for a
moment or two I could not answer because my eyes were
full of tears that I wanted to conceal, and my voice would
tremble if I spoke. But then, with a pretence of light-
heartedness, I said, 'Yes, heaven, whatever it's called. But
is it Shetland?'

'We found our way,' he said. 'We're lying in Hammar
Voe, and there, in that little copse or spinney – trees don't
grow very well here, do they? – there's the house where
Mungo Wishart lives. But without a boat I can't quite see
how to put you ashore.'

It is tiresome, I know, to speak again of my physical
condition; but I was, in fact, little better than an invalid –
our short voyage had quite undone me – and my frailty
must be noticed, because it prompted the next chapter of
the story. I said to Silver – disguising my weakness – 'Give
me an hour or so to make myself presentable. I can't go
ashore till I've washed and shaved and found a clean shirt.
Are you coming with me?'

'No,' he said, and spoke, in too much detail for me to
remember, of the damage his ship had suffered, and what,
under his supervision, might be repaired, or patched. 'I'll
join you later,' he said, 'but I think you should have a talk
with Wishart as soon as you can. There are boats on the
shore over there, and I'll try to attract someone's attention.'

Discipline came to my help again. I shaved, and put on a
clean shirt, and made myself – though hollow-eyed and

gaunt of cheek – as respectable in appearance as I could contrive; but I felt on the edge of fainting as I stood before the looking-glass. I went ashore in a boat that Silver had summoned – a little, neat, two-ended skiff – and as if in a dream said 'Thank you' to the boatman and set off towards the house in the trees – it was no more than a mile away – like a character in some tawdry, modern imitation of a folk-tale. But the land rocked under my feet; the solid land, after our witches' dance on the waves, seemed to quake and tremble, to climb and rush down in a mill-lade; and I had to sit on a broken stone wall and take my head in my hands to anchor my tumbling mind.

When I looked up I saw, on the field of winter grass before me, perhaps twenty yards away, two children on Shetland ponies. A girl of eleven or twelve, and a boy a couple of years younger. They were dressed alike in rough grey jerseys and corduroy trousers, and the girl was dark-haired, the boy fair. She had untidy, crow's-wing, breeze-blown locks, and he a rain-defying thatch as pale as straw. They came towards me – their stubby, round-barrelled ponies shaking their big heads – and the girl asked politely, 'Are you not feeling well?'

She had a beautifully modelled, lively, and sympathetic face – when I thought of her, later on, it seemed to memory like the face, in her childhood, of the woman in Renoir's picture called *La Loge* – and her voice rang light and high in the Shetland intonation.

'I think you should go away,' I said. 'I'm afraid I'm going to be sick.' – And as I spoke I got down on my knees and in utter wretchedness pressed my forehead to the cold, wet ground; for the world was going round me, and only by close contact with it could I find some measure of stability.

In my humiliation – through the whirling confusion of my weakness – I heard her say to her brother, 'Get down and help him, Olaf! O God, the poor man's ill! My pony is the quiet one, so we'll put him on her, and you'll go home as quick as you can and tell mother to get a bed ready for him. – Now help me pull him up.'

I felt their young, hard hands upon me, and it was shame, I think, that stirred me to recovery. Without much trouble I mounted the girl's pony – it was so small, my feet were hardly six inches from the ground – and the fair-haired boy set off at a gallop, the fat haunches of his pony working like pistons, and he, with a boy's romantic affectation, flailing it with a little heather-stick as if he were riding to warn the neighbours of an Indian raid.

I said to the girl – I was oddly deferential, as if she were my own age – 'I'm very sorry to give you so much trouble, because there's really nothing the matter with me. Except that I've been in a great storm at sea, and it's taken all the strength out of me.'

'I am frightened of the sea myself,' she said. 'I love it, but it fills me with fear. And a storm at sea, in the middle of the sea, must be a dreadful experience.' – She looked at me with a stately gravity in her childish face. Her face, I must admit, was rather dirty, and her lank, long hair needed a comb, and perhaps washing. But her expression was serious, and in her young and fragile features there was a tenuous, fine solemnity. I felt no hesitation, no incongruity, in telling her about the storm, and as she walked beside me she listened with a close intelligence.

'I want,' I said, 'to go to Mr. Wishart's house.'

'He is my father,' she said, 'and my brother Olaf has gone to tell my mother you are coming. But my father is out walking – he is a great walker – and he may not be back before night.'

Had I been in normal health, of mind and body, I think I would, at that moment, have found some pretext for resigning my part in Silver's plan; or even have turned about and insisted that he abandon it. Though I am not one of those who would betray their country rather than a friend, I have in me nothing of the blood-hound's nature, to relish at every loping stride the scent of guilt in the offing; and to hear that our quarry was the father of this solemn, pretty child destroyed whatever scrap of pleasure I had previously taken in the chase. – But I had no strength in me. My mind had lately been flogged by destructive news, my body (more recently) flung to and fro by the sea, and I felt no impulse to leave the course I had been set, though I was aware of new dislike for it. Silver had told me to find Wishart and talk to him, and I had accepted Silver as my leader. Almost from our first meeting I had recognised in him the power of decision that I lacked — that I envied – and now the minor forces of my attraction to him had been strengthened and thickened by an admiring gratitude. The light assurance of his literary judgments – the nonchalance with which he shook a female novelist out of her petticoats, and put a male author in his proper place – had delighted me in our early conversation – for under my mother's influence I had regarded authors more seriously – and since then, by his seamanship, he had possibly saved my life and the lives of all whom he commanded. Throughout the gale Silver, with mind alert and confidence undimmed, had been master of his ship, and master of the envious waves.

I was Silver's underling, and did his will. And now I know that I was right to obey him and, had I been in perfect health, in full control of my faculties, my own faculties might have led me astray.

The girl led the pony, and to entertain me told me little pieces of country gossip: that Old Maggie So-and-so lived in that cottage under the hill, whose cat, though very small, was the best ratter in the district; and the boat down there belonged to her son Willy, but Willy was at the war, and the boat had lain on the beach since he went away.

She talked without shyness or affectation. In her manner she was grown up, a little old-fashioned, but her interests were still childish: over there was a litter of puppies, of which she had been promised one, and what did I think would be a good name for it? – A thin rain was falling, and now from a darker cloud on a swifter draught of wind came a shower like needles of cold water. The rain beaded her thick jersey and flattened her wild hair; but she paid no heed to it. She was used to rough weather.

The little wood of bare, spindly trees that surrounded the house gave us some shelter as we approached it. A tall grey building, three storeys high, it was a big house for Shetland, but of no architectural interest or beauty: it was solidly built, it had good windows, and that was all that could be said of it. We went to the back door, and the girl's mother came out to meet us. Until the girl called her 'mother', however, I thought she was the housekeeper: she was a rosy-cheeked, brown-haired, trim and buxom woman of thirty-five or so, and might have been the wife of a well-to-do small farmer. She had eyes of great beauty – a luminous, dark brown – and her expression showed clearly that she was worried.

She told me to come in, and her voice, though sympathetic, was reluctant. The girl left her pony at the door, where her brother's stood – patient, and sheltered from the wind – and we went into a big, well-lighted kitchen that was furnished, like a farm kitchen, to be lived in. I began to apologize for the trouble I was causing, but in another attack of dizziness I lost my balance, and a moment later I was on my knees again, desperately clutching the back of a wooden chair while the room went spinning round me like a top. – I heard the girl, with childish earnestness, insist that I was ill and must go to bed, and her mother reply, 'But what will your father say?'

I wanted to tell her that all I needed was an hour's rest – somewhere to lie down for a little while – but the thought of a bed, of soft pillows in a tranquil room, so deeply tempted me that I let them argue. Presently they led me into a dark hall, smelling of damp, and up a broad, shallow staircase to a cold corridor hung with steel engravings in mahogany frames. A door stood open – one of several brown varnished doors – and a drift of peat-smoke came from within. The boy was already lighting a fire in a high, old-fashioned grate behind a brass fender, and his mother, now more obviously kind, gave me well-washed, white-flannel pyjamas. The girl brought up a stone hot-water bottle.

Olaf, she said, would go back to the ship and say I was not very well, but there was nothing to worry about . . . And as I fell asleep I remember thinking (as I had thought on my first visit, in the spring of the year) that as linguists the Shetlanders were not only clever, but remarkably courteous. Among themselves they talked in a *patois* that I found quite incomprehensible, but to strangers they spoke English: no rough or whimsical dialect – nothing that could be called 'Scotch' – but good English with an agreeable and distinctive intonation.

The sound of it was in my ears, like waves on a beach, when I woke and found Mrs. Wishart at my bedside with a plate of soup; and that I ate half-dreaming, so that now I remember it as if it were some rich and foreign food that I read about in a children's story. I slept again, and the next time I woke there was lamp-light in my eyes.

The children stood staring at me: Gudrun with a tea-tray in her hands, Olaf carrying an oil-lamp. I had thrown back the sheet, and my pyjama-jacket was unfastened. They were looking, with wondering eyes, at the crumpled, radiating scar on my right breast.

'Were you wounded?' asked the girl, and put down the tray.

'In a real battle?' said the boy.

I sat up in bed, feeling suddenly well and hale: luxuriously tired, but well again. We had some conversation, and as if it were a fairy-tale I told them about the retreat to Dunkirk, and the great fleet of little boats coming in to rescue us. They listened very seriously.

'It must be dreadful to be a soldier,' said the girl, 'but it's what I would be myself, if I was a man.'

She hoped I would enjoy my tea, she said, and if I had now slept enough, she had brought me something to read.

She took from the tray a thin volume, well bound in dark blue buckram, and gave it to me. 'It is all about *us*,' she said.

CHAPTER SEVEN

I KNEW SOMETHING about limited editions, for several of my mother's novels, in a green and gold binding, had been so honoured; and the book which Gudrun had brought me was handsome enough even for her exacting taste. It was excellently bound and admirably printed (by an Edinburgh firm) on hand-made paper. On a fly-leaf was the inscription: 'Of this edition of THE WISHART INHERITANCE twelve copies only have been printed for the Author's private requirement. This is Copy number 3.'

There was a spirited dedication, *To the Persistence of Human Folly*, and the author's name was printed with a territorial flourish: 'By Mungo Wishart of Weddergarth.'

I began to read it with a lively curiosity. . . .

THE WISHART INHERITANCE

(I)

Of the several hundred islands that cluster under the outer flanks of Britain, the remotest, most northerly, and least indebted to her are the Shetlands. Until recent years, when in common with the urban proletariat we have had our share of common doles, of grants for the so-called education of the young and the quarter-comfort of the old, for the limbless men of unnecessary wars and the workless men of a mismanaged economy, we received no smallest benefit to mind or body from our alliance, at first with Scotland, then with that two-backed beast of a forced marriage called Britain.

Scotland inflicted on us an 'ascendancy' – a little copy of the English 'ascendancy' in Ireland – of grasping merchant-lairds, largely out of Fife, who reduced the native peasantry to economic serfdom. This I know well, because my own ancestors, of whom I am not proud, were members of the 'ascendancy'. And when the itch of poverty compelled Scotland to accept in her political bed the great belly of John Bull, Shetland was stript of her manhood – prime sailors all – to serve the British fleets. In Nelson's day there were three thousand Shetlanders in the Royal Navy; and what historian has ever given Shetland credit for its share in victory? None! Shetland lies beyond the pale of London's interest.

But I put no blame on London. London is no worse than Lerwick, our puny capital: a smug little town infested by Scotchmen. London is merely bigger. Both of them need a purging of their inferior blood and a new flux from the north.

This by the way, but let my descendants mark it if they will. It is for them I am writing this late and lamentable chapter of our saga. It is for their instruction I shall expose the matter of a domestic quarrel, that by steady application to the law reduced two families to poverty and did no good to anyone but a pack of rascally solicitors in Edinburgh who for three generations lived on the milk of starving crofters and the unceasing bile of my dim-witted ancestors.

No one, as yet, has made a proper explication of these matters. But now, without fear or favour, I propose to do so, and to make a beginning I must introduce the Montague and Capulet of our divided island in the year 1747, when much of Scotland was still sore after suppression of the second Jacobite rebellion. Most of the Shetland gentry were Jacobites, but only at their dinner-tables. They were talking Jacobites, they drank the health of 'The King over the Water', and drank enough to float him home again. They stood for Episcopacy, and scorned the Presbyterians. But Episcopacy got no honour from their adherence, and the King no help.

Only one of the talking lairds, so far as I know, ever drew sword for the Stuarts, and he was Andrew Pitcairn of Sandwick: Old Andy, or Dandy, as he was known. As a

young man he had been out in the rising of 1715, but got
home again and lay low, and escaped punishment. For
thirty years he lived on the credit of having fought, for half
an hour, in the scramble at Sheriffmuir, and maintained
the reputation of a soldier by drinking enough for a
sergeants' mess. By 1745 the last of his wits lay drowned
in liquor, but his tongue still flapped like the foresail of a
boat in irons. He was hot for the Prince, and damned King
George to hell a dozen times a day. Others of his sort
showed some discretion, and chose their company before
they disclosed their loyalty; but Dandy Pitcairn wore the
white cockade and spat on Hanover no matter who was in
sight or hearing.

His lands of Sandwick marched with the estate of
Weddergarth, and Gideon Wishart of Weddergarth was
the greatest man in Shetland. He was Steward to My Lord
the Earl of Morton, who by act of the Hanoverian parliament had also the Earldom of Orkney and Lordship of
Shetland; and before the abolition of heritable jurisdiction
Gideon, on behalf of My Lord, held two head courts a year
and a circuit-court in each parish once a year. He was a
man of ruling influence, rich by the standards of the time
and, unlike the majority of the lairds, a Presbyterian and
supporter of the King in London. He had, moreover, a
wife; and the Lady Weddergarth, as she was called by the
common folk and the sycophants around her, was a woman
of formidable character. She had lands and money of her
own, and somewhere in Scotland an uncle who was a
baronet. To her shame, however, she had, nearer to hand,
another uncle – her mother's brother – who was Dandy
Pitcairn the Jacobite.

The Shetland lairds of the eighteenth century were little
despots in the islands. Most of them were merchants, fish-
curers, and shipowners in a petty way, as well as proprie-
tors of sour, thin land which they neglected. The sea paid
them better than the land, and under pain of banishment
their tenants must go to sea and fish for them. Haddock,
cod, and ling was the catch, and much of it was paid for
with Hollands gin. When ashore the fishermen were rarely

sober, and whether afloat or ashore never out of debt to the lairds. Merchants from Hamburg and Bremen came in the summer months, set up their booths, and sold fish-hooks and tar, lines and linen-web, spirits and tobacco. Meal and malt were bought in Orkney. Fish paid for most of the purchases, but there was some profit also in whale-oil, rancid butter, woollen stockings, and ponies. The gentry dressed well and lived better than their own sort in Scotland; the commons lived as they could and forgot their grief in drink.

Such was Shetland in 1747, when news came that the Prince had been routed at Culloden. Most of the talking Jacobites sat still and frightened, wondering who had heard them; but Dandy Pitcairn was in a drivelling panic, for everyone had heard him. And Gideon Wishart saw his opportunity.

Gideon Wishart, being wealthy, naturally wished to be wealthier still, and being a landowner was greedy for more land. Dandy's estate lay west and north of Weddergarth, marching with it on two sides, and Dandy had some of the best fields in Shetland. Dandy, however, stood in great jeopardy now, and if Gideon Wishart, My Lord of Morton's Steward, should name him as an open, stubborn Jacobite, his estate would certainly be forfeited. But that, as Gideon realized, would be a scandalous waste of good land, and a black shame to the Lady Weddergarth, who was Dandy's niece.

So Gideon invited Dandy to talk things over and, having first of all reduced him to abject fear by some reference to the gallows as well as forfeiture, proposed a pretty, neat little plan to preserve all that fine land for Dandy's own use and enjoyment, and save Dandy from any tedious, embarrassing questions that government agents, whom they might now expect, would otherwise ask him.

All Dandy had to do, said Gideon, was to make a will and name him, Gideon, as his heir. True, Dandy had a son, called Young Dandy, and he would suffer. But was it not written that the children of the kingdom shall be cast out into outer darkness – that when the fathers have eaten sour grapes, the children's teeth are set on edge – and who was Young Dandy to complain of so ancient a rule? And who was Old Dandy to suppose he could avoid all punishment for the sin of thinking treason and the folly of talking it?

Old Dandy wept and prayed, and wept and cursed, and then gave in. Gideon Wishart, being deputy head of the judiciary, had a document all ready, a seal to be applied, witnesses waiting; and Dandy in a trembling hand signed away all his many acres. He went home, and for some while, as rumour spread of the fearful vengeance that the Duke of Cumberland was taking in the Highlands, and of the bitter reprisals against all Jacobites, real, suspected, or potential, that the government in London was meditating, he felt happy to be safe, contented with the bargain he had made, and lucky to be living still on his own land.

But Young Dandy, his son, was a tall and handsome boy, of cheerful spirit and better wit, or so I have gathered, than anyone could have expected. And presently Old Dandy, in his few hours of sobriety, felt an ever-deepening remorse for the ill deed he had done him, and an ever-rising anger against Gideon Wishart who had driven him to it.

He took to visiting the house and policies of Wedder-garth, and abusing Gideon more loudly and intemperately than previously he had praised Prince Charlie. To all who passed he said the laird was a liar, thief, and perjurer, a hypocrite and blackmailer; a man of gross personal character whose vices were unusual and hardly credible. When no one was there to listen he would stand in the twilight and shout and yell abuse of the most violent sort. He would call the laird a fornicator, cuckold, bastard; an adulterer within the prohibited degrees; a man who openly robbed his servants as well as habitually committing incest with his daughters. And for many weeks Gideon Wishart took no action against him, neither private interference nor legal process, but sat whitefaced enduring it all, his will imprisoned by consciousness of his own guilt. What Lady Weddergarth thought of it all, no one can tell; but it may have been she who counselled inaction. And later, perhaps, she gave counsel more dire.

Suddenly the shouting stopped. There were no more twilit imprecations, uncouth, wild, and obscene charges from the wall of the kailyard or the shelter-belt of scraggy trees that Gideon had planted. No more was heard from Dandy, for Dandy disappeared.

To begin with, no one was surprised, and certainly no one was upset. It was commonly supposed that he had ridden off to drink with some crony in the northern parts of the island, or in Lerwick. But as week followed week, and no word came of him, Young Dandy and his household – his mother was dead – grew alarmed and began to make inquiry. But inquiry came to nothing, and the vanishing of Dandy became a mystery that had everyone talking. Talking to no purpose, however, for nothing was ever learnt of what had happened to him. The only possible clue to his disappearance, and that a poor one, was provided by a Dutchman in Lerwick. The Dutchman said he had seen a man fall out of a rowing-boat in the harbour, and drown; and the man looked something like Old Dandy. When asked why he had not gone to help him, the Dutchman answered that he would have done, and gladly, if he had been sober enough.

After six months this evidence was sufficient for Gideon Wishart, who, by the exercise of his own judicial authority, accepted the presumption of Dandy's death and, declaring the will, took possession of the lands of Sandwick as Dandy's heir. Give him credit, however, where credit is due. He tempered his justice with mercy, and took Young Dandy into his own house.

I cannot find evidence enough to resolve Young Dandy's character. He may have been less intelligent than I suppose. I cannot think he was a rustic lout, a mere bullock of a boy, but he may have had less sensitivity than I credit him with and, dismissing the problem of his father's death as insoluble – shrugging-off his disinheritance as unalterable – he may have taken what comfort he was offered as being better than no bread. This could be the explanation, but I am inclined to think he knew more than I do – or suspected all that I suspect – and went into Wishart's house to add to his knowledge or fortify suspicion, with, it may be, the purpose in his mind of finding means to regain his inheritance. But perhaps it was only because Barbara Gifford lived there.

Gideon Wishart and Lady Weddergarth had given to the world a family of five boys and four girls. Three, however, had died of small-pox in a fierce and sudden epidemic, and now the family consisted of three brothers, the oldest of whom, Henry, was twenty-four, and three sisters, the youngest being fifteen or sixteen. Lady Weddergarth had also adopted a cousin of hers, an impoverished cousin, not from that side of her family which was crowned by a Scottish baronet, whom she called her companion and used as a lady's maid and sewing-woman. Barbara Gifford, as well born as Lady Weddergarth, had a poor and lowly status in the family, but a handsome figure, a pretty face, and a stubborn, unscrupulous character.

Henry, the eldest of the sons of Gideon Wishart and his heir, was blindly, sullenly in love with her. So was William, his younger brother. No one – no one except Barbara – suspected that Young Dandy shared their passion. He was clever enough to keep that secret, and so was she. Young Dandy was a landless man, and there was no point in loving him. Not openly, that is. But Henry, though a heavy-footed oaf and as heavy of mind as of foot, would come into a great estate.

To give his family some sort of education, Gideon Wishart kept a tutor in the house, a shambling, weak-kneed young man called Abel Mouatt, a licensed minister of the Church of Scotland, who even at the dinner-table could not carry his liquor; for he fell from his chair one day and cut himself deeply on a bottle that broke in his hand. He had an impressive voice, however, and a gift for extempore prayer; and he may have taught the younger children to read and write well enough for their simple needs. He, too, had a hang-dog affection for Barbara Gifford, and was very much under her influence. She was something of a honey-pot; but there was gall in the pot as well as sweetness. In a young-lady-like way she

could paint in water-colour, and with a pen that was far
from lady-like she drew portraits.

She kept her portraits as secret as her love-affairs, and
secrets they remained till I found them – forty-seven of
them – in a little portable writing-desk of yellow mahogany
and mushroom-coloured leather that was known in the
family as 'Barbara Gifford's desk'. We had, and still have,
other of her belongings. She was a good needle-woman,
and in the latter years of her short life, when she lived alone
in Lerwick, she added to her income – perhaps even kept
herself – by embroidery and such-like diligence; some
pieces of which have been preserved, and are admired
by women who claim a knowledge of fine sewing. Some
of her water-colours also survive, and show a sentimen-
tality not otherwise apparent in her life.

No one in my family, for five or six generations, has had
much equipment of intellect or more than a functional
intelligence, and it was left to me to discover that Barbara
Gifford's desk had a hidden compartment. It is a pretty
piece of cabinet-work, but the difference between inner
depth and outer is fairly obvious, and it was not very
difficult to find the release and expose the cavity. There
lay the portraits she had drawn, and three of the old quill-
pens she had used. They are on odd scraps of paper, yellow
with age, the most of them fly-leaves torn from books. I
suppose Gideon Wishart had a library that she despoiled.

Some of them are sketches of Lerwick people done in the
years when she lived there: vapid, silly young women in
smart attire, as they considered it, and the hard, gross men
of the islands' 'ascendancy'. A few good portraits, too, of
simple people, fishermen with faces carved to bony
strength and stark endurance of the sea, and women, young
and old, endowed with the character to sustain a season's
unhappiness and a lifetime's work of breeding sons for the
rich to exploit and the sea to drown.

But the earlier drawings, of the Wisharts of Weddergarth, are of more interest, and from them I discovered
something of the truth that the Edinburgh lawyers had
hidden under pages of pettifogging argument and flatulent

deception. There is, to begin with, Lady Weddergarth herself: five pictures of her, and a domineering, tyrannical, breeding bitch of a money-proud, over-fed figure of malignant femininity she is in every one of them. Then there is Gideon Wishart: four of him, a lanternesque, long-jawed, dismal schemer, a Hanoverian time-server in every line of him; but he had a prize bull's ability to mark his young. All the family are there, those that survived the small-pox, and each of them, with his or her minor difference, is as much a copy of their calculating, swindling, undershot father as the calves of a prepotent Shorthorn.

Henry, the heir, a drooping pull of the sire, is simply a lout with a cunning gleam in his eye. William and George, the younger brothers, are wily hobbledehoys, too well-dressed for the indignity of their look, and their protruding under jaws make them ludicrously like their father. Of the daughters I can only say that they look like kitchen-maids in an age when kitchen-maids were ill-fed, unwashed, rarely saw daylight, and mated only in the dark with wandering packmen; but these three, being well dowered, all found husbands, or had husbands found for them.

Barbara Gifford did not spare herself. She left three self-portraits of her youth, and in all of them she has the eyes of a thief. Pretty, yes, and the sort to reduce to the service of her body better and cleverer men than the ungainly offspring of Gideon Wishart and his wife. But dishonest. The eyes of a liar and seducer, and the broad untroubled brow of a girl who instinctively knows how to make use of her power. A girl who could make men plead and whimper their desire, and judge the note of their desperation by her mind's own tuning-fork. A girl of strong decision, and honest enough to know herself.

There is one drawing of Old Dandy, the drunken Jacobite, that shows him as a kind of romantic scarecrow: a dissolved nobility, the dilapidation of a youthful ideal, a caricature of youth's impulsiveness; a wild uncomely creature draped about the broken pole of a once handsome spirit. But of Young Dandy there are three portraits, different from the rest because they are tender in mood, romantic in execution. Young Dandy is the figuration of a girl's love, yet drawn with a certain honesty. He is tall of carriage, bold of feature, curiously like his dissipated father; and, as if with insistence on a private joke, the tip of his nose is always bulbous. The drawings of Young Dandy are exercises in love, with a small malicious twist to give them reality and preserve through time his bottle-ended nose.

Of the Rev. Mr. Mouatt there are two drawings, and I have never seen a more dismal and lugubrious shepherd for a Christian flock: a figure of ignoble despair tormented by a gross and sensual mouth. – There, then, are the actors, and now for the action.

On a night in May 1749 the Rev. Mr. Mouatt, the three sons of Gideon Wishart, Young Dandy and the grieve at Weddergarth, a man called Gilbertson, were rowing home from Hillswick, a bay on the west coast some fourteen or fifteen miles north of Hammar Voe, where they had been shooting seals. They had also been drinking too much, and someone had been telling them stories of shape-changing. Stories of seal-women who come ashore to love, and bear male children who take to the sea again with a seal's dexterity and the torture of a human mind showing in its eyes. Stories of a sort that is the common property of all the western lands from Finisterre to Muckle Flugga. Or so I infer, from the tale they told when they came back to Weddergarth.

They had gone to Hillswick by boat because at that time there were no roads in Shetland, and nearly all far travelling was by sea. It was a good boat of the Shetland sort, the persistent, double-ended type that the vikings invented, and with thwarts for six rowers, and, six to row, they made good progress till they came into the smooth waters of Hammar Voe. It was a calm, still night, overcast but not dark, and there was no movement in the water except the creep of the tide on the shore. The voe is four miles long, and narrow. A ribbon of water between familiar shores. There is no more innocent and safe an arm of the sea in Shetland than the Voe of Hammar.

But suddenly, they said, as they were rowing strongly, the boat was stopped as if an anchor had been thrown out and taken fast hold in the sea's bed. They could not go forward, and when they backed water they could not go astern. They were held fast, by some invisible anchor, in the unbroken calm of the voe; and in the aftermath of drinking they fell into panic.

The Rev. Mr. Mouatt got down on his knees and let his gifted tongue unpack their fear in words. Though young and physically ill-favoured, he was already widely known and much admired for the power and fluency of his prayers, and with his life at stake, as it must have seemed, he probably excelled himself. The dark waters of the voe must have heard, that night, a remarkable exhortation, and God can seldom have been addressed in more moving terms. They were, quite literally, moving; for presently the invisible hold on the boat was broken and a light breeze carried her slowly forward. Then one cried out in horror, and pointed to the water, where three dark shapes, like great seals, were swimming away. Or so the young men said, when they reached home.

Gilbertson the grieve, who may have drunk less than the others, said he thought they had run upon some piece of submerged wreckage. Old timbers cushioned with weed, or a small boat floating awash, and there they stuck till a rippling breeze blew them clear. But the young Wisharts were sure they had been in the grip of some supernatural force, and the Rev. Abel, whose prayers had released them from it, had no doubt whatever of their miraculous escape.

Within a few days Gilbertson's sober explanation was quite discredited, and there was general agreement that their strange experience had been a sign or admonition to them, or so intended, and their recklessness in disregarding it was long deplored. They were loose livers, dissolute young men, who had been given fair warning to repent and mend their ways; but in the pride of their youth they paid no heed, and the calamity that soon befell them was self-invited.

Such, at any rate, was local opinion, and the Presbyterian

ministers of the county preached many remarkable sermons in which, together with much long-winded and dubiously honest sympathy for the bereaved parents, they denounced with equal vehemence the prevalence of hard drinking, the continuing habit of fornication, and the sin of going to sea on the Sabbath day. For it was early on a Sunday morning that catastrophe came.

Three days after their return from Hillswick, two of the Wisharts, with Young Dandy Pitcairn, the minister, and the grieve, rowed across the voe to drink and sup with Sam Louttit of Hammar, another member of the family who, as well as being cousin to Gideon Wishart, was his tenant-in-chief in Hammar. George, the youngest of the brothers, would not go in the boat, being still frightened of seals and deep water, but saddled a horse and rode round the head of the voe, a distance three times as long as the short sea trip of a mile or so.

How they spent the day, and what was spoken between them, is not known; but twice there was open quarrelling between Henry Wishart and Young Dandy, and once they came to blows. They, and everyone in the house, drank long and deeply, but no one, it is said, was dead-drunk or even hog-drunk. But they lost all count of time, and it was near midnight before they thought of going home. And then they found that George's horse was missing. Presumably it had got tired of waiting and was already in its own stable again, but they wasted an hour looking for it, and it was Sunday morning before they embarked. George, having no other choice, went with them.

There is total darkness over what happened next, but none survived that little crossing of the sea. There is no more than a mile of water between Hammar and the west side of the voe, and the weather was calm; but no one reached the other shore. Perhaps they took more drink with them, and fell to quarrelling again. A scuffle, a clumsy attempt to separate the brawlers, and suddenly, with all that drunken weight lurching to one side, the boat goes over and they are in the water. The water is still cold in May, and none could swim. No one swam in those days.

And a man who is full of drink, and cannot swim, will not live long in a cold sea.

That, or something of the sort, is probably what happened, though no one on the shore heard, or admitted to having heard, a shout of anger or a cry for help. But at that time of night everyone would be fast bedded, the crofters in their box-beds, the gentry with their windows shut, and anyone half-waking and hearing a scream in the darkness would only pull his blanket round his ears and hope the trows were not looking for him.

On Sunday, at some time in the forenoon, a messenger from Weddergarth came to Hammar, riding George's horse, to ask why the young men had not returned. Then the search began, and before long the boat was found, ashore and half full of water, at the southern end of the voe the outer end – where the tide had taken it. Young Henry's hat lay in her, and a walking-stick he often carried, but nothing else.

By then the whole parish was searching, men, women, and children raking the shores, and boats dragging the voe. It was early evening when young Henry's body was found, and soon afterwards the body of Gilbertson the grieve. But the sea kept all the others. The tide got them, and the Atlantic buried them.

Young Henry's body was carried ashore below the house of Weddergarth, and Barbara Gifford came running down, with a wild expression on her face, to ask who it was they had found. They told her, and without another word she pushed aside the men who stood about him, and kneeling down beside him, fumbled at his neck. She was in great distress, but not, as it seemed, overcome by grief, and when she had found what she wanted she rose with a look, it was said, both tearful and defiant. And went back to the house.

The search was continued for many days, long after all hope had gone of finding survivors, and the whole district lived in gloom and superstitious fear. Gideon Wishart and his wife 'turned into stony images of what they had been': so, many years later, declared an old woman whose mother had served them. In public they did not give way to grief, nor even admit it; but as if grief had opened private wounds, through which they bled invisibly, they were drained of human quality. They had lost three of their children by small-pox, and now their three sons had been taken by the sea. An empty cask was Gideon Wishart, but held together by hoops of iron; and Lady Weddergarth a stony well-head above a spring gone dry.

For some time no one dared tell her of Barbara Gifford's behaviour, when the body of young Henry was carried ashore; but the moment she heard of it, she sent for Barbara, and sat waiting for her in the parlour. There was a fire burning on the hearth, though it was now the second week of June, and on the far side of it a girl of eleven or twelve years old, picking nervously at some sort of embroidery frame. She was a daughter of Gilbertson, the dead grieve, whom Lady Weddergarth had taken into the house to teach her the useful domestic arts.

Lady Weddergarth at once demanded to be told what Barbara had been looking for, under a dead man's shirt, and after hesitating a while Barbara opened her bodice and took from her own neck a tape on which two rings were threaded.

'This,' she said, pointing to a plain silver ring, 'was what I had given him, and what he was wearing. And this other he gave to me, and I have worn it ever since. We were man and wife, legally married, and I can prove it.'

'A pretty piece of news,' replied Lady Weddergarth. 'Too pretty, I would have thought, to keep to yourself.'

'I was too frightened to tell you,' said Barbara.

'But you can tell me now! Has something cured you of fright?'

'I am carrying his child, and I cannot be frightened for ever.'

There was silence at that, a long silence, before Lady Weddergarth, with a great bitterness in her voice, said, 'So there have been games of sluttery under my roof!'

But Barbara answered defiantly, 'They are not games a girl can play alone!'

'No, in faith! And we have had bastards in the family before now,' said Lady Weddergarth.

'But this is no bastard! This was legally begotten in true marriage.'

'A likely tale.'

'But I can prove it! I have lines to prove it.' And Barbara, now 'greetin sairly', as Madge Gilbertson remembered, ran from the room.

For a few minutes Lady Weddergarth sat by the fire, making no move, said Madge, except once to clear her throat and turn her head, and spit in the flames. And Madge sat as still as she, not daring to draw attention to herself.

Then Barbara came in again, breathing as if she had run a long way, but now, on her flushed face, wearing a look of triumph. And she gave Lady Weddergarth a sheet of paper; who took it, and stood to read it in a better light.

Her lips moved as she read, but she read in silence till she came to the last words, and these she spoke aloud, very scornfully: ' "By me, Abel Mouatt"! And what,' she demanded, 'did you give Abel Mouatt to write this rigmarole? What bribe or freedom of your body?'

'They are my lines,' cried Barbara, 'and neither you nor anyone else can dispute them.'

'Abel Mouatt,' said Lady Weddergarth, 'could raise his voice in prayer like a cock crowing, but he had a poor, whimsical, bedraggled spirit. I was never edified by a word he uttered in exhortation, nor felt one jot the better for his intercession. Yet I had not thought he would stoop to this.' And she tore the paper across and across again.

'My lines, my lines!' – Barbara screaming in despair – 'Give me my lines!'

But Lady Weddergarth, holding her back, threw the torn paper into the fire, and struck her twice across the face. Then, with scorn and anger in her voice, exclaimed, 'Go back to your sewing! Is there not work enough for every woman in a house of mourning, with new clothes to be made for all of us? For the girls shall wear black, and nothing but black, till I have found a husband for the last one of them!'

I had read so far when I was interrupted by a buffet on the door, and before I could speak it was thrown open by a tall, heavily built man who wore a dark dressing-gown over white woollen pyjamas. He came round the foot of my bed, into the little area of lamp-light, and stood looking down at me with an expression, as it seemed, of ponderous ill-will. I made some small, trivial remark – I began, I think, an apology for my presence – to which he paid no attention.

'I've been out all day,' he said, 'and when I came in I had a bath. Then, when I was going to get a bite of supper, my wife told me we had a guest, an unknown guest, in the house. Well, who are you, and what's the matter with you?'

I sat up and, as I did so, concealed, half-instinctively, the book I had been reading. I was somewhat alarmed by the great size and immediate unfriendliness of my host, but I was ruffled by his rudeness, and my manner, as I told him something of our misadventures, was by no means apologetic.

He listened for a while without comment, and I remembered Silver's description of him; who had said that he looked like a survivor from the Indian Mutiny. There was indeed something in his features reminiscent of the righteous arrogance, the intolerant assurance of their own rectitude, that marked, and gave distinction to, so many Victorian soldiers and the pro-consuls of our eastern empire. His hair grew thickly – a grey pelt above his wide forehead, a curl of silver at his ears, and a heavy moustache, still dark, over an invisible mouth and a square, strong chin – and this abundance reinforced the Victorian likeness. But in his eyes (though now I may be fanciful) there was a look of injurious, resentful anger that to me seemed wholly modern.

His costume – the thick brown-flannel dressing-gown and the white pyjamas – gave him a somewhat monastic appearance; or would have done but for two additions. He wore also a Fair Isle jersey, patterned brightly in green and yellow, and he carried a large tumbler of brandy and soda.

I finished my explanation, and roughly he asked, 'What were you doing in the Faeroes?'

He was not entitled to an answer, but I saw no harm in telling him I was a Welfare Officer.

'Welfare!' he exclaimed. 'By God, what an army! Do you take a troop of nurse-maids round with you?'

'The problems of a modern army have to be handled in a modern way.'

'How are you going to win a war with a modern army that won't fight? That's your only problem.'

'I don't think we're worrying very much about that—'

'You've been kicked out of Norway, thrown out of France, and now the Japs are rolling you up in Malaya. If that doesn't worry you, what will?'

It was difficult, at that time, to defend our conduct of the war, and impossible to take pride in more than a few episodes. (My own regiment had fought well.) If I was to remain on speaking terms with Mungo Wishart – and it was for that purpose I had come to his house – I could not continue an argument in which, for lack of logic, I should be driven back on emotion; and I made an attempt to escape it by saying, 'We began the war in peculiar circumstances. In very difficult circumstances.'

Wishart sat himself down on the side of my bed, and asked, 'Are you a regular soldier? Well, in that case I may put up with you. You're a mercenary, you do what you're told and draw a wage for it. But God save me from volunteers! Those fools who got into uniform after Munich had made war certain. I can get on with skulduggery and open vice, but folly above a certain temperature drives me mad, and to volunteer for a war that was lost before it began – a war in defence of Poland, that we couldn't reach by land or sea or air – in God's good name, wasn't that stark lunacy? Not that I give a twopenny damn for Poland, but I was brought up to respect good sense, and make no promises I couldn't keep.'

There was no useful answer I could find to that, and Mungo Wishart sat in silence too. A silence in which, quite visibly, he wrestled with angry and unhappy thoughts. 'There's dry-rot at the heart of it all,' he muttered, and then, more loudly, 'What do you do when the centre collapses?'

'Patch and repair – or find a new centre?'

'That's occurred to you, has it? Do you ever read the poetry of W. B. Yeats?'

He pronounced the name very distinctly; doubtful, perhaps, if I had heard of it. And I was, indeed, surprised to hear it in these surroundings. 'Some of it, and sometimes,' I answered.

> When all the wells are parched away,
> O plain as plain can be
> There's nothing but our own red blood
> Can make a right Rose Tree!

He quoted the lines in a sombre, ritualistic voice; then asked me, abruptly, 'What was your father?'

'A soldier.'

'Alive or dead?'

'Dead.'

'A soldier, and the son of a soldier. Then we needn't argue about politics, and I'll put up with you for a night, though I don't like your uniform. Wait a minute, and I'll bring you a drink.'

He finished, at a gulp, his brandy and soda, set down his glass, and walked heavily from the room. I pushed *The Wishart Inheritance* under the pillow, and waited, a trifle uneasily. That my reluctant host had a reputation for eccentricity I could now well believe; and the half-promise of friendliness was not firm enough to expel completely my anxiety.

Presently I heard his ponderous tread – he had left the door open – and the clink of glass. He came in carrying a bottle of brandy, a siphon of soda-water, and another tumbler. He filled both glasses with a tropical generosity.

He drank again, and with a chant in his voice – as if he were going to church with poetry – he declaimed:

I came on a great house in the middle of the night,
Its open lighted doorway and its windows a'l alight,
And all my friends were there and made me welcome
                                                    too;
But I woke in an old ruin that the winds howled
                                                through.

'I don't know that one,' I said.

'You're too young,' he answered. 'But that was the Britain that I first knew; a great house with a lighted doorway. And when I had dreamt my dream I woke in an old ruin, and the latest architect of ruin was still held in honour by the people whose good name, or what was left of it, he had dragged in the mud.'

'Who was he?' I asked.

That opened the sluice-gates, and I shall not pretend to remember all he said, or indeed anything but a fragment of it, and that uncertainly. For he took me back to the first war, at the end of which he had served for some time with (I think) the North Persia Levies, and been drawn into a confusion of politics in the Caucasus. There, as he asserted, we had encouraged the good, simple, and warlike tribes of Armenia, Azerbaijan – and perhaps Georgia? – to assert their independence, and armed them to do so. Then, when they had aroused the anger of Turkey and the new, still ragged power of Soviet Russia, we betrayed them and left them to their fate. And for this betrayal – which, he said, made the name of Britain stink in every Caucasian hamlet – he chiefly blamed Lloyd George.

In our recent, or fairly recent history, as he dramatized it, Lloyd George was the leading villain, and his hatred of him defied reason, and almost certainly derided truth; but another villain, in a smaller role, was Balfour, whose determination to establish a Jewish national home in Palestine had only been realized by breaking our most solemn promises to the Arabs. About these two 'blood-boltered images of perfidy', as he called them, he told such tales as would have made the name of Britain stink, not only in Caucasian hamlets, but – if they were true – throughout all history. I could not believe a quarter of what he told me, but neither could I refute it; for he was well informed about the Near East, and I knew very little. He had been for many years in the Consular Service, and he had travelled, he told me, from the Gulf of Aden to the Caspian Sea.

It is, of course, characteristic of us – of the English and the Scots, I mean – to form a deep attachment to some distant people in a little known land; but Mungo Wishart had gone too far. He had fallen in love too often – with Armenians, Azerbaijanis, Arabs of various tribes, perhaps with the Georgians – and this promiscuity (in a political sense) had left him incapable, in his later years, of resisting the notorious appeal of Irish nationalism. Not until he retired, however, by which time the Irish were their own masters, had he taken any interest in them. At the time of the Easter rebellion, and in the days of the Black and Tans, he didn't, as he admitted, care a snuff for Ireland: his heart was then engaged with the Arabs or the Azerbaijanis. But in 1930 he had retired to Shetland and his six thousand unprofitable acres, and discovered in a growing library yet another romantic cause which, though by then extinct, gave him fresh reason to hate Lloyd George, and more evidence of English tyranny, English perfidy. All his love-affairs required an equivalent hatred, and a lost cause demanded his savage contempt for all who would not mourn it. Even of his fellow-islanders he was now contemptuous, especially of those who lived in Lerwick – because, perhaps, they cared so little about Azerbaijan?

At this time, with a distance of thirteen or fourteen years between us, I can write calmly enough about Mungo Wishart and his maniacal affections; but that night when, for three or four hours, I listened to his diatribe and felt his passion vibrating on my nerves – I sitting up in bed, in borrowed pyjamas, with a quilt round my shoulders – that night my mind was less placid. In a legal or medical sense he was certainly not mad; but there was madness in him. The madness of a fixed idea, the temper of a fanatic. And yet, while his interminable harangue went on and on, and filled the world with chicanery, lies, and people betrayed, I could recognize in him a perverted goodness, and in his face see a wild nobility. Years later a poem by D. H. Lawrence suddenly reminded me of him. I cannot quote it exactly, but only as near as I remember: 'Holbein and Titian and Tintoretto could not paint faces now, because the faces they painted were windows to strange horizons. But faces now are only grimaces, with eyes like the windows of stuffily furnished rooms.' – But Holbein and Titian could have painted Mungo Wishart.

In the flood-waters of his anger two things came to my rescue: his brandy, which he poured lavishly and divided fairly, and Ireland. I have never been able to disentangle Irish politics, and his belated passion for the Irish cause stirred me no more deeply than his concern for Azerbaijan; but in discovering Ireland he had also discovered Yeats, and every now and then his voice would lose its fierceness and take on the sound of chanting, that he considered proper for reciting poetry. Once, as he refilled my glass, he announced:

> A proud man's a lovely man,
> So pass the bottle round.

And again, when some remembered iniquity filled and over-filled his tormented mind:

> Grant me an old man's frenzy.
> Myself must I remake
> Till I am Timon and Lear
> Or that William Blake
> Who beat upon the wall
> Till truth obeyed his call.

I have not, I think, exaggerated his passion; though in my mood at that time, having just recovered from a storm at sea, I was, perhaps, unduly susceptible to it. The storm in the bedroom woke some echoes of the Atlantic. – But I had decided, or very nearly decided, that the deposit of madness in his mind was harmless enough – a sort of historical deposit – and that Silver was far off the mark in supposing he had any active connection with German or Quisling agents, when he spoke once more of Shetland and its people, and roused again a doubt in my mind.

He had been talking of Ireland and its woes, and of Roger Casement; whose execution by the English he regarded almost as a personal affront, because Casement, like himself, had been in the Consular Service. 'He was executed for bringing arms to his own people: that was all his crime,' he said. 'And I hope to God that I would have the courage to do what he did, if ever my people should want arms. For we have a history of injustice too.'

He thought for a while, and exclaimed, 'Take English history!' – I groaned, and thought I must endure till morning, but he was mercifully brief. What he said, in effect, was that all the achievements of England were due to men of Norman blood; to men who had some inheritance of flesh and spirit from the Norman conquest, or earlier settlements from the north. But now, he said, all England, and Scotland too, had lost that potency, that will to explore and conquer and create in their own image. And the reason? The last dregs of Norse blood had run out, and there was no hope for Britain unless its heart could be replenished.

Breaking a long silence, I said, 'I can't see where you're going to refill it.'

'There are sources,' he said darkly. 'Sources I know.'

I never learnt where they were, however, because my ordeal was now at an end, and Mungo Wishart interrupted himself; or his belly did. A loud, rumbling, abdominal noise startled us both, and with innocent surprise he exclaimed, 'I've had no supper! Not a bite to eat since noon. Good God, it's late, and I must go. I'll take what's left of the brandy.'

Gratefully I said good night, and at the door he paused, and in a deepening voice declared, 'You must study Irish history. It's of paramount importance, for Ireland showed the way:

> What gave that roar of mockery,
> That roar in the sea's roar?
> *The ghost of Roger Casement*
> *Is beating on the door.*'

I WOKE IN the morning with the assurance that Mungo Wishart was innocent of anything worse than an old mad mind and intolerable verbosity. I had slept soundly, dreamt no dreams, and that was proof, I thought, that he had told me nothing to disturb my inner mind: the mind that sits in judgment after the light goes out.

I dressed and went downstairs, and met Mrs. Wishart. We exchanged compliments and she said, 'I hope you won't mind having breakfast in the kitchen with us. It's where we always eat, though Mr. Wishart takes his meals in his own room.'

There was no comment in her voice – no inflexion of resentment – as she let in that ray of light on his domestic manners, and I, with an equal lack of emphasis, replied, 'I had a long talk with him last night.'

'He would enjoy that,' she said. 'He doesn't get enough company of his own sort.'

The children, looking very tidy and well-washed, were waiting in the kitchen, and Gudrun gravely hoped I had slept well and was feeling better. I thanked her again – her and Olaf – for having taken pity on me, and then such good care of me, and we sat down, at a long table of scrubbed oak, to a good breakfast of porridge and bacon and eggs.

Mrs. Wishart was much easier in manner with me than she had been the day before, and I guessed that during the night she had waited, with some anxiety, for the result of her husband's visit to my room; and then, having discovered that I was not to be thrown out, but kept as an audience, she had felt a grateful relief. I could not believe that her life with Mungo was happy – I wondered how she could tolerate him – but she did not look like a woman who had suffered unduly, and now, in her composure, she showed a very agreeable, easy dignity. She had, too, a shrewd intelligence, and in our table-talk there was no drag or strain of pretended interest. The children had evidently been warned to be on their best behaviour, and neither spoke much, but both watched me with a gentle, hardly deviating interest.

Before I said goodbye, however, Gudrun found opportunity, when her mother was out of the room, to ask if I had read the book she brought me; and when I told her that I hadn't been able to finish it, she said, 'Then take it with you. Oh, please! It's mine, you see, and I would like you to have it. Father gave one to me and one to Ólaf, and he has more in his desk. I know where they are, and I can easily get another for myself.'

Her manner was urgent, and I let her run upstairs to fetch the book; which, indeed, I wanted to finish. I put it in the pocket of my coat and, with more gratitude than one usually feels for a night's lodging, said goodbye to Mrs. Wishart. Despite the storm in my bedroom, and the brandy I had drunk, I was well again, and walking back to the ship I felt, like a convalescent, a fine renewal of strength. The wind had gone down, and grey clouds blew leisurely over the low brown hills that guarded the voe where, nearly two hundred years before, the dissolute young Shetlanders had been drowned.

The children on their ponies rode beside me, and beyond their mother's restraint chattered tirelessly. They were such handsome, charming, and lively children that I felt truly sorry to leave them, and on the shore we shook hands in a solemn, rather emotional fashion. They had rescued me, I think they regarded me almost as their property; and I promised to write to them. The boatman who had brought me ashore, put me aboard again.

I found Silver on the bridge, talking to Finch, and learnt that repair was almost complete, and we should sail in the afternoon. As soon as Silver was alone I told him there was no foundation for his suspicion of Mungo Wishart, and we must give up the idea of confronting him with the dead man from the Faeroes.

He made me repeat, as fully as I could, what Wishart had said to me; and I remembered, with perfect clarity, the whole course of the argument – if it can be described as such – except the political detail. 'But that doesn't matter,' said Silver. 'I'm not interested in Lloyd George and the Armenians. Tell me again what he said about Shetland and Roger Casement.'

We talked for an hour, and then he said, 'It's your belief that he isn't mad, but there's madness in him. Well, that's no proof of innocence. I should rather say it's a presumption of guilt. There's usually a background of near-madness behind the guilt that we suspect—'

'That you suspect.'

'All right, that I suspect. – And that's because the major kinds of guilt require a touch of madness: a patch of inflammation on the mind. Or on the soul, perhaps. – No, Chisholm, you're a good counsel for the defence, but you haven't established your case, and I'm going to have him aboard.'

'You don't know him. You haven't listened to him—'

'But I shall.'

'You haven't seen his wife and children.'

'No, and if they're attractive I don't want to. I want to keep my judgment cool.'

For the first time since I had met him I felt antagonism between us. In the Faeroes he had out-argued me, persuaded me (or willed me) to accept his point of view and adopt his plan; but that he had effected, as I thought, by a natural talent for taking the lead, and his charm of manner – though by 'charm' I do not, of course, imply anything deliberate or calculated. Now I saw, beneath his charm, a quality of ruthlessness that I had not suspected. He was looking, too, extraordinarily well – hard as an apple and as cheerful in hue – and I said to him, 'You seem to thrive on a storm at sea.'

He relaxed at once, and said, 'I slept for eleven hours, and Finch and the others, bless their hearts, went on working while I lay unconscious. I forgot all about you, and when I woke up I came on deck stamping like a drill-sergeant. In one way or another we've done a good job; but we haven't been working trade union hours. And having done a good job in the ship, I'm going to top it off by personal trial and investigation of Mr. Mungo Wishart. We'll have a gin party for him at twelve noon.'

He paid no more attention to anything I said, but roused his Number One and told him to prepare for the entertainment of a guest. 'We'll have you and Finch, who deserves a compliment more than any of us, and Tórur if he can make himself look respectable, and Captain Chisholm and myself; that's plenty,' he said. 'And now I'm going to call on the laird.'

He went ashore, and I wasted half an hour on regret for my ineffectual mind and too pliable character. I hoped, I remember, that Mungo would be stiffer than I, and refuse his invitation. But in giving way to that hope I under-esteemed the power that Silver exercised on people of all sorts. About noon I saw them walking together towards the ship: Wishart looking the old-fashioned country gentleman in Edwardian knickerbockers and a deerstalker's cap.

They came aboard, and in our tiny wardroom the First Lieutenant and Mr. Finch were introduced, and the steward, wearing a jacket in honour of our guest, offered gin and sherry on a silver tray. Mungo Wishart was astonishingly genial, and it seemed clear that he, as well as I, swung like a compass needle to Silver's north. Among men so much younger than himself he made a burly joke of being outmoded in thought and speech, and Silver played up to him with lively humour. He fell into conversation with Finch, who at one time had served in some small vessel in the Persian Gulf, and could talk about Bahrein and Kuwait. And to me he referred in the most amiable way as a visitor who kept him up half the night talking politics and spouting poetry. – I was embarrassed by this reversal of the parts we had played, and did not know how to reply. But our First Lieutenant, whose leading interests were music and horses, came quickly in with two questions, like a right and left: 'Do you read modern poetry, sir? And don't you feel that what it lacks most is melody?'

'I'm not a literary man,' said Wishart, 'and my opinion wouldn't have any value. Captain Chisholm and I were discussing Yeats last night, and I don't even know if he's a modern poet or not. But tell me what you think of this.'

He assumed his chanting voice, and quoted:

> When I was young,
> I had not given a penny for a song
> Did not the poet sing it with such airs
> That one believed he had a sword upstairs.

'That's good,' said Finch. 'That's what poetry ought to be like.'

'I'm inclined to agree,' said Number One.

Mungo Wishart took another glass of sherry, and Silver, who had been standing beside me, moved away and looked through a port-hole at the ruffled sea. He had, I think, been about to admit that our guest was innocent, our suspicion vain. – I, out of vanity perhaps, now had no doubt of that, and felt that I was responsible for his present geniality: I had been his patient audience, and into my lap he had shot his load of remembered injustice and grief. So now, having rid himself of that memory, he had the gaiety of an unencumbered man. – But the emotion of the Irish verses, the tremor of belief in his voice as he spoke of 'a sword upstairs', woke a doubt in Silver's mind again.

Then Tórur came in, looking like a provincial gangster dressed for the dance-hall. He had been told to make himself respectable, and he had borrowed, from various members of the crew, a dark blue shirt, a yellow tie, a tweed jacket with exaggerated shoulders and narrow waist, and chocolate-brown trousers. He had shaved to the bone, and smoothed and polished his hair with oil. He clapped his heels together, bowed, and introduced himself.

'A volunteer from the Faeroes,' said Silver, 'and a damned good man at the wheel. We were very glad to have him aboard when we ran into bad weather.'

'To my infinite regret,' said Wishart, 'I can't address you in Faeroese, and my Danish is very poor. But do you understand the *landsmaal*?' – And like a bad actor overplaying his part, he spoke a few sentences.

Smiling broadly, Tórur replied in the same tongue, and Silver, having allowed them a few minutes' conversation, interposed, 'You speak Norwegian very fluently, sir.'

'Why shouldn't I?' said Wishart. 'I have killed four hundred Norwegian salmon, and I daresay I've known as many Norwegian people. I'm very fond of Norway, and everything in it.'

Silver took his opportunity, and said, 'It's long odds against your being able to help us, but if you've spent a lot of time in Norway, there's just a chance you may have seen our prisoner somewhere—'

'A prisoner? Who's he?'

'A Norwegian we have aboard, sir. We think he may be a German agent—'

'Then I can't help you. Though I knew a lot of people, my circle wasn't as catholic as you think.'

There was an edge to his voice now, but he was smiling.

His posture had stiffened, and he looked down at Silver – he was almost a head taller – with something like condescension. With, perhaps, the cold forgiveness of a superior person who has been offended by someone who knows no better. And Silver's manner, in reply, was lightly worried, airly apologetic.

'No, sir,' he said, 'I didn't suppose he would be a friend of yours. But if you had ever seen him, in Oslo or Bergen or Andalsnes, it might help us to know where.'

'Where did you get hold of this man?'

'He got out of Norway and came to grief in the Faeroes. That's all we really know about him, so far. And there is a possibility – a chance in ten thousand – that you might have come across him. In a village post-office, perhaps. He might even have been your gillie when you were fishing.'

'I had the same gillie for seven years.'

'Well, that cuts that out. Probably. But I want to explore every lead, and as you know so many people in Norway—'

'I know a great many.'

'Well, sir.'

'I'm not going to interrogate him, if that's what you want.'

'No, sir, it isn't. I only want you to have a look at him, and say if you've ever seen him before.'

Wishart took his time to reply. We stood round him, waiting, I fear, with too obvious an interest for his answer. He met our eyes, in turn, and grew superbly confident. He appeared to become, in fact, the dominating Victorian that he looked. 'I am your guest,' he said, 'and if you feel that I'm under any obligation to you, pray let me discharge it.'

'This way, sir,' said Silver quickly, and led him on deck.

Still in its chair – to which, for its better balance, it was now more firmly tied – the body of the frozen man sat on the little after-deck behind the bridge. In milder weather his total rigidity had collapsed, and though *rigor mortis* – or some inward icicles – still gave him a certain stiffness, his outer parts were slack and soft, and his general appearance a dissolution – moral, it seemed, as well as physical – of human kind.

Mungo Wishart halted, and his head reared like a horse reined hard back, when he saw the body. He stared for a moment, his face darkening with anger, and exclaimed, 'By God and by God, sir, what monkey's trick is this? D'you think I'm an undertaker's man, or a body-snatcher? How else would I recognize a corpse?'

He seemed to grow in height, in breadth, and in outraged dignity. He dwarfed us all, and loomed above us in some outmoded dignity of wrath.

'That's the man, sir, of whom I told you,' said Silver. 'A Norwegian.'

'How long has he been dead?' Wishart stooped above him and pinched a cheek. It yielded like putty between his thumb and forefinger. 'The man's been dead for days. Who killed him? Did you?'

'No, sir,' said Silver. 'I've never killed anything bigger than a pheasant. All I'm trying to do is a little bit of police-work. A bit of detective-work.'

'And you're an officer in His Majesty's Navy, are you? Creeping round basements and peeping through key-holes looking for clues – eh? Well, God help His Majesty! I served his father, and gave up praying for the King after I'd seen too many of his subjects. But tonight, sir, I'll pray for the King, because I'd pray for any king who depended on officers such as you! And now, sir, will you be so good as to send for my boat, and put me ashore.'

'I'm sorry, sir, that you've misunderstood my request—'

'Listen to me, boy. I've known pimps in Basra and pimps in Baku, blackmailers in Smyrna and conjoint thieves in Kasvin, and I've never misunderstood any of them. Tell someone to fetch my hat.'

Our First Lieutenant ran down and brought up his

deerstalker cap, and Mungo Wishart, still superb in rectitude, marched (as if across his six thousand acres) to the side.

'May I beg your pardon, sir?' said Silver.

'No, boy, you may not,' said Mungo, and went down into the boat.

We did not sail until eight o'clock. Mr. Finch the engineer, whose work was not quite finished, recommended delay, and Silver, whose assurance was much deflated, made no objection. We ate luncheon (tinned beef and hard potatoes, semolina pudding and yellow cheese) almost in silence, and Silver thereafter went to his cabin – the cabin where I slept – and shut me out. Later, about six o'clock, he apologized and gave me a drink.

'I feel,' he said, 'that I have made a fool of myself.'

'We both have,' I said.

'No, it wasn't your fault. You tried to dissuade me—'

'But I didn't insist.'

'I'll take the blame,' he said.

'I'll accept my share of it,' I said.

'That's too quixotic.'

'It's mere justice.'

'There wasn't a flicker of recognition when he saw the body! No apprehension, no anxiety. Not a twitch. I was watching him, and his only response was a blaze of anger. O God, what a fool I've been!'

'He made us look like schoolboys caught smoking. Caught by Arnold of Rugby.'

'All right, don't rub it in. Have another drink. I can't, I'll have to be up all night. . . .'

I went early to bed; and after our great tossing and plunging in the Atlantic found no discomfort in the mild heave and descent of our southward passage to Scapa Flow. In accordance with our original orders we went east-about, between Fair Isle and North Ronaldsay, that is, and down to the southern entrance to the Flow through Switha Sound. A voyage, determined by the state of our rudder as well as distance, of some eighteen hours.

I settled, in my lifting bunk, to read the continuation of *The Wishart Inheritance*, and discovered to my surprise that Mungo had tied to his revelation of Barbara Gifford's pregnancy, like an over-heavy tail to a fallen kite, a long diatribe against the immorality of Shetland in the eighteenth century. I too, for personal reasons, am against immorality – it is emotionally confusing, and I think it makes emotion vulgar – but I don't enjoy reading sermons about it. So I skipped several pages, and went on to his Chapter Two.

(2)

I have before me, in two volumes, the printed record of some part of a suit at law which, by the stubbornness of both sides and the lawyers' cunning devices, was continued, in one way or another, for many years, and had no other result than to channel a vast amount of good Shetland money into the pockets of the legal gentry of Edinburgh.

One volume is entitled *State of Proof for Respondent* (Charles Pitcairn, Esq., of Gracechurch Street, City of London), and the other *State of Proof for Advocator* (Arthur Wishart, Esq., of Weddergarth in Shetland). Now shorn of all the tomnoddy decorations and obfuscations of Scottish Law, this means that Charles Pitcairn was trying to take from Arthur Wishart the property that Arthur held by the right of usage of three generations. The date of the action is 1833, and Arthur Wishart, socalled *Advocator*, is the grandson of the child that Barbara Gifford bore in scorn and tribulation; while Charles Pitcairn, described as *Respondent*, is descendant of the second of Gideon Wishart's and Lady Weddergarth's three slinking daughters. She married a nephew of Old Dandy the drunken Jacobite. His nephew, a plump fish-curer in Lerwick, was also correspondent of a rich firm of merchants in Bremen; – and by him alone that dismal trio of sisters had issue, for the eldest died in childbed of a still birth, and the youngest was barren.

These two faded volumes contain the evidence, for one side or the other, of some fifty people, many old and doddering, who had been summoned, at great expense of time and money, to Lerwick or to Edinburgh, to answer interminable questions which, in the way of lawyers, were aimed in all directions to find a single target; and the bull's eye they sought was the baby that Barbara Gifford bore, in a garret in the house of Weddergarth, some eighty-four years before. Was he the lawful son and heir of Henry Wishart, drowned in the Voe of Hammar, or was he a bastard? If a bastard, then Charles Pitcairn of Gracechurch Street – descendant of Henry's ugliest sister – might take from their possessor the rich lands and great estate of Weddergarth, Sandwick, and Hammar.

Not one of the witnesses knew the truth of the matter. None of them had been at Weddergarth when the boy was born. They could do no better than relate the gossip of the country, to which they had been brought up, and describe, so far as they had observed or been told of it, the manner of Barbara Gifford's life after she left Weddergarth and went to live in Lerwick. Some of the older ones had known her, by sight if not by real acquaintance, and not a soul on either side of the dispute could find harsher criticism than to say she carried herself proudly, was very lady-like, and did not easily associate with her inferiors. After the boy's birth there is no hint or whisper that she ever had friendship or association with any man.

The witnesses, for the most part, are a pathetic host. There are a few of the minor gentry, a doctor or two, and a brace of Presbyterian ministers; but small and humble people, stricken with years, are the majority, and in their faithfully reported statements one can almost hear their old and muddy wits fumbling for recollection of the great scandalous story that was told, over and over again, in ill-lighted smoky cottages where the women sat gossiping over their spinning-wheels; or in draughty stables where the men gathered, in rough friendship, and salted the same tale with bawdry. I am no lover, God knows, of our present world, but I thank heaven I was not born to the infinite tedium and frightful littleness – the dull restriction and the gulfs of boredom – of the world, as they knew it in the islands, two hundred or even one hundred years ago.

Here, for example, is some part of the testimony of Mrs. Janet Bruce, who gave evidence for the Advocator: the Arthur Wishart, that is, who flourished dimly in 1833 and was my grandfather. I omit the questions and that ridiculous solemnity of the report by which every trivial statement is introduced with the word *depones*.

'Mrs. Janet Bruce, being solemnly sworn, and purged of malice and partial counsel, *deponed* "That she understood that Weddergarth's three sons, and a young minister of the name of Mr. Mouatt, and a grieve on the property, were all drowned at once by the upsetting of a boat crossing from Weddergarth to Hammar.

"That she understood there was a young lady named Miss Barbara Gifford that lived at Weddergarth.

"That she understood Miss Gifford to have been a high-born and high-bred lady.

"That she has heard often that an honourable courtship had been noticed between Miss Gifford and Henry Wishart, younger of Weddergarth, previous to his death.

"That she understood that Lady Weddergarth had been violently opposed to a marriage betwixt them.

"That Lady Weddergarth was of a very proud and commanding character, and very violent in her temper.

"That she understood Miss Gifford to have a paper which some said was her marriage lines, and others a statement that she was with child to Henry Wishart on the promise of marriage.

"That she understood that this paper so far satisfied Lady Weddergarth as to make her bring up the child as the real heir of the family." '

But being interrogated for the Respondent, Mrs. Janet

Bruce had to admit, 'That she has not heard Miss Barbara
Gifford spoken of by any other name than Barbara Gifford, for Lady Weddergarth would not allow her to take
the name of Mrs. Wishart.'

There is the substance of Mrs. Bruce's evidence: Mrs.
Bruce, aged seventy years, and friendly to the family of
Weddergarth. There is the foundation of gossip that endured for generation after generation. But gossip spreads
out, and burgeons, and carries slander, filthy insinuation,
and little pious fruits as untrustworthy as the vilest nonsense.

Imagine, on the basis of Mrs. Janet's sober tale, what
was said of Barbara by unfriendly witnesses, and the gossip
that went on in the cottages where women were knitting by
the light of a cruizie-lamp, or in the sour, cold stables
where young men stood and guffawed at a shameful story
of their betters. Imagine too, more closely if you can, the
pain, and the agony of her mind, of Barbara Gifford in the
garret at Weddergarth while her bones fought her womb's
decision to show the tell-tale face of her child.

I do not know how loosely she had lived. I respect her
for her strength of will, but cannot like her for any belief in
her purity. The odds are all against her. By means known
only to her, she persuaded the lamentable young minister,
Abel Mouatt, to give her marriage lines or an affirmation of
some sort; and presumably she went to considerable
lengths to convince Henry Wishart, not only that she
was willing to marry him, but that he had some obligation
to marry her. There is also the remembered story that
Henry's younger brother was in love with her, and to
assume the truth of this makes it easier to understand
the general quarrel, the vulgar melee, that upset the boat
and in the narrow waters of the quiet voe drowned them
all. And the set of portraits that she left, in the secret
drawer of her desk, confess an attachment more vital than
any of her coarse flirtations.

The boy she bore had no likeness to Henry Wishart. He
had a fine broad brow, and according to the evidence of
some witnesses it was his forehead that first recommended

him to Lady Weddergarth; whose own brow was broad and fair.

Here are the words of the Rev. Mr. Cheyne, born in Delting in Shetland, and at the time of his interrogation aged seventy-four.

'*Interrogated*, "If he has always understood that it was in consequence of Lady Weddergarth's predilection for David (Barbara's son, that is) that Gideon Wishart was induced to declare and nominate him his heir?"

'*Depones*, "That he cannot expressly answer this question, but the lady was always said to have had a very great predilection for David, founded on his likeness to her family."

'And deponent adds, "That he has heard that the first time David was brought to see her, she laid her finger on his brow, and said, That brow should make a man of him yet, having immediately recognized the likeness to herself. . . ." '

The likeness to herself, be it noted: not a likeness to her son, the child's reputed father, who with all his brothers and sisters carried the glum stamp of his spear-side. To Lady Weddergarth, that imperious and handsome woman, it must have been a grievous mortification that every one of her children – save, perhaps those that small-pox killed, of whom there are no portraits – so faithfully copied their father's hang-dog and dismal features rather than her own bold glance and lordly bone. But here, in the sturdy child whose pouting lips were still wet with that hussy's milk, here at last she could recognize her own good pattern; and though she never forgave Barbara, she formed at once 'a very great predilection' for the boy.

I do not doubt that she had driven from her mind all thought of her late disreputable uncle, Old Dandy Pitcairn. But Dandy's bones, under the raffish disguise of dissipation, had been fashioned to the same shape as hers, and Young Dandy had flattered his father as closely as Gideon Wishart's brood copied him. If the child resembled Lady Weddergarth as doubtless he did, the resemblance came from a source she failed to guess; and of that I have proof – better than lawyers' proof – in the drawings that Barbara Gifford made.

There are eight drawings of the child, done as I think between the ages of six months or so and two or three years. There are three drawings of him as a little boy of, perhaps, five, six, and seven years. Barbara died, still a young woman, when he was seven, and she had been living in Lerwick, alone and parted from her son, for at least four years before her death. Now the last three drawings show a striking resemblance to the portraits of Young Dandy, even to repetition of the bulbous tip she gave his nose: that hint of caricature by which she redeemed her romantic view of Young Dandy is repeated, as if to proclaim his parentage, in her pictures of the boy David. This, of course, she did for her private satisfaction, for in public she maintained, at first hotly, and then with quiet persistence, that David was the legal offspring of her marriage to Henry Wishart. Even in labour with the boy, in the pangs of childbirth, she is said to have cried out, again and again, that she was Henry's wife and the child begotten of him. But Barbara, in her own way, had a character as hard as Lady Weddergarth's, and a great gift of secrecy. Her life, in the secrecy of her own mind, may have had strange satisfactions.

Throughout the evidence of the many witnesses who came to debate the boy's legitimacy, there is no hint, and apparently there was no suspicion, that his father was in fact Young Dandy. None of the witnesses had ever seen Young Dandy or his father, and in the gossip of their elders, from which they had got their clouded, legendary knowledge of the young men's drowning and the girl's tormented childbed, there had been apparently no glance at him, no ribald suggestion that it was he who had left a loaf in the oven. And for this there are two good reasons. The first is that Henry Wishart, as the heir to a great estate, was in the eyes of a hungry community the natural object of a poor girl's desire; and the second is a dream, or the widespread report of a dream.

It was commonly said, and generally believed, that some

time after his death Henry had appeared to his mother in a dream, and besought her to take care of the child that Barbara carried, for it was his. This old wives' tale, so manifestly the invention of a chimney-corner, got more attention in the country than young David's good looks, tall stature, and, as he grew to manhood, gaiety of manner – all the inheritance of Dandy Pitcairn – and nearly a hundred years later the lawyers still listened solemnly to the tale of a dream that their witnesses took oath about. You cannot blame peasants for being fools, when lawyers are no better.

Young David grew up to be a lively, popular, and extravagant young man who, when he succeeded to his property, lived in a style that several of the witnesses described as 'stately'. He, when they were giving their evidence in 1833, had been dead for five and twenty years, but still the circumstances of his birth were hunted as keenly as if they had left a living scent, and the ghost of his young mother was chased through the shadows.

Here is Andro Harcus of Northmavine, aged eighty-seven, *deponing* that Miss Barbara Gifford, when she lived alone in Lerwick, received from the Wisharts 'a mart (a fat ox, that is) every Martinmas, and in summer a lispund (or eighteen pounds) of wool'. – Though others say she kept herself by her needlework. – And Mrs. Mary Sand, of Delting, aged eighty-three, *depones* that Miss Gifford 'aye dressed like a lady, wore grey silk in her own house, and like a proper lady kept herself to herself'.

Christie Laing, now of Yell, aged eighty-two, says that when the body of Henry Wishart was carried ashore, 'Miss Barbara fell upon it with a loud shriek, and cried out she was five months gone with child and here was the father of it. And delving into his neck she fetched forth a paper on which was written her marriage lines'. – Though surely any paper that had been in the sea for a day, a night, and a day, would have been reduced to pulp.

Lawrence Williamson of Delting, aged sixty-nine, says that never had he heard a suggestion that Mr. David Wishart was anything but legally begotten and lawfully born, and the true heir to the lands of Weddergarth; while Grizel Irvine, now of Gulberwick, aged seventy-one, says her father often recalled a conversation in which he, having called Mr. David a bastard, was answered by the said David in high good humour, who assured him that half the grown men in Shetland might be so described, if only their mothers would tell the truth.

Little Madge Gilbertson, who had sat in a corner when Lady Weddergarth heard Barbara's confession, and burnt what may or may not have been a certificate of marriage, was dead long since, but two of her daughters gave evidence. Both were in their seventies, and like two old parrots they told, in identical words, the tale they had heard so often from their mother. They remembered every detail of it, but they remembered little else. Their wits had been wool-gathering for years, and because some of their statements contradicted the most reliable witnesses, what they told about the scene in the parlour was also doubted.

And so it goes on. The tittle-tattle of a half-starved countryside that throughout its long winters had nothing but tittle-tattle for amusement. – And there are the full-fed lawyers of Edinburgh drawing their fat fees, day after day and year after year, out of senile memory, dim-witted malice, and the pathetic loyalty of simpletons. To the lawyers all are equally valuable – tales of a dream, stories of marriage lines rescued from the dissolving sea, and solid assertion that Miss Barbara's yearly allowance was a fat ox and eighteen pounds of wool – because all are melted down to fit and fill the lawyers' pockets. Year after year the suit dragged on.

What could not be denied, by witness or counsel, was that Lady Weddergarth herself, though never reconciled to Barbara, had doted on the boy she bore, and made certain that he should inherit the Weddergarth estates. She ruled the house – there is no doubt of that – and at her insistence Gideon Wishart, an old man with no substance in him after the death of his sons, wrote to his solicitors in Edinburgh in 1752. He complained of the infirmities of age, and sorrowfully made known that 'it hath pleased God to remove all my sons by death, unmarried, and leaving no children after them, save only my eldest son, who left a girl with child. Whether he designed to marry her or not I know not, but the child promises to be a very promising boy, now about three years old'.

He speaks of his daughters, and their rights, but despite acknowledgment of them declares his intention: 'To entail the whole or the greatest part of my land estate upon my nearest heir-male; and although the child above mentioned labours under a legal inability to succeed to me in my estate, yet, as that defect may be supplied, I think he has the best natural right to stand first in the entail; and the necessary steps to be taken to clothe him with a legal title, I want to be informed anent.'

A year later it is noted that 'Gideon Winhart granted a general disposition of his whole heritable and moveable estate to David Wishart, a natural son of Henry Wishart, who was the granter's eldest son. . . .'

These business-like arrangements reminded me, uncomfortably, of my own obligations. I had a report to write that would require discreet and skilful phrases and a careful presentation of the facts. I would remember to spell Sergeant Fergusson's name with two 'ss', but could I count as accurately our motives, arguments, and half-reasons for taking Jón Jónsson's body aboard the trawler? – A dry recital, a simple narrative, a calm assumption that such-and-such was the obvious thing to do: there, most certainly, was the proper method. But the writing of the report must wait till the morning, for a morning light was needed for the selection of detail and a steady pretence of simplicity.

It was pleasant, next day, to look out on the starboard side and see the curious shapes and re-entrances of the Orkney islands, but I spent most of my time below, writing my story as scrupulously as a diplomat in time of crisis. I finished it as we approached the boom across

Switha Sound, and were let in, as if through the garden gate, to the barren garden of Scapa Flow. We were told to make fast to a buoy near Lyness and wait further orders; and there we lay as the light ebbed from the short afternoon.

At six o'clock, in darkness, Silver and I were instructed to come ashore and see the Intelligence Officer whom I had met before. We found our way, with some small difficulty, through the slum-like streets of that absurd but so-important, wooden-hutted, temporary village of Lyness, and marching down an echoing corridor, presently knocked at the proper door.

The I.O. whom I knew was sitting behind a brown-blanketed table – an iron stove close behind him – and at his side was a Commander with a hard, inexpressive face and smooth, black hair brushed sternly back from a widow's peak. The I.O., a lieutenant, conducted the interrogation. The Commander took no part in it, but merely sat and listened.

I put my report on the table, but the I.O. said, 'Just tell me, to begin with, what happened after you arrived in Tórshavn.' – And then, as tentatively I began, he interrupted me to ask Silver, 'Have you a written report?'

'Not yet, sir. My part in the affair was somewhat complicated by the weather. We ran into a Force 9 gale, and the ship took some damage. My report will have to be technical in parts.'

'I see. And I beg your pardon, Chisholm. Please go on.'

I told the story – the whole of it – to a silent audience. Neither the I.O., nor the Commander beside him, interrupted or made any comment throughout a narrative – I flatter myself that I kept it as short as possible – which began with my meeting Bömlo and Tórur, in Tórur's house, and ended with our discomfiture at the hands of Mungo Wishart.

The I.O. said, 'I shall have to see the man you call

Tórur. I think nine o'clock tomorrow morning would be the best time.'

'I'll see that he's here,' said Silver.

'You haven't made it quite clear – it isn't, at any rate, clear to me – why you took aboard the body of the man from Norway. It wasn't normal procedure; as you know perfectly well. But quite deliberately, it seems, you ignored the normal procedure and set off on this – oh, this adventure – which, if it didn't pay a dividend, would almost certainly land you in trouble. Now why did you do that?'

'I think I must deal with that,' said Silver, and very frankly admitting his responsibility for our disregard of convention, described most plausibly, as I thought his hope of proving a connection between the man who had called himself Jónsson and Mungo Wishart.

'You hadn't much evidence to go on,' said the I.O. 'You made a guess. You had, I suppose, some sort of expectation. Or anticipation—'

The black-haired Commander made his only contribution to the discussion. In a flat, uninterested voice, 'He had a hunch,' he said.

'Yes,' said Silver, 'I had a hunch. At the time it seemed a good one. But as things turned out, it wasn't.'

The I.O., with a question on his face, looked at the Commander, and apparently got an answer; though to me it was invisible.

'I've been in communication with Shetland all day,' he said. 'I knew you had run into Hammar Voe, and seen Mungo Wishart. I know – and for the last twelve months I have known – a good deal about him. At this moment I certainly know more than you do. I must tell you that last night, soon after you sailed from Hammar Voe, he committed suicide.'

I sprang to my feet, so clumsily that I knocked my chair over, and foolishly cried, 'Oh, no! O God!' – I saw in imagination the two children, and his wife, bereft and weeping. I looked at Silver and saw the ripe apple-colour ebbing from his cheeks, and a staring pallor remain. He sat still, he did not move, but he was pierced and shaken by the news as deeply as I was.

'He was prepared for suicide,' said the I.O. 'He took prussic acid – or a cyanide. They found another capsule in his dressing-table. In his stud-box. Made by a firm of German chemists. And the usual accompaniment in the fireplace: a pile of ashes.'

After a pause he added, 'Your hunch was a good one after all.'

'He had two children,' I said.

'They, I think, can be protected. They won't be told, that is, that their father committed suicide. We certainly don't want it to be known, and I don't think it will be. The doctor there is a man I know. He was worried, and got in touch with me before he told the police. So officially – and I hope public opinion will accept the official view – Mungo Wishart died of heart failure.'

IT WAS NOT until May 1942 that I got to North Africa, though I applied for a posting as soon as I returned to London from Scapa Flow; and that was on Christmas Eve. It was a desperately sad Christmas I spent, for the death of Mungo Wishart lay on my mind like a charge of murder. I have said – and I still hold to it – that I would, at any time, betray a friend rather than my country; but I had not realised, till then, the torment of guilt and the sensation of overwhelming sorrow that succeed, or may succeed, the bringing of death, not to a friend, but to a mere acquaintance. To a fellow mortal with whom, for an hour or two, one has lived and talked in some degree of sympathy: even partial, fleeting sympathy.

I admitted the probability – even the certainty – that Mungo Wishart was guilty of intended treason. But also I remembered him quoting Yeats, with endearing pomposity; I remembered his look of a hero of the Indian Mutiny; and I could not wipe from my mind the picture of his two tall and handsome children on the beach at Hammar Voe . . . I had played an equal part with Silver in sending him to his death. In contriving – as if he were another Roger Casement – his execution. An execution justified, I suppose, by the public need, but an execution in which my hand had helped push him to the drop; and still trembled for it.

It was I – it was Silver and I, but Silver had an English certainty of vision, an English ruthlessness, that I lacked – who had orphaned those two children and widowed their good mother. And by that action I had set myself beside

Cromar, who killed my brother Peter. I had joined the men of purpose, the men without feeling. The men in uniform whose hearts slept in their uniform. And in those trappings I did not want to live. I had to get rid of them, and there was only one way to do that. So for most of the next year I hoped to see myself killed. I had too much respect for my contract with the Army, and my allegiance to the King, to kill myself; but I should have been well pleased to be killed by the King's enemies. That is why, unscrupulously, I used every source of help that my father's name and reputation opened for me to get employment in North Africa.

The doctors disappointed me, by refusing to pass me fit for regimental duty, but at last I was promised, rather vaguely, a staff appointment in a division then fighting somewhere in Libya; and about the end of March I embarked in a troop-ship which, after seven or eight weeks at sea, set me down on a drab shore of Egypt.

It was an appropriate moment, for anyone in my mood, to join the Desert Army; for Rommel was about to attack in strength, and neither the French at Bir Hacheim nor the Guards at Knightsbridge would stand against him. Disaster was imminent at Tobruk, a sudden collapse with the loss of 20,000 men, and Auchinleck would have to pull back to El Alamein. – In such circumstances it would seem easy for a young man, on the losing side and eager to be rid of his life, to discard it. But I found difficulties in my way.

My first obstacle was the kindness of my old friend Pelly. A week or two after our conversation in the lighted room under Whitehall, he had been given a staff job in Cairo, and with it promotion to lieutenant-colonel. He had flown out, and arrived soon after Christmas; now, with the authority of nearly five months in the country, he was very much at home and appeared to know a vast number of people and the private intentions, as well as the personal habits, of all the senior officers both in Egypt and the desert.

He was, I think, quite genuinely anxious to be kind, and I had the feeling that he regretted having told me of Peter's death, and the hurt he had so obviously dealt me. He never mentioned Peter again; but entertained me with an unceasing stream of remarkable gossip. – We met by accident, and half an hour later were in the bar at Shepheard's, where he introduced me to several of his friends, all of whom, it appeared, had sources of gossip not inferior to his, and found equal pleasure in them. The next day he took me to Gezireh, to play tennis and swim, and with other friends match witticisms about the curious behaviour of exalted persons and ladies of fashion; or anecdotes, that I found alarming, of the Egyptians' continuous theft of our military stores and equipment; or opinions, no less disturbing, of the prowess of General Rommel.

If easy enjoyment had been my aim, I could have spent two or three very pleasant weeks in Cairo – before panic struck it – but in the temper of that year I hated the deep-rooted frivolity that characterized so many of the great horde of military tourists who had settled there. I disliked Egypt itself – its insensate geology and immemorial corruption – and I was nauseated by the loud display of an over-stuffed garrison and the absurdly swollen general, administrative, and pseudo-political staffs that had gathered so happily about its gaudy capital. I wanted to join my division in the desert, and though Pelly assured me that this would be the simplest matter in the world if I gave him a little time to arrange things – for my posting was a trifle irregular – his procrastination was so obvious that presently I asked him if it was deliberate. And to my surprise he answered, 'Yes'.

In the circumstances, he said, it would be wiser for me to wait a week or two. My division might be too busy to find room and occupation for a new and untried staff officer, and I must cultivate patience. – He was right, of course, but I would not admit it. I made friends with a young man, harsh in manner and appearance, who had just come out of hospital and was determined to rejoin his regiment by a quicker route than that through 'the usual channels'. He procured a vehicle of sorts, he found a sergeant and two troopers of his regiment who had also been sick – and now, having no money, were sick of Cairo – and with them, quite unofficially, I set out one morning along the dreary highway to El Amiriya: where the road forks right to Alexandria and left to Mersa Matruh and the frontier. We turned left.

By then the battle was almost at its height, but, from the news of it that was published, no one could tell what was happening. There was, however, heavy traffic on the road, and our progress was slow. I had my first experience of sleeping under the desert stars and waking – in the lee of an evil-smelling truck – to the exhilaration of dawn in the desert. But the next night the *khamsin* was blowing.

We drove on the road so well known by repute, in those days, and past names that sometimes had seemed to be making history – Mersa Matruh and Sidi Barrani, Sollum and Bardia, with the frontier between them. – But now history was overlaid by a multitude of signposts that pointed the way to this or that fragment of an army that sprawled, as it seemed, in irrelevant dissociation over five hundred miles of barren, sun-dazed, broken desert from the green luxury of the Nile to the bloody confusion of the battle that had begun on the minefields west of Bir Hacheim, and was now flowing sullenly to the east.

The ramshackle truck we drove in broke down, and was repaired. It broke down again, and my resourceful companions removed from a nearby wreck some part of its engine to renovate ours. The desert was littered with wreckage. Its ancient, stony face was scarred across and across by tank-tracks, and in the blinding haze of noon we seemed to be surrounded by the debris of uncountable traffic-accidents. Before turning south, we followed for some time the Trigh Capuzzo, on the long escarpment that runs from Bardia to El Adem; and intermittently the road was crowded. But here and there, beyond the traffic-stream – on the shore of the stream – we saw a curiously peaceful little gathering of men, like nomads pausing for refreshment and conversation.

They were men who had lost their way, or whose vehicles had broken down; and with the placid common sense of the British soldier they were taking life easily. They had their blankets and their rations. They spent their time sleeping, brewing tea, and – like their betters in Cairo – gossiping. Most of them had the air of plunderers, but some appeared to have settled down, as nomads settle for a while where their horses find pasture. They were all polite, good-tempered, and quick to supply information about the way to such and such a place, to this battalion or that brigade; and their information was always wrong.

Now we could hear the sounds of battle, and from worried officers in rear echelons got increasingly bad news. There had been very heavy fighting, and both sides had suffered grievous losses. Our estimate of German casualties, however, seemed to have been exaggerated, for always, when morning came, they joined battle again with sixty tanks that no one expected to be there. Our own tactics were unco-ordinated, and the German armour, instead of advancing across a defended minefield to a strongly held frontal position, had the disconcerting habit of finding an open flank; for such cunning we were quite unprepared. There was a rumour that the Knightsbridge box had been abandoned.

It was on our third night that we joined, at last light, a disconsolate and dishevelled company of troop-carriers, petrol lorries, and ammunition lorries. They had met on converging tracks, but some were withdrawing from battle, others advancing. Confused by conflicting reports of what had happened, and where the battle now was, they had decided to leaguer until morning. We were allowed to lie with them, and were roundly told that we were fools to be there. This was proved in the morning, when two German tanks, identified as Mark IIIs, opened fire on us from a ridge some eight hundred yards to the south.

About twenty vehicles were quick to move and get away; but twenty others were destroyed, and we were in the unlucky half because our patched-up engine would not start. A shell pitched in front of the bonnet, and the explosion threw our tired truck over. The sergeant, in the driver's seat, was killed, and I, in the back, was thrown out and lay stunned.

We had leaguered in a shallow depression to the right of a well-worn track, and to the left of the track there was a little curving ridge with a rocky crest, in the shelter of which three of the nomads of battle – three men whose lorry, with a broken axle, lay some fifty yards away – had made their gipsy home under a couple of spread tarpaulins. They were dirty, unshaven, cheerful fellows, remote from any compulsion of discipline, as it seemed, and quite divorced from the purpose of the war.

But when one of them saw me lying helpless, under fire, he came trotting across the open road from his snug shelter and, raising me with a fireman's lift to his shoulder, carried me into safety. Then we heard a cry from the young man who had been my companion – the young man harsh of voice and feature, and eager to fight – who now cried loudly that his leg was broken, and he could not move. Shells were still falling on the trapped and burning vehicles among which he lay.

The nameless soldier who had saved my life – the desert nomad – looked across at him, grimaced, and said, 'Aow, —— it!'

Then, running with head down, he crossed the road

again and, lifting the wounded lieutenant, turned to come back. There was a pause in the firing, as if the Germans were counting their score. But then two shells burst almost simultaneously, and one of them fell within a few yards of the nomad and his burden. . . .

I was picked up, unconscious, an hour or two later, and taken back to a field hospital from which, within a couple of days, I was removed to a base hospital in the Delta. The 8th Army followed me, and took up a defensive position between El Alamein and the sand-sea of the Qattara Depression.

There was nothing the matter with me except a delayed concussion and a gigantic bruise that discoloured all my back; but I was kept in hospital for three weeks, and during that time I thought of little, and nothing seriously, except the extraordinary behaviour of the idle, anonymous soldier who had saved my skin, and died in his attempt to rescue another man whom he had never seen before.

Why had he done it?

Why, for the sake of two strangers, had he risked his life, and lost it? Pity, I suppose, but why should pity move a man so strongly? I heard, in memory, the coarseness of his anger when he felt in him the compulsion of pity: he had gone to his death – for a stranger – with the soldier's word on his lips. He was a man of slovenly appearance, and probably of slovenly habit.

I could not discover his name, nor anything about him. I had felt some pain as he carried me across the road, and when he put me down I wondered, for a few minutes, if my back was broken. Then I lost consciousness, and what became of the other two nomads, under their tarpaulins in a cleft in the desert, I do not know. In the great turbid flux of battle it was impossible to trace them.

My life had been saved by an unknown man, moved to pity by an inscrutable force; and I could see no profit in his action. I had lost interest in life, and if I had been left to

die in the desert, I would have died without regret. I felt
no gratitude to the nomad; I was merely puzzled by what
seemed a quite irrelevant exhibition of pity and bravery.

There were jobs for everyone in the next few months,
when behind the narrow front on which we held the
Germans there was a vast, purposive activity – though
often it looked chaotic – as a new army was fashioned and
the great attack prepared. From hospital I went to immediate though humble employment, and in quick succession I commanded a depot company at a camp in the
Delta, I was adjutant of a transit camp, and instructor at a
battle school. Major reinforcements had arrived from
England, and the Highland Division was in Egypt. My
company commander in France was now commanding a
battalion. I called on him, and persuaded a doctor that I
was fit for active service. Even in training areas casualties
occurred, and presently I was posted to fill a vacancy in a
battalion of my own regiment. That was a month before
Alamein.

On the night of October 22nd I went with my company,
of which I was second-in-command, to an assembly area
behind the start line. We lay hidden all day in small
trenches well camouflaged, and with the return of darkness moved forward. There was a full moon shining.

On a forty-mile front nearly a thousand guns opened on
the German batteries, and the enormous desert moon was
hidden by dust and smoke. Through the nerve-shaking
din of the guns we could hear the pipers playing, and with
slow precision we began the long advance.

Except for the physical discomfort that I always feel
under heavy gunfire – as if the noise were rubbing a fiddle-
string in my guts – I was calm and almost without fear. I
felt quite sure that I would be killed within the next few
days, and there was nothing in the prospect of death that
could alarm me when, for close on a year, I had lived with a
distaste for life (my own life) so bitter that it had dissolved

– or so I thought – my sentient being, and left between my helmet and my boots only a serviceable, intelligent ghost.

Shell-fire and spandaus opened our ranks, and steadily we went forward into the battle of El Alamein. I felt a deep respect for the bravery of the men I led, for they, of course, hoped to survive the battle. I had the great advantage that I was confident of the imminence of death. . . .

Rather more than five months later, and about fifteen hundred miles to the west, I was leading a small but very unpleasant attack on the Wadi Akarit in such fear that I could hardly hold my head up and watch where I was going. I had survived the anabasis, the several battles and the great pursuit across the roof-line of Africa, and so far recovered my health of mind, and an appetite for life, that I had become acutely frightened of mortar-bombs and S-mines. But I was grateful for the change.

In the long advance, in the redoubtable comradeship that I now remember with pride, I had not been a popular officer; for a ghost contributes little to comradeship. But I 'got by', as they say, because I knew my job, I was efficient, and as our casualties increased I was widely recognized as lucky; soldiers like a lucky officer, even though he is cold and unfriendly. – Perhaps the first sign of my recovery was seen at Tripoli, where one day I heard the Colonel say, 'Good God, look at Tony! What's the matter with him? He's laughing!' But the proof came at the Wadi Akarit, where I, who had desired death, stood in a lather of sweat to see it close beside me.

That was the division's last battle in Africa, and a month later we were training on the Algerian coast for the invasion of Sicily. I had no part in that operation, however, for in Philippeville I met Pelly again; and Pelly, now red-tabbed, a full colonel and bursting with his importance, had to show it by taking charge of me and shaping my career.

'You're the very man I want!' he exclaimed. 'This bloody army is entirely staffed by well-behaved illiterates and heavily disguised civilians who don't know a loading-table from a landing-strip. What are you doing, and when can you come and work for me?'

'What would the work be?'

'You don't expect me to tell you that, do you? But the war's going to last a long, long time, and it can't go on without planning. That's what I've been doing from the start. – And you, what have you been doing? You're looking very well. More like an Arab than a Christian.'

'I went back to my regiment, and came with them from Alamein.'

'All that way? With the infantry? Well, it's high time you had a change. Your own table to sit at, and a chance to use your brains: that's what you need, and I need you.'

At Force Headquarters of the Allied Armies, as I learnt a few days later, there was already anxious thought and continuous debate about the next-but-one operation: where, after Sicily, should our divisions seek battle? It had been decided that a special planning staff was needed to organize the invasion of Sardinia, and Colonel Pelly was in charge of its British half. He invited me to be his personal assistant with the rank of major.

After six months of war in the infantry I felt the attraction of the Army's upper levels – of military intellectualism – and as a regular soldier I did not despise promotion. So I joined him, and for many weeks an Anglo-American staff at Bouzaréa worked hard to ensure a smooth and successful invasion of Sardinia. As it happened, our work was wasted, for the Germans abandoned Sardinia without fighting; and Pelly, out of sheer disappointment, fell ill with diarrhoea and was sent to South Africa to recuperate. I have not seen him since.

It was while I was working in Bouzaréa – an incurable shortage of landing-craft was my problem at the time –

that I got news of my wife's death. She had taken a large overdose of sleeping-pills, and if one were charitable one could pretend that she had done it by accident. So my mother pretended, who wrote at great length about the wretched life the poor girl had led since I went abroad: lonely, unfriended, without purpose or comfort. My mother had always favoured her, and blamed me for my lack of understanding.

By the same post, however, came a letter from the young man who, for some time, had been living with my wife. He wrote in grief – genuine, overwhelming grief – and protested, again and again, that he had loved her. Only a love that could not be denied had allowed him to live – shamefully, as he knew well – with a girl whose husband was fighting in the desert while he, more conveniently, served his country in the Air Ministry. He appeared to think that he was the first of her lovers.

I sympathized with him, for I too had loved her in the heights of trust and the depths of folly and the ignorance of youth – it was not till we heard of his death that I discovered she was one of Peter's discards. She herself was very young, and very pretty. When she had misbehaved, and been found out, she came with spaniel eyes and the sorrowful, wriggling insinuation of a spaniel to be forgiven. The first time, it was quite a pleasure to forgive her.

She was, poor girl, a coward as well as a liar, and she had swallowed all those sleeping-pills when she knew, past hope or doubt, that she was pregnant by the young man in the Air Ministry; who would certainly have married her if she had had the courage to face divorce, my mother's hysterical surprise, and eventually a labour ward. I felt his sorrow spilling over, and infecting me. But within a few days I was aware – and ashamed to admit it – of a sense of relief that was oddly like dawn in the desert.

I remembered that on my voyage to the Faeroes, under

the shock of hearing about Peter's death, I had thought of telling Silver both my troubles – Peter's shame and my unfaithful wife – but for some forgotten reason I had never done so. And now I was thankful that I had said nothing to him.

CHAPTER TEN

I WAS NOT allowed to forget Silver, for when I went to Italy as D.A.A.Q. of a brigade then fighting uncomfortably towards the Winter Line, I met a young man named Poynter, a subaltern in an infantry battalion, who introduced himself to me as Silver's cousin. But he was like Silver neither in appearance nor manner, and the ebullience of spirit that could be discerned under his engaging shyness was no cousin-in-kind of Silver's hard and cheerful confidence.

I learnt, for the first time, that by friends and relations Silver was called Dick; that he was now in the Eastern Mediterranean; and that to the Poynter family he had talked a great deal, without telling them much, about our grotesque adventure in the Faeroes, and a storm at sea which, to them, he had described as the Atlantic's deliberate attempt to assassinate us.

Poynter was tall, fair-haired, and promised to be very good-looking when he had learnt what to do with his features. They were, at that time, too lax and mobile; too much at the mercy of shyness or enthusiasm, of ribaldry or sudden doubt. He was an easy talker, and for that reason I, who made few friends in Africa or Italy, found it easy to be friendly with him: I am not very good at initiating conversation, but I am willing to respond; and often – because of my difficulty in finding for myself the quite ordinary, agreeable, small topics that make up the most of conversation – I respond very gladly. We did not, of course, see much of each other, but I drove him to Naples just before Christmas, when I had to settle a dispute with an Ordnance depot at the docks, and he had a day or two's leave. On two successive nights we dined together at a black-market restaurant in Posilippo – and I developed a new anxiety.

I saw in him, or thought I saw, a likeness to my brother Peter. Not a physical likeness, but some resemblance of mind or character . . . The fidelity with which his expression reflected his mood, and the flux of expression, suggested not only extreme sensitivity, but instability. That was the resemblance I saw, and feared; for if he had any kinship of temperament with Peter, the winter war in Italy would certainly defeat him, as Peter had been defeated.

We had been told that a Mediterranean campaign would let us strike at 'the soft under-belly' of the Axis powers; but their belly was tucked up high above the long, lean, hard and hairy, drenched or frozen, hind leg of a wild goat. We had to climb the mountainous, cross-grained, kicking leg of Italy before we could strike at softness.

The scenery was magnificent; and the better the scenery of a country, the better its prospects for defence. The rivers ran furiously and full; and all the many rivers ran across our path. The winter cold was fiercer, more inimical, than the desert's summer heat; and the Germans in defence were as lethally efficient as they had been in attack.

I was fortunate, however, in having a job that rarely gave me any time for the luxury of contemplating our difficulties: I lived too close to them for contemplation. And I was doubly fortunate in that I found my new work of such compelling interest that I needed nothing else, and scarcely wanted anything more. There are, I know, many who pretend that the work of the 'Q' staff is dull, laborious, and mechanical: that only those who are shopkeepers at heart can be happy in it. But it was we who kept the campaign moving. We fed and maintained the gunners and their guns, the drivers and their transport, the gen-

erals and their tactics. We gave life to tactics – we made
tactics viable – by the punctual delivery of petrol, ammunition, and bully beef. For every new advance, or shift of
troops from one front to another, we devised a new arterial
supply and the proper pipe-lines for evacuation of the
wounded.

If our job was shopkeeping, it was shopkeeping of a
superior sort, for our customers lived in some very curious
and dangerous places, and our trade-routes were as open
to fire as they were. We had, indeed, to spend much time
on tedious calculation; but in all our calculations there was
no concern for profit. Sometimes, however, we had to be
as economical as a parson's wife with a large family; for we
in Italy were not always given our full requirements,
because in England they were hoarding for the invasion
of Normandy. But even the exercise of economy – the
problem of feeding a hungry family on a slender income –
gave me a certain anxious pleasure. Perhaps I am a shop-
keeper at heart?

Or am I romanticizing my duties as the 'Q' staff officer,
at first of a brigade, then of a division? It is possible. For
the last few months, in my present employment in the very
different world of 1955, I have been making an intensive
though tentative study of the means of supplying an
international army equipped with nuclear weapons; and
after trying to analyse the extraordinary requirements of
our new tactics, it is perhaps forgivable to be romantic
about the vanished past – the old forgotten world – of the
Italian campaign.

This, moreover, is an egotistical record, and the humble
part I played in that campaign, from my arrival in Italy in
September 1943 till I was wounded a year later, did a great
deal for the restoration to its proper health – to sanity, I
had better say – of the lamentably bruised ego which I had
brought from Shetland and taken to Africa. The anabasis
of the 8th Army had saved my reason, and a year of

shopkeeping from the Volturno to the Gothic Line gave my ego a fair degree of confidence; even robustness. Behind a constant professional anxiety for others, I found an inner calm.

It was not, however, immune from accident. There were occasions when emotion broke through the normally watertight bulkheads of my *métier*, and in January, soon after Poynter and I dined together in Posilippo, I was subject to great distress.

We had a plan to cross the Garigliano, the river that runs round the southern promontories of the Auruncian mountains into the Gulf of Gaeta. It was to be a corps attack, and three infantry divisions would be committed. At that time of year the Garigliano ran wide and deep through its alluvial plain – a hundred yards across and too deep for fording – and a great quantity of bridging material, with rafts and assault-boats, had to be found and carried forward. It was a major operation of great difficulty, and casualties were heavy.

In addition to my share of the general anxiety, I suffered acutely from a private fear. Poynter was with one of the leading companies, and as the battle went on I became almost obsessed by an increasing dread that Peter's tragedy would be re-enacted. I could not believe in Poynter's capacity to survive, in his strength to endure the stark physical horror of fighting in such conditions, and the mental strain of watching death come more narrowly towards him. He would crack, I was sure of it.

The landscape was dank and miserable and sinister. The sodden fields of the plain were cut by criss-crossing irrigation ditches, and beyond the river rose the darkly clouded Auruncian hills. The desolate coast-lands lay drably on our left, and to our right and behind us rose the grim shape of Monte Camino, where there had been some very bitter fighting. On a clear day – and it did not rain all the time – you could see Monte Cassino, and the shadowed door to the valley of the Liri. But often the sky came down in curtains of sleety rain, and the view was confined to a wretched patch of mud, water, sullen batteries under their sodden camouflage, incongruous vehicles, and still more incongruous men. In such a landscape it was quite absurd to find so great a multitude of men; and parts of it were crowded with men. Soaked and angry, determined and noisy men. Foul-swearing men – and about the river the more blasphemous clatter and roar of small arms, mortars, and exploding shells.

At the bridges were the points of desperation. A large number of soldiers had crossed to the farther side, but most of the supporting weapons they needed were still on our bank, because the flimsy bridges were easily cut by shell-fire, and the approaches to them were quagmires of mud. The real men of the day – the scaffolding of tactics – were the infantry on the other side, and the ever-enduring, filthily complaining sappers on both banks.

I knew that Poynter's company was – or should be – on the flank of his division, and I went down one evening, just before dark, to see if the bridge that was his lifeline had been repaired. But there, in that segment of the battle, there was no communication with the farther shore. The wind was whining out of the coming night, the thin rain was icy cold, the river dark and sinister, and beyond its sombre flood were the crash and rattle of the continuing fight. Only our guns could bridge the river, and from time to time the air above us was full of the sound – like the sound of wings – of their rushing shells.

Normally I do not drink, except at guest-nights and in situations where drink is necessary: as with Bömlo and Tórur in the Faeroes. But I have a hard head for drink, and that night, at midnight after three or four hours' hard work, I needed half a bottle of whisky – in shameful, solitary drinking – before I could enter the calm matrix of sleep. But I woke at six, and went down to the river again.

Before the grey dawn appeared – a corpse-grey dawn with a shrill cry of wind about it – I found that the bridge had been mended, and a sapper officer, snapping cold fingers, peppered me with details of his men's achievements. A thin, miserable light gleamed on the swollen river as sullenly the winter night receded, and with insensate clamour the battle on the farther bank was renewed. A few shells fell near us, exploding in the soft ground with an obscene, flatulent violence. And then a great and burly, drenched sapper came in, half-carrying a listless young officer with a wounded arm: the big man was ruby-red, a simple-looking giant who was, perhaps, less simple than he seemed, and the little officer was the dingy grey of a used dish-cloth, with a faint unshaven bristle of gold on his cold-pork chin.

'Poor bugger fell in, right at this end of the bridge,' said the sapper. 'I had to go in too, and fetch him out, and it's running —— fast, it is. What he needs is a nice glass of rum, and so do I. No more bathing in —— Grigglyano for me.'

We were in some half-ruined farm-buildings, where the dwelling-house was in use as a Regimental Aid Post. The young officer had his wound dressed, and his clothes taken off, and the enormous sapper was given some appropriate comfort, too; for I heard his voice as he went away, and it was loud with satisfaction. I was still watching, in witless anxiety, the far side of the river, the spirting flashes in the thick grey mist and the occasional, incomprehensible movement of men, when the Medical Officer, a juvenile and harassed lieutenant, came in and asked me, 'Are you going back soon, sir? I shan't have an ambulance for another couple of hours, and that chap from the other side's a bit nervy, a bit on edge. I've dressed his wound – it isn't serious, but he's lost a lot of blood – and I've given him some rum, and I'm going to give him some more. But I'd like to get him out of here, and if you're going back—'

'Almost immediately,' I said. 'I haven't had breakfast yet, and I've a day's work to do.'

'Well, sir, I'll hand him over to you, and if you'll give him another ten minutes to settle down—'

'Then I'll take him back.'

'That's most kind of you.'

The young man came in, dressed in a vilely ill-fitting battle-suit – except for an arm in bandages – smelling of drink and carrying an enamel mug with half an inch of rum in it. The winter-grey, battle-grey of his cheeks had cleared a little – showed the faintest flush of dawn – and he began to talk in a chattering, high-pitched excitement.

'We're all right now,' he said, 'We're sitting pretty now! I wouldn't leave them till I was sure of that. But God Almighty, what a difference he made!'

'Who?' I asked.

'The Colonel,' he said. 'The colonel of the battalion in the div. next door to us. Our colonel was dead, and this other colonel came right forward to where we were. "Hang on," he said. "You've done bloody well," he said, "and I'll help you if I bust a gut." That's what he said. And twice in the night he came up to us, and helped us. He helped us beat off a big attack. He went right forward, roaring like a stag in rut. I was close behind him, and he killed three of them. Then he picked up my sergeant, and carried him in. My sergeant was a bloody good man, the very best. I cried like bloody hell when I saw he was dying. Then the Colonel said again, "I'll see you're all right. You've done magnificently, getting as far as this, and I'll see to it that you get support." Then he left us. By God, what a man! He sent a platoon of his own battalion across to us, and I talked to their sergeant.'

'Who are you?' I asked. 'What's your battalion?'

He told me, and I asked him, 'Do you know Poynter?'

'That bastard!' he answered. 'He's the bastard who sent

me back. Told me to get to hell out of it before I died on his hands. Just because he's three weeks' senior to me.'

'Is he all right?'

'Sitting pretty, I tell you! With three anti-tank guns behind him now. Nothing to worry about at all. And the Colonel did the whole thing. He went down to the bridge, he made those bloody idle sappers work all night, he got the guns across, he was up to his neck in water, and he brought them into position himself. I've been talking to the sergeant he gave us – the sergeant of the platoon he gave us – and the sergeant said, "He's the best C.O. in the British Army, and he's got the temper of a tiger with a dose of clap." And I believe that. The sappers down at the bridge were talking about him, too. He said to them, "There's half a company up there" – that's us – "that's the only —— company in the Army today that Wellington wouldn't be ashamed of, and by God I'm going to save them, and so are you, if I have to drown the —— lot of you to make a bridge for the guns to come over."

'And when the guns came over he brought them up, he went forward himself to make another recce, and there in sight of us all he was killed. And I broke my bloody heart.'

'Who was he,' I asked, 'this colonel from the other div?'

'Cromar was his name. The best C.O. in the Army, his sergeant said, and I believe him. I broke my heart when I saw him dead.'

'Cromar – are you sure?'

'Of course I'm sure!'

'And Poynter: you say he's all right?'

'Right as rain. Sitting pretty. All because of the Colonel. . . .'

Poynter survived the battle, and was decorated for gallantry. He survived the whole campaign, and was decorated again for a very spirited action in the fighting for Florence. He learnt to control his features, and is now a popular and aggressive Member of Parliament in the

Conservative interest. Only in the most cynical temper could I pretend that my fear for him, my terrible foreboding, had had any substance or justification.

But what was I to think about Cromar? I made inquiry, and found that he was indeed the Cromar I had known, the Cromar who had been Peter's company commander. And how was I to reconcile my old conception of him as the brutal executioner of my brother – the jumped-up drill-sergeant to whom a human life was of no moment when weighed against discipline and military propriety – with this self-sacrificing man who, in his final revelation, was moved by a compassion so extreme that sympathy grew hot as wrath, and who died in a wrath of love? For surely that was the truth, the motive and cause of his behaviour. . . .

I did not know, I could not think. I had too much to do. Poynter survived, and the pale young man who had talked so much volunteered for some cloak and dagger work. He survived, too. I stuck to shopkeeping, and presently we moved on to Cassino, and the horrible, overcrowded valley of the Liri. . . .

In June, after the fall of Rome, one of our war correspondents got into trouble for writing that the 5th Army, the Americans, had taken the city as a reward for the 8th Army's hard fighting. It was untrue, of course, for the French Colonial troops deserved an equal share of the credit, but certainly it was the opinion held by many of our soldiers, and they were very bitter when Rome became, for a while, a sort of American colony, and they were denied its pleasures. That, however, was only a soldier's grievance, and a soldier has so many that one more or less matters little in the eye of history. A greater and more general grievance – and a grave dislocation of what should have been our history – was the American decision to remove from Italy three of their own divisions, and the

French corps, to form a new army for the unnecessary invasion of the south of France.

The armies in Italy were deprived of the strength on which they had counted for their attack on the Gothic Line of the Apennines, and their advance thereafter into the heart of Europe; but they decided, in spite of mutilation, to go ahead with their plan; and though the decision was of doubtful wisdom, they were, to begin with, remarkably successful.

On the Adriatic side the Gothic Line was broken in a week of battle – but that was the prelude to prolonged and savage fighting in very difficult, mountainous country. The mile-long ridge of Gemmano became a thing of horror, and such names as Croce and Montescudo still make evil memories. After the first few days it began to rain; and it went on raining. There was a week of fighting in the rain in which every day we lost a hundred and fifty killed and six hundred wounded.

I went forward one night to watch, on my divisional front, the delivery of ammunition. There was a road that ran down one side of a valley, and at a hairpin bend crossed a bridge to climb the other. The bridge had been captured intact, and the Germans shelled it regularly. It was a dangerous and difficult corner, and the lorries had to make their run between the bouts of shelling.

The road down to the bridge went through a small cutting where there was shelter for a jeep or two, and a few sappers; who were for ever patching and mending the approaches to the bridge. I had been there for perhaps an hour, and the lorries going forward – carefully timed and keeping a proper distance – had safely run the gauntlet. It was a dark night, and I wondered, as often before, at the skill and endurance of the R.A.S.C. drivers – and at the night-bird's vision they seemed to have. The valley was noisy with gunfire echoing and re-echoing among the hills, and the rain was cold. I grew impatient for the return of the empty lorries; and so, unhappily, did a couple of their drivers.

One came down too fast, and on the far side of the bridge went off the road; or perhaps a wheel found a soft patch where a shell-hole had been loosely filled. The following driver, too close behind, struck the overturned lorry, and a moment or two later the German guns – five full minutes before their proper time – sent over a salvo of shells. After the multiple crash of their explosion I heard a thin, tearing scream of pain, and with the vision in my mind – the intolerable vision – of men trapped and bleeding in the wreckage of their lorries, I ran towards the bridge.

The driver of my jeep tried to stop me, shouting 'Not yet, not yet!', but I paid no attention to his good sense, nor thought him sensible, till I heard the next shell coming.

I went down flat, but there was no cover and its explosion blew me off the road.

CHAPTER ELEVEN

NOW I KNEW, because I had experienced it myself; I had submitted to it.

That grimy nomad in the desert, dying with a shabby word on his lips, had known it; and so had Cromar, bellowing his anger on the shell-torn bank of the Garigliano. – I had doubted their motive because I could not understand it. Or, to be precise, I could not believe it had such power. That they had felt pity for neighbours in distress was fairly evident; but I could not realize that compassion was their only motive, because I had not known the strength of compassion, and in the narrowness of my spirit I had been unwilling to admit the possibility of its strength. But now I knew.

It was pity expanding to indignation – to an indignant refusal to allow such pain to cry for help, unanswered – that had broken down the persistent coldness of my temper, the caution of my spirit, and sent me headlong to the rescue of those trapped and suffering drivers. Unavailingly, alas. For compassion did not endow me with that curious combination of audacity and wit – that dextrous audacity – which the very best of soldiers have in reserve. My father had had it, and so, in a lesser degree, had Cromar: Cromar, though he died in doing it, had saved Poynter and the remnant of his half-company. I had saved no one – but for the trifling cost of a broken leg I had made myself whole.

I had submitted to the impulse of compassion, in circumstances that menaced me with death for doing so, and though I had failed to achieve anything – and my failure, and the thought of those poor drivers dying of my failure, recurrently twisted me with sorrow – I recognized, with enormous gratitude, the nature of my impulse; and for the first time in my life – I think this is true – I felt I was a whole man.

Physically, of course, I was far from being that. There was a ten-inch gash in my right thigh, and the lovely smooth surface of my right femur had been split and broken. I suffered a good deal of pain, and on either side of me were men who suffered more. My self-satisfaction dwindled as gradually I became aware of what the nurses and sisters were doing: their permanent and dreadful intimacy with suffering required a steadfast compassion of which, I knew, I was quite incapable. I was saved, by them, from any swollen-headed, puffed-up conviction of a suddenly acquired spiritual superiority. They had it – they won it anew every day – and as often disowned it in the humility of their tasks.

I fell in love with all the nurses, all the sisters, and as I was moved from one hospital to another I fell in love with each succeeding batch. Many of them, if they were judged by their conversation, were silly women; but judge them by what they did, and they were all compact of beauty and virtue. They thought me a model patient because, in my new openness to life, my new gratitude for life, I was so appreciative of what they did. We formed a mutual admiration society, my nurses and I, and I was almost imbedded in a sort of gelatinous contentment when Dick Silver, with a broken ankle, was carried in.

He had changed – in appearance slightly, perhaps more in character – but the change was so subtle that I cannot properly describe it. His confidence was undiminished, and buttressed, if it needed help, by a Distinguished Service Cross and bar. But he had lost something of his old gaiety of assurance. He had a thinner look and a thinner voice, and after a day or two he showed a cynicism of which he had been quite innocent in the Faeroes.

He had been serving with an irregular force known as K Force – its commanding officer's name was Kaye – and his experience with it had persuaded him that whatever happened by way of battle, surrender, or negotiation, we would morally be on the loser's side when the war was over.

'Germany may crumple tomorrow as Italy crumpled last year,' he said, 'and the politicians of our time, and the history books of the future, will pretend that we were the victors. But you and I won't. Not if we're honest and realistic. We're losing the war now – morally speaking – and we're going to go on losing it because we're not fighting *for* anything. We haven't a purpose in view or a cause to believe in.'

'Survival?'

'Not enough.'

'But if we had gone to war for a cause, we should have been as bad as the Germans. It's the lack of a cause that has kept us innocent.'

'The Germans are fighting for Germany. But are we fighting for Britain? Search all three services, and how much real patriotism would you find? Enough to fill a pipe.'

'There's no explicit patriotism, but there's a strong impulse to finish the war and go home.'

'Yes, we all want an easy life. A cosy, comfortable, easy life in the country we prefer. In our own country. And we're fighting the Germans because they stand in the way. They're an obstacle, they're a nuisance. But we don't feel any moral compulsion to fight them, and we haven't any larger purpose than going home. The people who are going to win the war—'

'Are the Russians?'

'Yes. Because they have a purpose.'

'You're very conventional. We all admire the Russians. It's the fashion this year.'

'We should be a lot better off if we had something of their energy and discipline. Something of their seriousness.'

'I've heard K Force described as "an extravagant frivolity" – but it was one of our stuffiest generals who said that. The sort of general I shall be.'

'He was quite right. K Force and all the other irregular forces are both frivolous and extravagant. We're quite irrelevant. We probably give our own side more trouble than we give the Germans.'

'You haven't been completely idle.'

'Are you admiring my decorations? Uniform needs a touch of colour, doesn't it? And twice my conduct has been politely mentioned – oh, in the rubber-stamp phrases that describe an hour or two when sheer funk lets loose pure recklessness, and mother-wit shows you how and where to do a lot of damage. But the background of those two occasions was eight or nine months during which I lived very comfortably, in very little danger, and doing very little work. My decorations have cost the taxpayer a great deal of money.'

'If you have such a poor opinion of K Force, why do you stay with it? Why don't you go back to the solid Navy and earn an honest living?'

'No fear!'

'Then what are you grumbling about?'

'Nothing at all. I'm merely dissecting – myself, among other things. I'm as bad as everyone else in these fancy brigand-parties. Worse I imagine. For I'm honest enough and intelligent enough to see and admit what I'm doing; but many of the others are either pure romantics or gifted self-deceivers. As an Englishman I'm well above the average, so it's very lamentable when the truth about me is that I have no faith in my country, and no respect for myself.'

We spent Christmas together, in a very pleasant convalescent hospital near Sorrento, and from time to time Silver, with what seemed to be a quite cheerful acceptance of his own moral decay and the moral collapse of his country, talked with a hard-hearted assurance of the futility of the victory that was now close at hand. Nothing, he said, would persuade him to live in England when the war was over.

'Where are you going?'

'Do you remember what I told you about Grierson? In the Faeroes?'

'Grierson? I never heard of him.'

'Yes, you did, but you've forgotten. He's the rich man whose yacht I was in when I saw poor old Mungo Wishart talking to Vidkun Quisling in Oslo. – Well, Grierson's in K Force, too. He's one of the few people who aren't escapists. He was in the first war, and he's too old for the work we do – the work we occasionally do – but psychologically he's a Siamese twin: a romantic and a realist on the same blood-route; he's very brave as well as rich. He reads the future as I do, and neither of us feels much attracted to England as England is going to be.'

'So you're going to look for a coral beach. Or calypsos and planter's punch in the West Indies?'

'On the contrary! We're thinking about the Far East. We're not going to give up the struggle for existence, but we're going to struggle exclusively for ourselves. We're going to fish in troubled waters, and after the Americans have whipped the Japs, there's going to be troubled water from Sumatra to New Guinea. Do you know anything about the islands? Nothing at all? – Well, wait. I've a book somewhere. You might like to join us.'

He gathered his crutches and went limping briskly to his

room. When he came back he was carrying, clutched under his arm, a thick volume, official in appearance, and another, much smaller. It was the latter he gave me, and said, 'This is yours, and I'd forgotten all about it. You left it aboard my ship, and I didn't know where to send it to you. I kept it in the hope of meeting you again somewhere – and then, like a fool, I forgot it.'

The book he gave me was the slim, privately printed volume called *The Wishart Inheritance*, that I had read in part in the house of Weddergarth in Shetland. I opened it and saw, in her childish handwriting, the name *Gudrun Wishart* – and remembered, with a sudden clarity, how she and her brother, on their ponies, had looked on the shore of Hammar Voe. I had sent them Christmas presents, and written to Gudrun perhaps half a dozen times; and to each of my letters she had replied with a bundle of local news and gossip that meant, in fact, very little to me, but touched me by the friendship it so ingenuously offered. Now, with her book in my hand, I felt a curious emotion: an absurd impatience with the Mediterranean. I was tired of the Mediterranean, and I wanted the cold grey sea that laps the Shetland isles.

'I've read it three times,' said Silver, 'and he was mad as a hatter. Look at his last chapter – here – and read that.'

He pointed to a paragraph beginning: 'Wordsworth was wrong. Diametrically and absolutely wrong. Wordsworth wrote:

> Not in entire forgetfulness,
> And not in utter nakedness,
> But trailing clouds of glory do we come
> From God, who is our home.

But they are no clouds of glory that we drag behind us. They are the black and evil clouds of poisoned memory. Memory is the curse of man, the curse of nations. No man who remembers, no country that can never forget, has ever lived happily or ever will. All my life has been haunted by a memory of lies and murder, fraud and violence, and the sins of humankind that compete – and compete in vain – with the overwhelming strength of its indurate and indomitable folly.'

'Mad as a hatter,' Silver repeated. 'I was wretched for a month after that day when we heard that he had committed suicide; but then I decided it was the best thing that could have happened. For he was mad, and madness isn't static. It gets worse. . . .'

I spent the rest of the day with *The Wishart Inheritance*. Most of the latter part was dull. I had read – in the trawler going south to Scapa Flow – some of the evidence of old men and women that had been taken in Edinburgh in 1833, and Mungo Wishart had included, in a subsequent chapter, the testimony of other witnesses at other times; all of it repetitious. The dispute between the Wisharts of Weddergarth and their relations the Pitcairns – their quarrel for possession of the estates of Weddergarth – had dragged on and on, or been renewed by appeal or the discovery of more evidence, over a period of forty years; and its conclusion was a verdict in favour of the Wisharts that an intimation of appeal to the House of Lords had threatened but never reversed. For neither the Pitcairns nor the Wisharts could now afford the cost of that appeal.

In his last chapter Mungo Wishart spoke with a curious malice of his father and grandfather, both of whom, as it appeared, had lived honourable lives, the one in the service of the East India Company, the other in the Indian Army. Both had died fairly young, and neither had won distinction in his career, or made any money. That was partly the cause of his contempt for them; but there was a deeper reason.

He admits that both his father and his grandfather felt doubts of their entitlement to the estate they owned, and whose rents (of falling value) they enjoyed. As the cost of living rose, and a landowner's income remained what it had been, they found the estate insufficient to support them; they had to go oversea to make a living. But the possession of their land still encumbered their spirits, and for this – as well as for their failure to make a fortune – Mungo despised them.

He despised them because he despised himself for the same reason. He was oppressed by the doubt that had troubled them, and a page or two after his quotation from Wordsworth he had written: 'If ever I found proof, if ever I could be certain, that Gideon Wishart murdered Old Dandy Pitcairn, then I might, I think, live happily in Weddergarth. For murder is the great evil, and requires great punishment, demands great recompense. If Gideon murdered, or caused to be murdered, Old Dandy, then the child that Dandy's son begot on Barbara Gifford was entitled by natural law to the estates he got, and that his descendants kept, by the lesser justice of Scots law. Murder would legitimate our title, and if murder could be shown forth, I would sleep more easily. . . .'

Silver left hospital a week or two before I did, and we dined together in Sorrento on the eve of his going. He spoke again of his intention to live 'sensibly and quite selfishly', as he said, in the Far East; but he would not tell me what he and Grierson proposed to do.

'There are several problems to be solved before we'll know for certain that we can do what we want to do,' he said, 'and till then, we're saying nothing. But our plan's a good one, and if and when it's properly launched – that may give you a hint – I want to talk to you about it. I might persuade you to join us.'

'That isn't very likely.'

'You may think differently when you know more. And you would be very useful to us. We must have someone who can organize and – well, maintain supplies, let us say. That's your line of country, and apparently you ride it very well.'

He pointed to the new ribbon on my tunic: I had recently been given an O.B.E.

'No,' I said, 'I'm not an adventurer, and whatever your scheme is, it's evidently – is unorthodox the word? And that wouldn't suit me. I'm orthodox – in the social sense – because I need orthodoxy. I believe in traditions, because without them I wouldn't know what to do. I don't walk alone, I take tradition's hand and go where I'm led.'

'I'll lead you, if that's all you need.'

'I prefer tradition,' I said.

'Wait till the war's over. It's been going on so long, you've forgotten the horrors of peace. Let us have another bottle of wine.'

'You won't persuade me that way.'

'I don't expect to. But next year – some time next year – I'll write to you. . . .'

I had the good fortune to rejoin my division in time to share the exhilaration and the sweeping movement of the victory that brought an end to the war in Italy – and then, near Vicenzo, in a Palladian house that would have raised her voice to ecstasy, I got word of my poor mother's death. She had been staying with friends who lived near Salisbury, and on a fine afternoon, at tea on the lawn with a bishop most suitably beside her, she had taken suddenly ill, and died before midnight. . . .

I had spoken of her to Silver. I had told him that she, writing under her maiden name, was one of the female authors with whom he had consoled himself in northern seas; and I had listened with interest to his admiration of her.

'She doesn't despise a good old-fashioned plot,' he said. 'Indeed her plots are all very old and quite out of fashion – till she goes to work on them. She treats people, and situations, too, as if they were onions. She peels them. Peel after peel comes away – you had no idea there were so many – and the cruelty of it brings tears to your eyes. Is she cruel?'

'Not intentionally.'

'But she enjoys peeling. And at last, when you think there's nothing left, she exposes the heart of the situation. It looks white and small, and translucently candid – and the flavour is what the flavour at the heart of an onion should be. Is she candid?'

'That's an understatement. She dramatizes all her moods. . . .'

It was when I was about thirteen that I began to look at her objectively. I had realized already that she and her 'temperament' were the cause of the recurrent gloom and unhappiness to which my young life, and Peter's, were subject. They came and overshadowed us – these periods of misery – like the storm-clouds that pour across a hill in the West Highlands, and suddenly darken the bright valley below. And she was the storm-centre. Always.

Objective vision, which I was certainly developing by the age of thirteen, discovered that she enjoyed the storms she sent out; and this, at first, astonished me. For Peter and I, in our misery, had until then been made more miserable by the thought that our gracious, most tall and beautiful mother was suffering, too. It was a great relief when I perceived what bunkum that was. It was she who brewed and precipitated the storms, and took her pleasure in them. She watched the performance of the drama she had concocted, and as her own Bernhardt revelled in her own performance.

Objectivity and my first acquaintance with Chaucer came together. The study of English literature is indeed

the proper base of education, and from Chaucer I learnt
that mysterious and whimsical word 'cuckold'. Both Peter
and I had been puzzled by the relationship to the family of
old Charles Aytoun; who sometimes stayed with us in the
Highlands, and with whom my mother seemed to spend
much of her time when she was in London. My father, to
my mother, always spoke of him as 'your admirer'.

But what exactly was an admirer? It was an unclassified
addition to the cousins, uncles, and aunts whose precise
connection with us had sometimes been as hard to understand as algebra; 'admirer' was even more bewildering.
There were, we knew, people who admired pictures,
poetry, or a view: we could not understand why admiration of these things gave them a recognized status, but we
accepted it as part of the irrational world we were beginning to explore. But why should our mother – as if she
were 'The Thin Red Line' (a picture we revered), or
'Lepanto' (a poem we recited with rapture), or the Coolins
of Skye (a view that everyone told us was magnificent) –
why should she have an admirer?

Then, by wicked association of two mysteries, I asked
myself: Was an admirer one who cuckolded? That meant,
of course, that my adored and noble father was a cuckold –
and, though I did not know what a cuckold was, it was
clearly something exposed to shame and derision.

At the thought of this possibility I was quite overcome
by dismay; and for some time I regarded my mother with
horror. From this estrangement I was rescued, as from
many other predicaments, by my father himself; who, I
had to admit, continued to show, not merely that he was
fond of his wife, but extremely proud of her. And therefore, I told myself, it was impossible to suppose that she
had done anything to his dishonour.

My mother always claimed that she was descended from
an uncle of the poet Shelley; and, in consequence of this,
that her literary aptitude was natural, hereditary, and

would reappear in me. My father took her pretensions seriously, and felt quite sure that she was – as she certainly believed – a great writer, secure of her place in the tradition of English writing. His respect for her genius gave him great happiness.

Charles Aytoun also respected her: of that there is no doubt. But I am not quite sure of the value of his respect. For a quarter of a century he reviewed books – biography was his favourite subject – for a Sunday newspaper, and his critical essays were always erudite, urbane, and regretful of the past. The memoirs of a lady of fashion who had known Napoleon III – a book about the Goncourts or the pre-Raphaelites – these were always sure of his wistful and most polished regard; and on a Sunday morning blessed by such a topic one could hear him purring like a plump, well-fed, and favoured cat before a clear, bright fire.

A tom-cat? I really do not know.

CHAPTER TWELVE

SEVERAL MONTHS AFTER the end of the war I was in London, on leave, and met Charles Aytoun in Button's, who promptly asked me, 'And what are you going to do now?'

'Whatever I'm told to do,' I said. 'I haven't much choice.'

'But you're not going to stay in the Army?'

'What better can I do?'

'You have such abilities, my dear boy! Abilities you have never developed. Surely the Army is mere waste of time now? You could write, if you cared to – your mother always said so, and your dear mother was never wrong.'

'And what ought I to write?'

'What we're all waiting to hear! What only you young men can tell us. You young men who have been fighting this war that has kept us alive. How did you manage to keep us alive? And for what purpose?'

'I don't know,' I said. 'I've often wondered, but I've never found an answer.'

'You don't mean to say it was a useless war?'

'It was an unnecessary war, but it wasn't useless. It did keep us alive – but about what we're going to do next, I've no idea.'

'So you can't help us?'

'Only by staying in the Army.'

'And what good will that do?'

'We'll continue to protect you, and give you a chance to make up your minds about the future.'

'But you must have a voice in the future.'

'No, I don't think so. We supply the accompaniment, that's all. We're the scaffolding, and we'll hold you up while you build. We're soldiers, not thinkers, and it's not our job to design the building. That's your job. But for God's sake don't under-esteem us or under-pay us, because you can't do your job without us. The best architect in the world can't do anything without scaffolding.'

'Oh, my dear boy,' said Charles, 'how quickly you've grown up! You used to be such a nice, amenable child, and now you have a mind of your own – and frankly I don't like what you're saying. How old are you?'

'Twenty-nine.'

'No, no! Your mother – your mother was so young, till the day of her death. Oh, dear me, I'm out of touch, I fear.'

He did indeed look very old, and rather pathetic; but only with the pathos of a natural decline. Under his silky crop of white hair his face, though shrunken, was still pink and white, and his body, though diminished in height, was still erect. I brought him another brandy, and presently, with a little cackle of laughter, he said, 'Well, I've had a good life, I can't deny it, and I hope, my dear boy, that you will live as long, and enjoy your years as much as I have. – But do tell me, Tony, what the young men *want* us to do?'

I wanted to tell him to shut up; but that, of course, was hardly possible. All the old men of his sort I now found boring, because they seemed so helpless. Many younger men, too, affected a foolish air of resentment and regret: resentment against the Russians, against the Socialists who were now governing us, and regret for a life of vanished riches which, in fact, most of them had never known.

I, to begin with, supported the Socialist government. Its foreign policy was inept, in its domestic policy it foolishly neglected book-keeping, and most of the Socialist Members seemed as loudly and lushly pleased with themselves as actresses; but they were trying to reform society, and heaven knows that a social reformation was overdue. When I went back to the Army in Austria I was quickly labelled as a very red Socialist for saying this, but as a lieutenant-colonel I could afford to show some eccentricity, and in spite of it I found myself living more easily with my fellow-officers – on lighter and more genial terms with them – than for some years past. My second wound had done me a lot of good.

I spent about a year in Klagenfurt, and then, with inevitable reduction in rank, went to the Staff College. There, after the first couple of months, I complained that we were merely being taught to fight the battle of Alamein over again, and discovered, to my surprise, that in the upper reaches of the Army criticism was no longer resented. I learnt a lot, and on the whole enjoyed my two years as a student.

From there I went as second-in-command to a battalion in Germany, and found day-to-day discipline, training, and routine rather boring. – I read, a year or two ago, an English translation of de Vigny's *Servitude et Grandeur Militaires*, and from an introduction to it (as good, in parts, as the best parts of de Vigny) I copied out the following passage:

> The army is more than an occupation, more than a profession; it is a way of life, a dedication. Within its ranks there is room neither for the undisciplined enthusiasm of the volunteer nor the impotent reluctance of the conscript. They are merged in the common mould of discipline, become indistinguishable in the uniform of abnegation. And this personal surrender to a dedicated way of life has, like every mystery, its visible signs and ceremonies. The donning of the vestments by the priest, the sacred dance before the altar, the chanting of the ritual are at once the symbols of initiation and a rhythmic, almost hypnotic, control of the physical which must precede all essential spiritual experience. So it is with the soldier: his uniform,

his music, and his drill are all means to an arcane ideal, the state of military grace. They set him apart, mark him as a member of a dedicated sect and thereby exact the tribute of emotion. For the wail of the shell is implicit in the sound of the bugle calling across the Park, the roll of musketry in the beating drums, and the beautiful precision of the ceremonial on the Horse Guards Parade echoes the tramp of dead feet marching down alien roads.

That is perfectly true, and admirably said; but I have no great liking for ritual. I am, by nature, a staff officer, not a regimental officer – and in a battalion I realized, more and more strongly, that it was the 'Q' side of staff duties that really had my interest. I was, then, immensely pleased when, in 1950, I was offered promotion and a posting to Hong Kong as D.A.Q.

I did not, however, take up my appointment. The war in Korea began about the end of June, and twice my sailing orders were cancelled. Then, in November, my promotion was positively deferred and I was sent to Korea to study and report on the system of supply which our 27th and 29th Brigades had had to evolve, or adopt, in the large American army in which they were serving.

I was flown out, but the Army's air transport is sometimes hardly as quick as a steamer, and Christmas was near at hand before I reached Seoul. I was, I thought, prepared for the sub-arctic weather, against which I had been warned – both mentally and materially prepared – but I had never imagined the cold ferocity, the lethal malignity of the Siberian wind that blew, not always, thank God, but every few days, and went on blowing for two or three days at a time. That took me by surprise, and frightened me; and the country and its wretched people assaulted me with sheer dismay.

I shall not try to describe Korea – neither the war there,

nor its people – for the sufficient reason that I have not the skill to put in words what only Goya, perhaps, could have put in drawing. How horrible life was in that stricken land! There, it may be, was the only campaign in history in which soldiers, who are notorious grumblers, complained primarily, not of their own discomforts, but of the agonies of the refugees who came flooding down from the north. What could be done for them? Very little, and that was made more difficult by the abominable policemen. Our soldiers had to face, not only Siberian wind and a multitudinous enemy, but the knowledge that their own allies included people as malignant as any the Communists could produce. On the other hand, there were many South Koreans who were civilized, courteous, charming, and kind; and they, whom we had come to help, did not like us. It was a confusing war.

On a frozen desert, under some white hills north of Seoul, I spent Christmas Day with the 29th Brigade, and at night returned to my tolerable (though not inviting) quarters in the city. Seoul had only a few more days to live, and the peace of Christmas did not last. By January 1st the Chinese had broken through positions held by a Korean division, and presently, after a day and a night of fighting, of initial loss and successful counter-attack, the 29th Brigade was ordered to withdraw. The 5th Fusiliers broke contact successfully, but the Ulsters were heavily attacked in a long, curving, narrow valley through which they had to march, in darkness, on a slippery track between frozen paddy-fields.

I had gone forward on the main road as far as the entrance to the valley, where transport waited for the battalion. The greater part of it came out before midnight, but still in the valley were the battle patrol and a missing platoon, some mortars and their crews, and the reconnaissance troop of the 8th Hussars: they had been fighting a rearguard action, and the battalion had lost touch with them.

I drove along the road to the last rearguard positions of an American regiment and, while I was talking to a sergeant there, a few men came down from the hill above us, out of the invisible dark, and were challenged.

'Ulsters,' they replied.

There were about a hundred in all, under an officer of their regiment who had taken command in a burning village. Its narrow road was blocked by a tank that had shed a track, there were Chinese all round them – voices crying from the dark, mortar bombs whistling, bursting, in a continuous din – but with three remaining tanks they fought their way out of the trap. They marched a little farther, and were halted by a burnt-out tank that lay athwart their path – the slippery path between frozen rice fields – and their running tanks could neither shift it nor pass it. They set fire to their three runners, turned west, and took to the hills; and in gross darkness their officer led them safely down to the road.

There was a wounded man who had collapsed after crossing the hills, and I offered to take him into Seoul. A tall and well-built young Rifleman was looking after him, and he came too, to support the wounded man in the back seat of my jeep. We drove slowly along the jolting, abominably rough road, and the Rifleman gave me a very clear and well ordered account of the fighting in the valley. Or rather, he began to give me an account of it; for after a few minutes I interrupted him to ask, 'Are you Irish? You don't sound like it.'

'No, sir,' he said. 'My home's in Shetland.'

'Where?'

'Shetland, sir. Do you not know where it is?'

'I do indeed. Do you live in Lerwick?'

'About twenty miles from Lerwick. On the west coast.'

'Anywhere near the Voe of Hammar?'

'That's just where it is, sir. Have you been there?'

I felt a curious tension, as if a strand of excitement were

about to snap; and for a moment I did not want to break it. I leaned back to look more closely at him, but it was too dark to see him properly. Then I asked his name.

'Wishart. Rifleman Wishart, sir.'

With a sudden uncontrollable anger, as if the broken strand of excitement had slapped me on the face, I demanded, 'What the devil are you doing here?'

He was, not unnaturally, astonished at my tone, and a little gruffly he replied, 'I volunteered. I thought it was the proper thing to do.'

I apologized to him. 'I really didn't mean to speak like that,' I said. 'But, of course, you don't know who I am.'

He was not much surprised when I told him. He had seen too many surprising people and surprising things in the last few months to be excited by a chance meeting with the man whom he had last seen, nine years before, half-dead on a Shetland beach. There was no background of emotion to his small memory of me. I, who had helped push his father to his death, fell inevitably into angry consternation when I found Olaf in a country where death lay in ambush round every corner for boys of his sort; but he regarded our meeting as nothing more than a coincidence that gave him the sentimental pleasure of talking about his calf-country to someone who knew it. He remembered that twice I had sent him a Christmas present, and he told me that Gudrun was in her final year at Edinburgh University. I had to do sums in time to persuade myself that she could be old enough for that, for our exchange of letters had not continued, and when I had last heard from her – about the time of our breaching the Gothic Line, I think – she was still a schoolgirl, and young for her years.

My intention was to take the wounded man to a field ambulance, and return Olaf to his battalion, if I could discover where it lay. But I was able to do neither of these things, because the wounded man died in Olaf's arms, and that night Seoul went on fire.

We stopped to let the Rifleman die in peace, and the last of the Americans drove past us – the rearguard that had been holding a position on the road. They had, I suppose, the remnant of the Ulsters with them. We laid the dead body on the floor of the jeep, and Olaf squeezed into the front seat between me and my driver. A little while later, puzzled and alarmed by small-arms fire ahead, we turned off the main road on to a miserable, rough track, and got lost. Eventually we returned to the road, and again got lost in Seoul, when a burning street barred our way.

Who set the town on fire I have never learnt. It was generally supposed that Communist agents of the advancing Chinese, or Communist sympathizers, were responsible: and there was a tale, which few believed, that patriotic South Koreans had destroyed their capital to prevent it falling into the hands of the enemy. Cynical observers – or realistic observers – declared it was deliberately fired by gangs of hooligans who saw, in the retreat of our army, their opportunity to loot. The population of Seoul, swollen by a vast number of refugees, was well over a million. There was room in that multitude for hooligans, and certainly when the fire had taken hold there was an orgy of looting. Twice, as we drove through burning streets, we had to shoot our way past little mobs of yelling, violent ruffians. Many of the streets consisted of small, wooden-framed shops and houses that caught fire quickly and soon burnt out; but elsewhere larger buildings burnt fiercely and long, and the scarlet and orange flames, the black smoke, danced in a wild extravagance over snow-covered roofs, white lanes, and parti-coloured roads.

Thanks to my driver – in civil life a publican in Hull – we found our way at last to the north bank of the wide, the dreary, the frozen, and densely packed bed of the river Han. The ice that filled it was crowded with refugees, for a whole population was in flight, and the American bridge across the river had been blown up. The 27th Brigade was covering the retreat, and a couple of their military police-men, as confident and unperturbed as a pair of constables in a football crowd at Wembley, told us there was another bridge to the west, by which we could cross if we hurried. A company of the Argylls was holding the northern end and, not long after we went over, that bridge was blown, too. I decided, in these chaotic circumstances, to go to Suwon, where I knew I could find shelter of a sort.

When I think now of those days of agonized cata-strophe, I often feel a sense of guilt. Not, however, because I did nothing to help anyone, for there was nothing I could do. No, it is simply due to the fact that in a tragic moment of history I failed to use my chance to watch and record the passing of the moment. I have a confused, impressionistic memory of fire and snow, of slowly moving crowds and small frantic crowds, of a petrol dump roaring to the sky in orange and black and an ammunition dump exploding in a dangerous *feu de joie*; of the nightmare on the Han, as if a world had died and the Styx had frozen for its passage into hell, of the two stalwart Red Caps, and the dour, un-flinching Argylls about the bridge to the west. – But I should have gone about closely observing, mapping the scene, and noting details; for it is not every night (thank God!) that a capital city dies in a convulsion of terror.

My failure to be more closely observant was due to pure selfishness. My mind, against that awful background, was more intent on my own affairs, on the turning pattern of my life that now included, as if in the scroll-work of an intricate design, the boy I had first seen on a plump Shetland pony by a northern beach. In that blazing, gun-shooting, frozen nightmare my thoughts were tied more closely to Olaf Wishart than to burning Seoul and the Koreans. I felt, with great intensity, that I was re-

sponsible for him. I felt that I had inherited (by killing his
father) the onus of protecting him; and the burden made
me proud as well as anxious. In that night of chaos, where
all was flying loose, two pieces had come together in an
emotional relationship which one piece gladly acknowledged. I saw myself as Olaf's foster-father.

I have usually taken my strength from other people –
either by following or resisting them – and so it happened
next morning. I took strength from Olaf. He, with the
resilience of youth, seemed none the worse for his two or
three days of fighting, the ambush in the valley, his march
over the hills and our bewildering journey through Seoul.
In the cold, harsh light reflected from a snow-covered land
I saw him as a very handsome copy of his father who, by
genetic luck or the innocence of his years, had escaped his
father's faults: his expression was wholesome, candid, and
gay.

My driver too – Ben Wills, the publican from Hull – was
a source of comfort. A little man with a bony, red face and
small, sapphire-blue eyes, he had served throughout the
larger war and volunteered at once when trouble started in
Korea. 'Family life's a cramping thing. I get restless,' he
said, 'and the wife's better on her own, too. Individualist,
she is. She'll look after the business all right.' So now,
having learnt the roads of northern France, and navigation
of the desert, and all the roads between Sicily and Austria,
he was learning the vile tracks between Pusan and Pyon-
gyang and was undismayed by them.

I was, for once, in a quite unscrupulous mood, and
having failed to find the Ulster Rifles, I had no intention
of looking for them again, until I had had more conversation with Olaf. I told Ben something of my rough voyage
from the Faeroes to Shetland, and the three of us sat down
deliberately to waste the King's time and talk. Ben Wills
was a great help, for he took a lively interest in any part of

the world he had not seen, and his many questions loosened Olaf's tongue.

There was one thing about which I wanted to reassure myself, and presently I found an unobtrusive chance to say, 'It was the night we sailed that your father died, wasn't it?'

'The same night,' he said, and looked at me so frankly, so entirely without animus – no emotion in his voice or eyes – that I felt sure he had never imagined any connection between our visit and Mungo Wishart's death. I felt relieved, and happier – and, strangely, more responsible for him than before. As if his innocence demanded protection.

He told us that he had been at school in Edinburgh when the Korean war began. His school had a Junior Training Corps, and Olaf was a sergeant in it. He had joined the Ulsters before he was eighteen, and without his mother's knowledge. I could not understand why he had gone to Belfast to enlist, and he was unwilling to tell me; but he let slip the fact that he had been friendly with an Irish sergeant-instructor in his J.T.C., and the sergeant-instructor, I have no doubt, knew someone at the depot who would see that Olaf made no mistakes when he filled in his papers. And after that his height and his strength, and his cadet-sergeant's knowledge of weapons and drill would be all he needed to assure him of a place in the troop-ship.

'When did you tell your mother what you had done?' I asked him.

'Just as soon as I'd passed the doctor and drawn my kit. I didn't give her any anxiety, I promise you that.'

'She wasn't anxious when she heard you were coming here?'

'She didn't like the idea of it. She wasn't happy about it, I've got to admit that. But I told her as soon as I could – I didn't leave her in doubt.'

'You were a bloody fool,' said Ben Wills, 'and so was I. But you've got more excuse: you're eighteen, and I'm forty. – Why the hell do we do it, sir?'

'You're restless and he's romantic,' I said, 'and if no one had ever suffered from such irregularities, we'd still be living in caves.'

'A good cave would be a lot more comfortable than a fox-hole,' said Ben.

With the access of an emotional fatherhood, I had realized one of the problems of real fatherhood. I wanted to keep Olaf with me, to shelter him from the danger of battle; and though I knew that my desire was both hopeless and wrong, it was still persistent. It was he who exposed my fault – and, in the long view, my impotence – by soon showing an impatient desire to go and find his battalion. I kept him with me for another half-hour, and by then his civility was strained, he was beginning to look unhappy. Though he had been with the Ulsters for only a few months, the community of his own battalion already drew him.

So we went to look for them, and found them, as Ben Wills said, 'just round the corner'. They, too, had come down to Suwon, and were already making ready to go back another twenty miles or so, down the coast road to Pyongtaek, which became the left-hand anchor of the allies' new front.

I had a talk with Olaf's company commander, who was still very tired and showed no interest at all in the fact that I, a visiting officer, had discovered an old acquaintance among his men. His interest was sternly confined to his own company and the neighbouring fringes of the companies to his right and left; to visitors from the outer world he was polite, but he could not hide his belief that they were idle and irrelevant people. That is the common, the inevitable, temper of infantry officers when they are in contact with the enemy – when they have lately been in action, or are on the point of action – and it is a nice demonstration of the total demand that battle makes. I myself, on the long advance across the roof of Africa, had often felt exclusive to the world that did not know what we were doing.

The young captain in the Ulsters did, however, speak well of Olaf. 'A good soldier, cheerful and efficient,' he said. For a moment, indeed, he grew almost warm, he nearly betrayed some feeling. 'I'm very glad you picked him up and brought him back,' he said. 'I'd have been damned sorry to lose him.'

I had to be content with that – as if it were a favourable report on a boy's first term at school – and say goodbye to Olaf, and go back to my own affairs: to the supply and movement, in conditions unlike those I had known before, of petrol and rations, of ammunition and the wounded. I succumbed to the spell – the spell of my *métier* – and by hard, professional work the emotional luxury of foster-fatherhood was worn away, and left nothing better than a submerged anxiety.

Before I left Pyongtaek I had to endure the extraordinary cold which fell upon us, not like some disorder of our normal climate, but like a disease of supernatural origin: a stupefying and terrifying cold. I heard of an officer who put a silver flask to his lips, and tasted blood as he tasted the mouthful of whisky: for the skin of his lips came away on the flask. There were men who put their hands on the steel side of a tank in the morning, and their hands stuck to the steel. Beer was brought forward, frozen in solid bottles. Machinery froze too, and before the Hussars could move their great Centurion tanks, they had to melt the fluid in brakes and bearings. The lowest recorded temperature was, I think, sixteen degrees below zero Fahrenheit, but in the Siberian wind there seemed to be a malignancy beyond measurement. Yet in this weather our men lay out in fox-holes stuffed with straw, with a brazier in the wall to warm the air about their legs.

And through the cold still came a stream of refugees, stumbling, stinking, and dying. The Gloucesters made a bridge across the river that runs in front of Pyongtaek, and all one day handed across a whimpering half-frozen column of fugitives from the north. There was shelter of a sort for them in Pyongtaek.

In mid-March I went to Japan, which I disliked; and when I came back, in mid-April, it was to a country I had not seen before. The first movements of spring had preceded me, and the air was genial and dry. Not warm, but light fingered, not welcoming, but exhilarating. The snow had gone, and some of the hills, among the winter-brown shabby scrub that covered them, showed the pink flush of little wild azaleas. Pusan already stank to heaven, but farther north there were people who seemed less miserable than before, and in the ruins of Seoul — such drab and horrid ruins, under a stony peak of hill to the north, and dominated with monstrous incongruity by their surviving, pretentious Capitol — I saw a bold outpost of returning civilization: on the veranda of a ramshackle house on the road to Inchon sat three heavily painted, marvellously decorated young women. A brothel had been established.

The Chinese had been pushed far back from the line that, in the cold of January, had been anchored to Pyongtaek, and our army was again on, or near, the 38th parallel. It was almost ready for a new advance when the Chinese forestalled it, and made a massive attack across the river Imjin, where our 29th Brigade stood astride the traditional route of invaders from the north: the road to Seoul that ran through the grotesquely squalid, burnt-out village of Uijongbu — about which, though it looked like a dead suburb of an abandoned world, a few glum peasants were working in their rice-fields.

On April 22nd, I was at main headquarters of the brigade, on the road to Seoul. West of us, in wild country where there were hardly any roads, was a confusion of very steep hills, most of them small and sloping as sharp as a roof, with the surly bulk of Kamak-san – it was 2000 feet high and could be called a mountain – dominating the landscape. On the far side of Kamak-san were the Gloucesters; their battalion headquarters about five miles west of the road, and a little more than three miles south of the river. Before midnight on the 22nd their forward positions were under persistent, heavy attack, and in the battle that developed the Gloucesters bore the hardest pain and won most of the honour. They were stiff and stubborn men, and they held their ground with such adamantine valour that the whole intention of the Chinese was stopped and defeated.

The Gloucesters bore the palm, but the rest of the brigade should not be forgotten. The Gunners, indeed, were admirable – I spent much of my time with them – and we had a very good Belgian battalion attached to us. The Belgians, with one troop of a mortar battery, were north of the river when the battle started, and the 5th Fusiliers and a squadron of the 8th Hussars just south of the Hantan ford. The Ulsters were in reserve. On the 23rd, St. George's Day, the Fusiliers and some of the Gunners went into action with the roses of England in their buttonholes.

But this is not a tale of war. It is only the story of a man who, fearing and detesting war, has seen something of it, and survived its perils as, so far, he has survived the more familiar pains of what is called peace; and therefore I shall only say that the remainder of the brigade 'imposed on the enemy the necessary delay' – I think that is the customary expression – and then 'withdrew to conform with the tactical situation'.

A swarm, a bursting hive of running, shooting, bomb-throwing, insanely buzzing, cotton-clad Chinese were all about us: that was the tactical situation, so far as I could see it, when finally I withdrew – or was withdrawn. That was on the 25th, when, I must admit, I had no good reason for being where I was. To begin with, my reason had been adequate: I was interested in the expenditure and replenishment of ammunition. But latterly, as the infantry were driven from their hill-tops – driven in upon the road, from either side – and gradually we went back through a road-block that a company of the Ulsters held – why, then I had no better purpose than a ridiculous and sentimental desire – but a passionate desire – to find Olaf Wishart.

After our first meeting, and before going to Japan, I had seen him only three or four times, never for more than a few minutes except once, when I took him to dinner with two American war-correspondents whom I knew. They, a friendly, cynical, knowing pair, were pleasantly amused, or so pretended, to find a British major and a British private on friendly terms; and in their expansive company Olaf showed something of his quality.

They were kind to him, generous, and prompting; and about me they made the proper sort of fun to put him at his ease. They made it clear that they recognized him as the guest of the evening, and encouraged him to talk.

It was a very youthful mind that he showed, but it was brave and good. He revealed a happy innocence, and a firm belief in the prospect of bettering, by human effort, all mankind. He was by no means priggish: just hopeful, and romantic. About his reason for volunteering to serve in so unpleasant a war he was reticent and vague, but that, we supposed, was due to shyness or a proper modesty: he did not want to declare anything so embarrassing as a high purpose or a sense of duty. – The Americans, those cynical, all-knowing men, made much of him, and I could hardly suppress my pride.

He lay wounded, when at last I found him, and by then my own left arm hung useless, the elbow shattered by the bursting of a grenade. I knelt beside him, and he said, 'The bleeding gets worse when I move.'

'Where is it?'

'Here.' He opened the top of his trousers, and I saw the little, pouting gash in his belly. It looked harmless enough.

I had lost all sense of direction. The wild landscape of steep brown hills echoed and re-echoed the rattle and bursting din of battle, and I did not know where I was or whither we had retreated. We lay in a little patch of scrub and spindly trees, and I watched the Chinese, hundreds of them, running past: little Chinese soldiers in long-nosed cotton caps, cotton khaki uniforms, with rifles or tommy-guns and cotton bandoliers and stick-grenades hanging from their belts. They paid no attention to us.

Then, nearby, we heard machine-gun fire and felt the heavy vibration of an approaching tank. It was one of the Hussars' great Centurions, and a voice shouted from the turret, 'If you want a lift, this is your last chance.'

Someone helped us on to the broad deck behind the turret, where already three or four wounded men crouched or lay. The jolting, lurching movement began, and through the swarming countryside the tank fought its way out of the battle. A man beside me was hit, and died, but I had no thought for anyone but Olaf, who was dying too. He was bleeding through the anus, and nothing could be done for him. He lay still, grey-cheeked and seeming thin, and his lips trembled slightly.

The hard stammer of machine-gun fire, reverberating through the steel hull, beat intolerably on our ears. There was now another tank to the left, and between the tanks a group of walking wounded. The Chinese were attacking us, throwing grenades that fell short, and then, as the attack was beaten off, there was a spell of comparative quietness.

Olaf opened his eyes, and looked at me with intense gravity, but without – as I thought – anxiety. I bent low above him to hear what he was saying, and slowly and very faintly he said, 'Do you think – this – will make up – for him?' I had no idea what he meant, but he wanted acquiescence, and I cried, 'Yes, yes. Of course it will.'

I saw a change of expression on his bloodless face. It was small enough, but it gave him a look of peace. He whispered again, but I could not hear all he said. It was a message for his mother, and I promised to deliver it. Then he sighed deeply, and was dead, I think, soon afterwards. But I do not know, for I was by then in great pain from my own wound.

It was in a hospital in Japan that my arm was taken off, a few inches below the shoulder, and perhaps that is the true reason for my present belief that I disliked Japan from my first sight of it. To begin with, however, I did not resent my loss. I was foolishly glad of it, for it did something to medicine my grief for Olaf. He was dead, and part of me had died, too. I still was nearer to him than any man who had kept his full complement of limbs, and to have this sensation of nearness, this knowledge of my own loss, was a comfort in my sorrow.

It was not until sorrow had receded – as it was bound to recede! I had known him for so short a time that memory had not much to feed on – it was not till then that I resented the strangeness of being without an arm, and to an overwhelming sense of mutilation was added a dull fear that I could not manage my life, the daily tasks of living, with only one set of fingers left to serve me.

That phase did not last long. As soon as I had a little strength with which to combat it, I drove that fear out with scorn. I had suffered in my mind, and survived them, worse things than the loss of skin and bone and a few finger-nails. A very young man could be forgiven such a fear, but not I. I was thirty-five, and knew better. I did not, however, fully recover my confidence till I had been flown to Hong Kong, and thence to Singapore, where I lay for some time in a tall, sunlit room in a hospital that stood above a pale blue, glittering sea and had great windows open to rich and strange perfumes.

I remember Singapore with pleasure, with a glowing delight; and Japan with a profound aversion. In Japan I was ill with a major grief and a major wound, but in Singapore I got better. The flight between them is now, in memory, no more than an invalid's dream.

There were, I found, several people whom I knew in Singapore, and I had a sufficiency of genial visitors. One day, after I had been there for two or three weeks, Dick Silver came in. 'You look,' I said, 'like a character out of Conrad.' – And immediately I was sorry for my perception, and the rashness with which I had exposed it.

He frowned, and went to consider his reflection in a looking-glass on the wall. 'It isn't dissipation,' he said. 'I drink more than I used to, but not as much as most people here; and I'm respectably married.'

'It's your look of dash and elegance – the elegance of the Far East, of the South Seas – that took me by surprise,' I said. 'When I heard you were here, I suddenly remembered you, I thought of you, in your North Atlantic rig, your Faeroe rig – and there's a difference, isn't there? Do you still read mathematics?'

He was well dressed, well tailored, in cream-coloured tussore silk, with a white silk shirt, a dark red tie, and a scarlet flower in his buttonhole. His figure was lean and good, his face leaner than it had been; but he had lost his hard and healthy, ripe-English-apple look. His cheeks were yellow with the sun, rather than tanned by the sun, and his eyes, between wrinkled lids, less bright than

I remembered them. His air of dash and daring was carried now, as it seemed, on a rather tired habit of dash and daring; not, as before, on a constantly renewing impulse. – I was, however, a badly wounded man, recovering from his wound, but still looking at the world with the squeamish understanding of the invalid. I may have seen too much, or more than was there.

Silver, turning with a shrug from the looking-glass, said, 'I'm older than I was, and that's something none of us can help. And I've no time for reading now. But how are you, Tony?'

'I'm very well,' I said. 'How did you know I was here?'

'You're important enough, nowadays, to be talked about. I came in yesterday, and one of the first names I heard in the club last night was yours. By God, I'm sorry you got a knock like that! But you'll manage all right, won't you?'

For an hour or more he showed all his old charm of manner, and gradually my first impression faded, my old recollection of him returned. He made me tell him about the war in Korea, what I had seen and done, and what I thought of it; he said nothing of himself until I had unloaded my cargo of news, and to unload it into the hands of an old friend, eagerly attentive to it, was a great pleasure. Then I asked him about his affairs.

'We're doing very well,' he said, 'but not well enough. We need a man of your sort, as I knew from the beginning we should. As I told you we should. An organizer, someone to ensure supply and maintain supply to meet the demand that I can find. – Haven't you changed your mind yet?'

'No, not yet.'

'Look at these,' he said, and from his pocket took some photographs of a ship in Conrad scenery: a trim, well-kept, expert-looking ship of the sort the Dutch use in their coastal trade, and behind her grew feather-headed palm

trees, the tropic sun made her light and lovely – and here
were the thatched roofs of a village on stilts, and there
exuberantly manned canoes coming down a river to meet
the ship.

'Yes,' I said, 'they're very tempting. And you really
make a profit, too?'

'A handsome profit. We bought that ship in Holland
three years ago – or rather, Grierson bought her – and
we've done so well that now we ought to buy another. But
we can't – it isn't practical, I mean – unless we can find,
and persuade him to join us, a man we know, a man we can
absolutely trust, and a man with an organizer's brain: all
three in one.'

'How much of your trade is dishonest?'

'None of it. We pay for what we buy, and we deliver the
goods to those who buy from us. But we don't trade under
the British flag, and – well, we don't always feel bound to
respect certain political conventions. Why should we? Do
you respect the politics of this world?'

'No,' I said. 'But I don't like the look of that flag you're
flying. What is it?'

'Liberian. And *Liberia* means liberty. Don't you believe
in liberty?'

'Only when it's controlled by a few good English or
Scotch policemen.'

'You are a damned old Puritan, Tony. And what
makes it worse is that you're a sort of romantic Puritan.
Why did you go and get your arm shot off? In the job
you were doing there was no need to stay in the middle
of a battle.'

'It was an accident. The sort of accident that can happen
to anyone.'

'It wouldn't happen to me.'

'Do you sail as captain of this ship?'

'I do indeed.'

'Do you carry arms?'

'Only a few rifles, and a pistol or two. To prevent accidents.'

'And your headquarters are in Singapore?'

'We have an office here, with a Chinese manager and a Chinese accountant, but I live in Macao. I've a house there, and that's where my wife is.'

He showed me some more photographs: photographs of a Chinese girl. She had a precision of beauty, a delicate exactitude of beauty, such as hardly can be found in Europe, and within her beauty – which was the ultimate refinement of an old convention – there lived, if the photographs were true to life, an alert and subtle intelligence.

'You're a lucky man,' I said.

'Damned lucky,' he answered, and looked at one of the photographs with an expression I could not analyse.

'Are you married?' he asked.

'No.'

'Come and stay with us in Macao before you go home. She's got a sister living with us. A younger sister, as lovely as she is.'

I laughed and said, 'You can't bribe me that way.'

'It isn't bribery. I'd like to have you stay here, and I'd like to see you happy.'

'Does your partner – Grierson, isn't it? – live in Macao, too?'

'It's because of Grierson I really need you. I don't blame him, he's getting on for sixty, and he's a wealthy man. He's entitled, at his age, to take his pleasure. But he's a damned good business man – or he was – and I relied on him. And now, for the last six months, he's been living in Bali.'

'Is it safe to live there?'

'If you can spend money as he does, yes.'

'And he does no work now?'

'You don't feel much inclined for work – real work – in Bali. But with you here, in Singapore—'

'I'm sorry, Dick, but it wouldn't suit me. I'd be out of my element.'

'Shall I come in tomorrow?'

'Yes, do.'

'I'll leave these photographs: that's the ship in a river-mouth in Java.'

'Don't leave this one of your wife.'

'That's her sister.'

'I don't want it.'

'It won't do you any harm to look at it.'

It nearly did. . . .

Since my wife died, I had lived in a desert where there were no women, and the picture of that exquisite Chinese girl, with her promise of an utterly strange delight – the delusive promise that young men believe, and to which men who should know better, still listen – almost persuaded me. She, and the picture of the alert and lovely ship lying under the wind-blown, softly stirring heads of the palm trees. – But I knew it would be no good. I didn't blame Silver for cutting loose, for making his own independent life in contempt of the orthodoxy and the loyalties by which I was bound; I simply admitted that I was in bonds, and if I broke them – as I was tempted to – I should never be happy.

That I recognized, without much difficulty, but I found it harder to define the bonds which held me. No more than Silver did I believe in the wisdom of politicians or the moral compulsion of their policies. The function of history, as I saw it, was to catalogue and explain the mistakes made by dead politicians, and there seemed little prospect of its function changing. It was no political argument that told me my proper place was in the gap my father's death had made – a gap I could not fill, though I could stand in it. And why I wanted to stand there, I do not know. I am by no means sure that I did want to; but I felt an obliga-

tion, a compelling sense of propriety, perhaps a commanding instinct. Or it may be that all I felt was the domination
of my *métier*:

> What God abandoned, these defended,
> And saved the sum of things for pay.

The pay was not very good, but I had made a contract and
taken an oath.

I put away the picture of the Chinese girl, the picture of
the lovely ship – and could not sleep till morning.

Dick Silver came again, the next day and the next.
Cautiously he returned to his old argument, and discreetly
added to his offered bribes. I could not resent them
because I knew they were designed to secure, not only
a good business partner, but the company of a friend. I felt
that our friendship was stronger than before – because,
perhaps, he needed me now – and yet, though his friendship pleased and flattered me, I had little difficulty in
refusing it: or what it implied. I could not, I said, live
under the Liberian flag.

'Well, that's conclusive,' he said, 'and tomorrow I sail. I
think you're a fool, Tony, but you're the only damned
Puritan I've ever liked.'

It was then – the last time I saw him – that I told him
about Olaf Wishart's death in the Imjin battle. I don't
know why I had said nothing of it before – unless I was
reluctant to revisit an old emotion, or jealous of my
memory – but when he told me that he was going to
sea again, I felt it would be dishonest to let him go without
knowing the end of an affair in which we had been equally
involved.

He listened with an interest that I found improbable and
extraordinary. I thought that I alone had kept in mind
remorse for Mungo Wishart's death, and was therefore
unduly moved when Olaf died. But now I discovered that

Dick Silver, too, had kept a black memory of his share in the execution. As I remembered that bad old man drinking brandy and soda in his dressing-gown, and spouting Yeats, so he remembered his joviality when they walked together from Weddergarth to our sea-battered trawler; and Mungo's death still haunted him.

He made me repeat the story of my rescue from the battle, and Olaf's death on the after-deck of the tank. ' "Do you think this will make up for him?" ' he repeated. 'Those were his words?'

'Almost his last words.'

'There's only one thing they can mean.'

'They meant nothing when I listened to them. Nothing at all, except that he wanted me to agree with him. And I did, and I think he died happy. Or almost happy. But afterwards – after I began to get better – I thought about them, and now, I think, I agree with you.'

'He knew – he had discovered – that his father was a traitor, and committed suicide to avoid arrest. Olaf volunteered for Korea to expiate his father's guilt.'

'It looks like that.'

'So Mungo Wishart murdered his own son.'

'Isn't that going too far?'

'No! Mungo Wishart left a memory that Olaf had to wipe off the slate and, in the act of wiping it off, he was killed. His father left a heritage of death – and now I know that, my own conscience is clear. For the last ten years I've felt like a murderer, but now I feel like – what's his name? The fellow who took it on himself to shoot man-eating tigers. We killed Mungo Wishart and, if we hadn't killed him, what harm might he have lived to do!'

'Yes, I've thought of that.'

'That poor boy.'

'At the end – at the very end – he wasn't unhappy, I think.'

'But the misery he must have suffered! Oh, God damn Mungo Wishart and all those bloody egotists who take up causes!'

'Yes,' I said.

'Stay here with me, Tony. Marry a Chinese girl, make money, and enjoy yourself. And to hell with causes.'

'I haven't got a cause,' I said. 'I fight for permission to live without a cause.'

'Do you believe in God?'

'Yes.'

'Even after Korea?'

'I make no pretence to understanding.'

'Is blind faith enough?'

'It isn't wholly blind. There's a little light in the darkness.'

He stood at the window for a while, looking at the sea, and a weakness in me – a weakness of affection – tempted me again to make an impossible recantation of my – what was it? my faith, my instinct? I don't know – but from that he saved me by saying, with a sort of irritation in his voice, 'Do you remember Kingham?'

'Kingham? The I.O. at Lyness?'

'Not the statue out of Easter Island who sat beside the stove and didn't utter, but the lieutenant who talked to us: Kingham. Well, I met him again a couple of months ago. He's got a job in Brunei. Not a very good job.'

'He was a good I.O.'

'Yes. And he'd a sense of humour, of a sort. He wouldn't let us leave Scapa – do you remember? – till we'd attended the funeral of Jón Jónsson. We had to stand beside his grave in the Naval cemetery at Lyness while they shovelled in the dirt. Yes, Kingham has a sense of humour.'

'Does he like living in Brunei?'

'No, not very much. And if you won't join me, I think I may get him.'

We shook hands and said goodbye; but he stood in the

doorway, as if reluctant to go. 'That poor boy!' he said again. 'For ten years I've had a feeling of guilt about his father, and now, I suppose, I'll have an equally persistent feeling of pity for Olaf.'

I REMEMBER LOOKING at myself in the big glass of my sleeper from Euston to Inverness, and thinking, You've changed – changed as much as Silver – since the night when you were sick in the lavatory on a train to Scotland . . . I had, of course, the lopsided look of a man who has lost an arm, but in compensation for that my face had acquired a firmness that was, perhaps, too like severity; a little fullness, too, for in the eagerness of convalescence and the leisure of the long voyage from Singapore I had put on weight. It was a face very different from the ingenuous, quick, uncertain visage of my youth; and though in my heart I still felt, from time to time, the tremors and expectancies, the rawness, the tenderness, and even the hopes of a new-hatched subaltern – well, thank heaven I no longer showed them.

I washed, and walked through the long train to the dining-car, and sat down opposite a man of about my own age. I hardly looked at him before sitting down, but another glance brought me an absurd and most painful embarrassment. He was staring at me – glaring, rather – and was evidently in a temper. For by a ridiculous coincidence I had seated myself opposite another man who had lost his left arm, and the duplication of our dismemberment made us both look silly. And made us both angry.

But only for a moment or two. It was I who laughed first, and said, 'I beg your pardon.'

'I beg yours,' he said, laughing, too.

'Where did it happen?' I asked.

'On the Rhine,' he said. 'On their side, I'm glad to say. And yours?'

'In Korea.'

'Ah yes. We haven't yet cured them of madness. Do you think we shall?'

After that we fell into conversation which, beginning with, 'Did you know So-and-so?' – 'Yes, he was with them when Ginger Harlow commanded' – that sort of talk – presently developed, or expanded, from personalities to the world we lived in, and contracted again to our own interests. He was, I discovered, a fisherman; and he was on his way to a river in Sutherland where there was a run of sea-trout in September. It was then September 1st.

Those who are fishermen themselves will understand and sympathize with me – and those who are not, must bear with me and believe me – when I say, in all seriousness, that four months after the loss of my arm I felt no bitterness in mutilation except for the fact that it would stop my fishing. All my life, from the age of six or seven, I had fished – for little brown trout in the hill-lochs of the West Highlands, for bigger trout in bigger lochs, for sea-trout in tidal rivers, and salmon in our own short river (which carried only a few) or wherever I was invited to fish. It was not so much a passion, as a part of my life: running water and the wind-whipped water of a loch were features of my necessary scenery. And to be cut off from fishing was a mutilation of my life.

But now my train-companion – his name was Adrian Skene, and I was fishing with him this year in which I am writing – now Skene told me that he himself, faced with the same deprivation, had gone to a most ingenious man, who had a fishing-tackle and gunsmith's business in Inverness, and this man had devised for him a sort of harness that served his need to perfection. He used a light rod, and when he had struck a fish he pushed the butt into a socket in the belt of the harness, hooked the middle of the rod to an elastic bridle, and moved his right hand to the reel. He needed a gillie, of course, to net or gaff a big sea-trout or a salmon – but he could fish.

We talked fishing till we came to Crewe, where the dining-car went off; and exchanged addresses. Feeling much more cheerful, I returned to my sleeper and settled down to rehearse, yet again, what I had to say to Mrs. Wishart. For I was on my way to Shetland to tell her about Olaf and his death, and I did not like the prospect.

In the morning, at Inverness, I had another short conversation with Skene, then boarded the bus for the airport. The northern Highlands, under the spilt light of a clear sky, were a marvellous dappling of light and shade, of reddish moor, grey hill, and gleaming water, and the Orkney isles – I changed aeroplanes near Kirkwall – a calm and blissful mockery of war-time's rough, harsh memory. We flew on, over that low-spread, fantastically patterned archipelago, and came to the southern tip of Shetland, with the huge cliff of Fitful Head frowning superbly beside it.

I walked from the aeroplane to the modest shed where traffic was administered, and a girl in a well-cut tweed suit came towards me and said, 'Major Chisholm?'

'Yes, that's me.'

'I'm Gudrun Wishart.'

I saw her eyes turn to my lopped-off arm, and turn away again. I was used to that. I saw the beginning of a smile on her face – a friendly, welcoming smile – and I saw it fade and disappear. And I realized why. I was, I knew, looking at her with no friendliness at all, but with, perhaps, something more hostile than surprise. With resentment.

My thoughts had been dominated by memory of the girl on her pony – a girl with a grave and lovely face, but a rather dirty face, and wind-blown, unbrushed hair. I had not been so foolish as to suppose she had remained a child, but I was unprepared to find her so completely 'grown up'. Olaf in Korea had told me she was in her final year at Edinburgh University, and though Edinburgh has an excellent university its students are not, I think, notable for being well dressed. Certainly one doesn't associate, instinctively, Edinburgh students and good tailoring. I had expected to be met by a pretty but rather unkempt young woman – a well-grown but (I fancy) rather hoydenish girl in waterproof and muffler and dirty shoes. But Gudrun Wishart wore good clothes as if she were used to them, and she was better than pretty. She was entirely self-possessed, and she was beautiful.

So much I might have accepted with nothing worse, or more ungracious, than surprise. But what roused my resentment was that she had grown taller than I. In male company I have always had to admit that I am rather small. I am five foot eight – the same height as my father – and I have got used to the company of much taller friends. But among women, five foot eight is usually enough to give one a little sense of physical command; though my mother, who was five foot eleven, always seemed to tower above me. And now, to my shocked and irritated astonishment, I saw a Gudrun who was at least five foot ten!

I could not, I am ashamed to say, at once overcome my resentment, and I remember quite clearly that when I said, 'It's very kind of you to come so far to meet me,' my voice had an unpleasant, grating quality. – I had, after all, come a long way and been at pains to prepare a suitable style, or tone, for telling her and her mother about Olaf's death, and it was disconcerting to realize that the style I had meditated was unsuitable. She led me to her car, and there again – though this was a trifling mistake – my anticipation of what I should find had been at fault.

My knowledge of Weddergarth was confined to breakfast in the kitchen and a bedroom that was furnished well enough for the comfort demanded in 1900; and I had read in Mungo Wishart's story of the poverty to which he had been reduced by disastrous law-suits. It was not unnatural, therefore, that, when Gudrun wrote to say she would meet me, I had expected her to arrive in some shabby, clattering motor car that had been built about 1935; but the car she drove, though neither large nor luxurious, was brightly polished, neat, and new.

From the airport at Sumburgh to Lerwick is a distance of twenty-seven miles, and Weddergarth is twenty miles north and west of Lerwick. We had a longish drive together, and till we got to Lerwick nothing passed between us but arid question and answer about my journey, the weather, the crops, and so forth. But when, beyond Lerwick, we turned into a bleak hinterland, she asked me, with an abrupt and unexpected seriousness, 'How much do you remember of mother?'

That was a difficult question. What I remembered of Mrs. Wishart was, in the first place, that she had clearly been born and brought up in a social station very different from that of her husband. But within her own right she had a natural dignity, a more than agreeable appearance, and eyes of remarkable beauty.

I replied, with imperfect frankness, 'She was very kind to me, though at first she didn't want to be, and what I chiefly remember is her friendliness and hospitality – and her eyes.'

'She has changed a lot,' said Gudrun. 'Try not to show that you see how much she has changed.'

'Should I not have come?'

'Oh, yes. She wants to see you. She wants to hear everything you can tell her about Olaf – every word – but don't tell her anything to hurt her. She has been hurt too much.'

'There is nothing to hurt her except the fact of his death. He was, in every way, a son to be proud of.'

'And she lost him.'

I began to realize then why Gudrun, at twenty-one, was

so 'grown up'. I remember exactly where she said it: we were passing a small loch called Petta Water, which means, I suppose, the lake of the Picts; and the tone of her voice said clearly that she had matured in the grief that had aged her mother. Sorrow had carried her from the untidiness of a girl's estate to womanhood.

I think we said nothing more till we came to Weddergarth. I can remember no more words, but I remember the oppression of her sorrow. I think we were silent.

About Weddergarth my memory was accurate. It was a big, gaunt building, of no architectural interest, of no architectural value except for the fact that its windows were well spaced and of proportionate size. But its situation, on that bright autumnal day, was enchanting. It stood on the west side of the long, narrow firth to which, almost ten years before, Dick Silver had brought his trawler out of the storm, and from the shelter of its coppice of spindly trees it looked beyond the tongue of blue water to low, kindly hills that ran down to meet the sea. The enormous sky poured out its radiance on a tangle of land and water: land so fluent that it seemed to proclaim its cousinhood with the ocean whose bright arms enclosed it. Blue sea, a brown and yellow land, a sunlit immensity of sky. . . .

Gudrun drove to the front door, which we had not used on my previous visit; and we stopped on a cleanly raked circle of gravel. Mrs. Wishart was waiting for us, and I was thankful that I had been warned of the change in her appearance, for she had become an old woman. She was only forty-five – so Gudrun told me – but her hair was silver, her pink and pretty cheeks had fallen in, and her lovely eyes had become the eye-holes of a tragic mask. But her voice was firm, her carriage upright.

For the first few minutes it was she alone who talked, for I, distressed by her appearance, was tongue-tied. She welcomed me with grace and dignity. She told me how

kind I was to have come so far, for her comfort, and hoped
that my journey had not been too hard or tiring. Unlike
everyone else whom I had met in the last few months, she
seemed not to notice the fact that I had lost an arm – there
was no quick look, and look-away, and eye-flicker of
embarrassment – but to her, apparently, I was still a
normal man: a visitor who was so courteous as to come
and give her the news she wanted.

The room into which we went was a parlour, or drawing-room, on the right-hand side of the hall. It was
furnished curiously, but with a certain charm, in an
Anglo-Indian style that imperatively recalled our vanished
empire. There were chairs and sofas, a big table and lesser
tables, of intricately carved and fretted teak and other
Indian woods, and on cream-coloured walls, in thin ebony
frames, hung a great number of small, exactly drawn, and
brightly coloured Persian or Moghul paintings of mahar-
ajahs and court ladies, court scenes and hunting scenes.
But it was a comfortable room – cushions and rugs
abounded, as well as Benares brass and ivory – and on
a big hearth a peat fire burned. It was obviously the
creation and bequest of Mungo's father and grandfather,
who had spent their active years in India.

A plump, red-cheeked maid pushed in a trolley furnished for tea, and after an expectant silence I began to tell
them about Olaf. The tale lasted a long time, for when I
had told all I knew of him – now without any attempt to
qualify the narrative, to soften it for them – they plied me
with questions, intelligent and close questions not only
about Olaf, but about the circumstances of the war and the
unhappiness of the Koreans. I had not expected to say
anything about the war in its political relations, but I
found myself arguing warmly for the rightness of President Truman's decision to fight Communism. They
must never, I told them, think that Olaf's life had been
thrown away. It had been spent for a good purpose.

We talked till dinner-time, and dinner had to be put back for half an hour. We dined, very simply but sufficiently, in a small room that had been newly decorated, and again I found myself puzzled by evidence of a prosperity – a modest but manifest prosperity – that contradicted all I had previously seen of Weddergarth, and what I had inferred.

After dinner I had to rake my memory for every detail I could find of Olaf's appearance and the general habit of a soldier's life; for his mother was still hungry for any crumb of information that had in it some flavour of him. She was neither importunate nor tearful, but his death had turned her love to a land of famine, and in the desert I was her only source of manna. What gave her greatest comfort, I think, was my story of our dinner with the American war-correspondents. That they, from another and far distant country, had shown appreciation of her son, had seen his virtue and been kind to him because of it – this, more than anything else, gratified her motherhood. She went to bed, not indeed consoled, but with, as it seemed, a new buttress against sorrow.

I was exhausted when I went to bed, at half-past ten, and slept till half-past eight. I woke to another fine morning, and presently, with Gudrun, walked to the head of the voe; for we had had time, during dinner, for some little talk of fishing, and I had learnt that the burn of Hammar was one of the best sea-trout streams in Shetland.

While I waited for her I walked round the house, and saw everywhere the signs of renovation. My bedroom – the room I had slept in ten years before – had been redecorated, and the adjacent bathroom modernized. The whole house was newly harled, and there was a new iron gate at the entrance to the drive ... I was, at that time, rather sensitive to economic conditions, for I was not so well-off as I had expected to be after my mother's death. It was she who had owned our small estate. She had bought it as a wedding-present for my father, but prudently kept the title in her own name; and when she died she left me the sum of £2500, and the residue of her property to endow scholarships (or some such thing) for promising young novelists: scholarships to perpetuate her name as a patron of letters as well as a practitioner.

Our Highland property was sold, and I was homeless. I was quite well-off – I had an income of about £400 a year in addition to my pay, and in the simple fashion of my life my pay was sufficient – but I had thought I would be better-off; and I found myself taking a new interest in money, and other people's money.

When Gudrun came out she saw me admiring the new gate – it was a handsome piece of smithy-work – and she said at once, with perfect candour, 'Mother has had a lot more to spend since father died. He was very extravagant: a case of brandy every fortnight, and cigars, and books. He was always buying books: the dullest sort of books History, mostly. We sold his library a couple of years ago, and got over £900 for it.'

It was, I thought, a pretty piece of irony that Mungo Wishart's death had made his wife and daughter rich: rich, that is, in their own estimation. For in the assorted hatreds that dominated his life – hatred of his progenitors, of Britain, Lloyd George, and of himself – there had been a hateful contempt of what he regarded as his poverty; but, dying, he bequeathed abundance.

'His life was insured,' said Gudrun, 'and as officially he died of heart-failure, the insurance company paid up at once. If they had known the truth, it might have been different.'

I hesitated for a moment before asking, 'What was the truth?'

'You ought to know that,' she said.

'When did you discover it?'

'About a year after he died. People here aren't stupid, you know. They can put two and two together. He was anti-British, they all knew that, and then he died suddenly the night after two officers – one in the Army, one in the Navy – had been to see him. And I think the doctor talked. Not much, perhaps, but enough to boast that he knew more than other people, and could tell a lot if he was allowed to. And one day a girl at school, who didn't like me, said to Olaf and me, "Your father was a spy and ought to have been hanged. He would have been if he hadn't killed himself." – She was a bad girl, and still is, but somehow or other we felt she was speaking the truth. She lives in a cottage on the other side of that hill. She's had two illegitimate children since then, but she doesn't seem to mind.'

'Did your mother know?'

'Of course. We told her what the girl had said, when we got home, and asked if it was true. She said no, but there were many things we were too young to understand. She said father had been a great man, but very unhappy. So unhappy that often he said and did things that weren't wise; and that no one in Shetland was clever enough to understand him. – She knew, all right, and both Olaf and I saw that she was only making excuses. She was still in love with him.'

'What did you think of him?'

'Hated him! When he came back that day – from the ship you were in – he was in a blazing temper. Mother went out to meet him, and he hit her on the face and knocked her down. That wasn't the first time either. But mother was a crofter's daughter and father was a gentleman, a landed proprietor, and old enough to be her father. She was still awe-struck by the fact that he had married her. He was easily the best-looking man in Shetland when he was younger – and, when he was in a good mood, he could be very nice. Olaf and I never really liked him, because we could never trust his moods, but there were times when he simply enchanted us. And mother's a very good woman: she's got a much nicer nature than I have. She loved him on her wedding-day, and nothing he did after that could make any difference. It was after father died that her hair began to go white, though she was only thirty-five or thirty-six.'

All this she told me in a voice that was clear and cool. So cool, indeed, so void of emotion, that no great knowledge of human nature was needed to see that her composure was studied. She had acquired it over the years by resolute exercise of her intelligence and her will. It must have been after her father's death that Gudrun began to grow up; and her brother's death hastened the process.

'You must,' I said, 'have hated me when you realized that I had had some part in what happened.'

'Not you,' she said. 'The other man – the Naval officer who came – yes. We were furious with him because he was responsible, not only for father's death, but for making us contemptible. For that's what we thought! I've never in my life done anything more difficult than going to school the day after we'd been told the truth of the matter, and looking the other children in the face as if I'd nothing to be ashamed of. And for Olaf it was more difficult still. He was younger than me, and a boy. I remember him crying on the way to school – crying at the roadside – and saying he couldn't face it. But he did, and I don't suppose anything he had to face in Korea seemed much more unpleasant than that. – But we never blamed you.'

'Why not?'

She stopped, and looked at me, and for the first time since meeting me at Sumburgh, her composure was embarrassed. Her girlhood rose, to threaten its smooth surface, and, with a hint of laughter to go with it, a blush coloured her cheeks.

'You won't be offended?'

'Of course not.'

'Well,' she said, 'do you remember how we found you? You were sitting on a dyke, looking as cold and white as a plucked hen, and the first thing you said to us was, "Please go away because I'm going to be sick." And after that we helped you on to my pony, and took you home. And because of that we felt, you see – well, we had found you, and we felt, in a way, that you were our property. So we couldn't possibly blame you.'

'I see.'

'You're not offended?'

'No, it helps me to understand.'

We were, by then, not far from the head of the voe. The path along it was an old cart-track, separated from the sea by a strip of heather and black rocks half-covered with yellow weed. Ahead of us lay a short beach of cream-coloured sand, and while I was wondering whether I should tell her what I wanted to tell her – while I was tapping courage to tell her – I saw, in the narrowing bay, a silver fish leap from the water and fall on its side with a heavy splash; then another, that seemed to skate in a quick, wavering progress before it fell; and I let the human issue suffer postponement. They were sea-trout that were jumping.

'We've had no rain for ten days,' said Gudrun, 'and there isn't water enough for them to get up the burn.'

We saw a dozen fish jumping before we came to the beach – some of them big fish, of five or six pounds' weight – and with a quickened pace and rising excitement we walked on beside a run of tidal water that led us to a big pool below a series of rocky falls; above which a stone bridge carried a road across the stream. In the pool finnock were jumping, and occasionally a large trout came up with, as it seemed, an indignant, a contemptuous splash of sheer impatience. Beyond the bridge were two or three long, deep pools, peat-black between sheer black sides, and farther up the valley the sun shone on a yellow waterfall that filled another, rounder basin whose surface sent shivers to the shore as an unseen, great fish turned and swam quickly to the farther bank.

'But this,' I said, laughing in sheer excitement, 'this is paradise! Fisherman's paradise. Oh, if I had a rod, and could stay here!'

I told her, with an enthusiasm which may have been absurd, about my meeting with Adrian Skene, and the ingenious harness that would allow me to fish again; and she listened with at least an appearance of understanding.

'Olaf was like you,' she said. 'He used to dream about sea-trout.'

We lingered for an hour by the stream – by the yellow fall, and the long black pools, by the rock-falls and the curving sand-sided pool through which it entered the sea – and I decided at last to tell her what Olaf had said to me as he lay dying on the after-deck of the tank. They were the only words of his, which I remembered, that I had not told his mother.

' "Do you think this will make up for him?" ' she repeated; and suddenly all her composure was gone. She burst into tears, and ran from me.

'No!' she cried, 'no, don't come near me!' So I sat on the parapet of the bridge, and she, with her face averted, sat for a long time on a rock above the falls below me. She moved at last, and knelt beside a little pool, and washed her eyes in the water of the stream. She climbed to the road again, and said, 'Do you wonder that I hated him?'

We turned to walk home to Weddergarth, and presently she said, 'It's a dead hatred, thank goodness. I shan't make the mistake he did, and let hate poison me. He was a miserable man; poor father, and I'm never going to think of him again, if I can help it. But till you told me, I hadn't admitted to myself, I hadn't been honest enough to admit

why Olaf went to Korea. I pretended he was being
romantic in a much more ordinary way.'

A little while later she said, 'I'm thankful you didn't tell
mother. You won't, will you?'

I spent a very domestic afternoon with Mrs. Wishart.
She had assembled all her memorials of Olaf: photographs
of him as a child, school photographs of football teams, a
selection of his letters, and letters from his friends and
schoolmasters. I was not bored, and I was deeply relieved
to see some relaxation of the tragic intensity of her expression as we spoke of him. At tea-time she sat upright on
her chair, a Victorian rigidity in her back, and in her
posture I saw another hint of comfort. Pride was bringing
a little cushion against bereavement – an insufficient
cushion, but better than nothing.

In the evening we talked farming. She had two small
farms in hand, and was doing well with them. 'I was
brought up on a croft,' she said, 'and I've a closer knowledge of what's needed to make a farm pay than Mr.
Wishart had; who was used to a different way of life
altogether.'

Our conversation was quite unemotional, except for
some well-justified annoyance about the monstrously high
freight-charges that the island farmers had to pay; and I
went to bed with the contented feeling that I had done
something to mollify a good woman's grief. I could stay
with them no longer than two nights, but I promised to
return in a year's time and catch sea-trout in their splendid
stream.

In the morning, before leaving, I stood for a minute or
two with Gudrun on the east side of the house, looking
down at the long voe, and said with idle interest, 'You
should make a path to the beach.'

Their road turned left to meet the main road over the
trout-stream bridge, and to the right curved into a cart-

track. Below the junction – the house stood a hundred feet above the sea – there was a belt of peat and heather, and between that and the sea a slope of meadow-grass. By cutting through the peat a pleasant path could be made to the small beach that lay below.

'But that would be sheer extravagance,' said Gudrun, 'and we can't afford luxuries.'

She drove me to Sumburgh, and I repeated my promise to return in a year's time. In the meantime we had to continue our studies: for she, having taken her degree, was going back to Edinburgh to train as a teacher, and I had had the good fortune to be nominated for a vacancy in the Joint Services Staff College.

I began my studies with the advantage of a good conscience, and in the projection of such knowledge as I had acquired – a purely military knowledge, till then – into the larger field of world-strategy, I found, not only a justification of my *servitude militaire*, but a great extension of my interest in it. I have never known twelve months go by so quickly and with so rich a reward of knowledge. And a year and two days after my duty-visit to Shetland – on September 3rd, 1952 – I was again flying north to Weddergarth, now equipped with the fishing-harness devised by that ingenious man in Inverness, and a couple of light rods that I could use all day, single-handed, without tiring.

There was the usual little crowd of people, of travellers and their friends, on the wind-thrashed hillock above the black runways at Sumburgh, and Gudrun stood among them like a masterpiece of drawing in a students' exhibition. Now she woke no absurdity of resentment in my mind – no rebuff to her welcome – but as we drove northward we talked of small matters in the easy manner of old friends. The weather was rough, but when she told me that the fish were running I thought the gale-driven

dark clouds and the lean sides of Shetland looked wonderfully handsome.

At Weddergarth the atmosphere was pleasant and relaxed. The oppression of tragedy had lifted, and I had no
difficulty in talking to Mrs. Wishart. In conversation she
now showed a gentle humour, and she had a mind richly
stored with country legends, and knowledge of an older,
vanished way of life that she had got from her parents. She
went early to bed, and Gudrun and I sat talking for
another hour or so.

She agreed that her mother was much happier. 'But she's
far too old for her years,' she said. 'She's beginning to talk
about father as if he were still a young man when he died. A
gifted, and rather silly young man. She doesn't laugh at him,
of course, but she's like a mother talking about a brilliant
and quite irresponsible son. I think, now, that he was half
way to insanity. He used to go for tremendous long walks –
thirty miles over the hills: more than that, sometimes – and
not long ago she told me that he believed in what he called
'the familiar spirits of the country'. I don't know whether he
expected to meet them, and have a chat with them, or just,
perhaps, to feel and absorb them. But what he was always
hoping to discover – or to learn from his familiar spirits –
was where Old Dandy Pitcairn was buried. Even mother
laughed when she told me that. Walking all over Shetland,
looking for the body of a man who died two hundred years
ago! And then he would come home, and for three or four
days drink brandy and soda, and read, read, read. Sometimes I found him in his chair, dead drunk, with dozens of
books lying on the floor all round him.'

In the morning I went fishing, and Gudrun came to
gillie for me. But this is no more a tale of fishing than a tale
of war, and I shall not describe the tense, continuous
pleasure and recurring excitements of those wet and
stormy days. For the credit of the burn of Hammar I

must say that in three days I caught nine fish over two pounds in weight of which the biggest was a little better than eight pounds, and a dozen or so finnock; but to that cold statement, though I am reluctant to leave it, I shall add nothing. My story is of people, and after taking strenuous delight from trout and running water I have to record a painful and ludicrous misfortune in the more emotional world of human affairs.

It was late in the afternoon, and I was fishing the big pool below the bridge. I had taken a fish of four and a half pounds out of it, and there was another, as big, rising impatiently, every ten minutes or so, that I could not quite reach. But the wind, a blustery south-easter, was slowly backing, and presently I saw that from a rocky bank about twenty yards away I could cover the water quite easily. There were rocks all the way – rocks covered thickly with yellow bladderwrack and some patches of black ribbon-weed – and Gudrun warned me to be careful. She came, too. I, more intent on my objective than balance, slipped and tottered. Gudrun reached out to prevent me falling on my wounded side, and I, clutching her arm, brought both of us down on a wet, cold bed of sea-weed. We were not hurt and, recovering in a moment from the shock of the fall, began to laugh.

We lay as close, with legs almost as neighbourly as in a marriage bed – not quite, for all four were clad in rubber wading-boots – and, seeing her laughing mouth so near, I bent and kissed it. Gudrun made one small movement of evasion, and then, with hard intent, turned and kissed again. We lay like that, kissing closely on a mattress of cold bladder-wrack under a thin, pelting rain from a wildly blowing sky, for two or three minutes: more, perhaps. And then, from some disastrous innerness of my mind, I felt the flow of a chill revulsion – against myself and what I was doing more than against her, but against her, too – and pushing myself free of her arms, I sat up and said, with a

cruelty and *bêtise* that I shudder to recall – with a loutishness for which I should not be forgiven, and a blatant
pretence of speaking casually – I sat up and said, 'It's
hardly the place for this sort of thing, is it?'

I saw – and was hit to the heart by what I saw – the look
of total dismay, of youth's dismay, on Gudrun's face; and
then a look of indignant shame. But shame receded,
indignation stayed. She stood up, and angrily brushed
her wet coat. 'No, indeed,' she said. 'I didn't expect a
rough-house when I came out with you. I didn't think
you'd behave like a drunken medical student.'

'I am very sorry.'

'You've broken your rod,' she said, and picked it up. 'I
think, in any case, we've had enough fishing for today.
Shall I help you back, or can you manage by yourself?'

'I can manage.'

She left me, striding easily over the cushioned rocks,
and I followed more carefully. We walked back to Weddergarth in silence, and immediately after dinner she
pretended a cold, and went to bed. I found less interest
than before in Mrs. Wishart's stories of the old-fashioned
ways of Shetland, and was glad when I, too, could go to my
room.

I had a bottle of whisky, unopened till then, and with its
help I tried to repel the ghost of Mungo Wishart. It was
his ghost that had come between us when Gudrun and I
lay together on the yellow bed of the rocks, and kissed so
warmly. His ghost, beating at the door – the door of the
bridal chamber – had started the chill revulsion that
divided us. 'You killed me,' said the ghost. 'You came
from the sea and killed me, and to make love to the
daughter of the man you murdered is worse than incest.
There may be no great harm in incest, which is the coming
together of kindly blood, but fornication with the blood
you have spilled is a deadly sin.'

So some barbarous superstition in the uncharted deepness of my mind must have prompted me when I committed my act of cruelty, of incredible *bêtise* and loutishness, among the rocks; and whisky, when I sought its help, betrayed me and played me false. I drank greedily, seeking comfort, but grew more melancholy and thought the ghost spoke truly. Not at first sight – not when I came the year before – but this year, when I saw Gudrun standing in her tall and lovely distinction among the dull, the small, the ordinary people who were waiting to meet or wave goodbye to their friends at the airport, I had fallen suddenly in love with her: but with a delight so intense and pure that I had had no thought of physical possession. It was a love that took its satisfaction through the eyes and ears. Impractical and absurd; but, for a day or two, sufficient. And then, when our mouths met in kissing, it became real – and impossible.

Or so I thought when I heard the ghost of Mungo Wishart beating on the door. And so I still thought when whisky betrayed me, and reinforced my unforgotten guilt. I threw what was left of the bottle out of the window, and, sobbing drunkenly, fell asleep.

Seeming unperturbed, seeming bright and practical at breakfast, Gudrun said she had to go into Lerwick. 'But I've got a gillie for you,' she said. 'An old man called Willy Harcus. You won't find him very entertaining, but he'll look after you. He knows the burn better than I do.'

Willy Harcus was a slow, shambling, pessimistic man, with stooped and narrow shoulders, watery eyes, and a drop at his nose; but Gudrun was right when she said that he knew the burn. He took me to pools that I had not fished before, a mile above the bridge, and wherever he led me I rose a fish; and lost them all. I was full of gloom, my hand was unsteady, and though twice I had a good trout firmly on, I never expected to land it. But my repeated failure, though it deepened my gloom, seemed to lighten Willy's pessimism; he grew more cheerful as increasingly his pessimism was justified, and when at lunch-time we sat down to eat our sandwiches he told me, with relish, a dozen stories about notable and skilful fishermen who had been defeated by the wily, robust, and perversely natured trout in the burn of Hammar.

In the afternoon he led me far uphill to a small, wind-blown loch, in a wilderness of high moorland, where wading was difficult on a soft, uneven bottom; and there I caught three fish, the biggest nearly five pounds. They gave me wonderful sport – in open water they ran like porpoises – and my bruised and bewildered spirit began to revive and rise again. But Willy Harcus was again depressing.

My three fish were all very dark in colour, for in still, peaty water a sea-trout quickly loses its brightness and puts on a muddy, dull disguise; and Willy, looking at them, grew muddily philosophical. They came up to spawn, he told me – these fish, so glittering with lordliness in the sea – in dark runnels of the peat, in thick and clouded water, in almost stagnant pools.

'They are very nearly human,' he said. 'They have an impulse to breed that won't be denied, and an instinct for dirt that makes a nonsense of all their education in the good, clean sea. They are as stubborn as children, and wild as drunkards. They will do anything to get their own way, and what does that amount to? They go swimming up-stream, always up-stream, mile after mile up-stream, to no better end than wriggling in a mire of peat. They are as bad as human beings – but if you cook them properly, they will not taste as bad.'

At dinner that night Gudrun over-played composure, and I found the prospect of a weekend at Weddergarth quite intolerable. The next day was a Saturday, and if I did not go then – I had not intended to – I should have to stay till Monday, without occupation on Sunday: for in Shetland one is not allowed to fish on Sunday. So I discovered an excuse for leaving in the morning, that did not deceive Gudrun but made Mrs. Wishart very sorry for me. I must come again, she said, and have a proper holiday.

In the morning, on our way to the airport, Gudrun and I talked chiefly of the film-industry; about which I know very little. At Sumburgh, in the uneasy minutes before saying goodbye, she put aside for a moment her pretence of indifference, of composure, and said, 'Mother will be very disappointed if you don't come back. I hope you will.'

I was too slow in replying, and when I said, 'Yes, I should like to catch another fish or two' – the mask was on again, and with excess of brightness in her voice she exclaimed, 'And you'll stay with us, of course. You mustn't think of going anywhere else.'

I had slept badly, being over-tired by a long day's fishing in rough weather, and hard, uphill walking, and in the aeroplane I dozed and woke, and dozed again to catch fragments of ridiculous or tormenting dreams. After leaving Edinburgh, when we flew in darkness the longest leg of the journey, I fell into deeper sleep and a sequent dream that was compounded of fish and a river, of Mungo Wishart and Willy Harcus, and some commoner ingredients.

My dream began among symbols that no one who has ever heard of Freud can fail to identify. I was swimming up-stream, with earnest endeavour against every sort of difficulty, to reach at last a dark and perfect happiness which, I knew, lay hidden in a secret channel under cover of the heather. That was my whole intention, and I was vastly disconcerted when the narrowing stream became a current in the sky. I was no longer safe and snug between enclosing banks, but all at large in the upper air, and my goal was no longer darkness but a very bright and distant star. But head to stream I went on swimming; for the compulsion was still strong.

In dreams, as in a circus, clowns interrupt the drama on the high trapeze. I landed, quite suddenly, on a sand-bank where a group of lugubrious and bespectacled choir-boys were singing, out of tune, the well-known hymn:

'Time like an ever-rolling stream, bears all his sons
                                                     away. . . .'

Angrily I told them to be quiet. 'You are out of tune,' I said, 'and I'm pretty sure you don't know your geography. This stream that you're singing about: can you tell me its source? Can you tell me where it rises, and where it flows?'

'In the Book of Genesis,' said one of the boys. 'That's where it rises, in the far backward and forgotten sump of our beginning; and it flows inexorably towards our un-imaginable end.'

'What nonsense!' I said crossly. 'It rises in the future – it flows from the future – and we have to swim up-stream. Has anyone here heard of Mungo Wishart?'

'We knew him well,' said a choir-boy with a sad and sinister face. 'He used to quote Wordsworth to us:

Not in entire forgetfulness,
And not in utter nakedness,
But trailing clouds of foul and noxious memory we
                                                     come—

'Only if you swim *down*-stream,' I said. 'If you swim *up*-stream, as you should, as Willy Harcus says you must – though Willy Harcus is wrong in thinking you swim into darkness – then your trailing clouds of memory are carried away, and you're rid of them.'

The sand-bank dissolved, the choir-boys disappeared, and I continued to swim. But now I was swimming easily, in the rhythm of my breathing. I swam out of dreams into a sound sleep, and did not wake till the red landing-light went on. I woke, however, with the memory of my dream whole and fresh in my mind.

I am no intellectual, and I cannot really comprehend the modern theories of time: the linking, the inseparability of space and time; the non-existence of time without a determined reference-point; or an infinite series of different times. I understand what the theorists say, but I cannot bring their conclusions within the range of my own creative imagination. Within the scope of my own reference to them, I cannot accept them as real. In the common way, the traditional way, I have always thought of time as a stream; and I still do. But I no longer think of it as a stream flowing from the past.

In my dream it ran the other way, and the more I ponder my dream, the more I am convinced of its essential truth. Now I see time as a river rising in the future, and like – but contrary to – the lordly fish that swim from the light of the sea to the darkness of their spawning-grounds, we may swim up-stream from darkness towards the light of its undiscovered source. No compulsion leads us by the nose, but free will permits the choice.

In a progress up-stream, moreover, memory is not inseparable. Memories gather about us, but against the current memory can be let go; and the stream will carry it away. Mungo Wishart – of whose unhappiness I often thought – was right when he said there was no contentment for a man who remembered everything, for a nation that could forget nothing; and the obvious reason is that such a man, and such a nation, have no faith in the future. They go with the stream and their memories cling to them; they swim in a jelly of unhappiness. But the up-stream swimmer and the spawning fish can shed their yesterdays.

I am, by nature, distrustful of truth-by-revelation. I prefer truth that is the legal offspring of observed and known facts. But in the autumn and winter of 1952 I found myself accepting the revelation of my dream. I grew accustomed to the idea of living in a vast, invisible, impalpable Mississippi of the sky that ran through galaxies of stars from a fountain in the unpredictable future, either of time or space; and as I grew accustomed to the thought, the use of custom let me accept it without the labour of conscious decision.

I was, however, curiously slow to realize one of the advantages of accepting it. It was not until the new year had come in that I saw the possibility of declaring myself innocent, in this present, of Mungo Wishart's death. I had to declare my faith in the future, in the light that was our goal, and become an up-stream swimmer. Then I could rid myself of guilt, and go free. . . .

My military career, enlarged in understanding by my year at the Joint Services Staff College, was now enlarged in practice, and in purpose too, by my appointment, on the staff, to the Supreme Headquarters of the Allied Powers in Europe: which is part of the military body of the North Atlantic Treaty. A month after leaving Shetland I was in Versailles, and adapting myself with unexpected ease to a new concept of loyalty. I was now a servant, not only of the Queen, but of the United States and Luxembourg, of Greece and Turkey, of France and Iceland and all the other signatories of the Treaty. It was, from the beginning, an exhilarating feeling, and as I acquired some knowledge of our organization, and the difficulties, complexities, and possible rewards of our work, I felt as never before the importance of being a soldier in this make-or-mar century.

Others, unfortunately, realized their importance, too. Our necessary work was often imbedded in departmental pastry, and there were times when the pastry-cooks demanded more respect for their confectionery than for the game in the pie. But all organization corrupts, and great organization corrupts greatly; and in spite of that I found the atmosphere of Versailles more stimulating than that of any purely British headquarters I had known. I made friends, and learnt to talk with them in a mixture of French and English, with a polyglot addition of Dutch, American, and jargon.

I wrote to Gudrun, and after a few weeks she replied. I wrote again, and her answer came more quickly. To begin with, our correspondence was almost impersonal. She was now teaching in Lerwick, and her letters were a very pleasant mixture of sharp comment, unsweet affection for the little town and its people, and a humour I had not expected from her. I, in return, sent descriptions of my colleagues, the scene at Versailles, or a play at the Comédie Française.

By degrees, however, our letters grew warmer; and with decent reservation we spoke about ourselves. In February or March I told her not only of my belief that time's fountain was in the future, but how that belief had started. 'And if you can't accept my dream as revelation,' I said, 'at least you can laugh at it.' She wrote to say she was an immediate convert to my view, but when I told her that I no longer felt guilty of her father's death, she replied: 'If you worked out a new theory of time merely to prove yourself innocent of that, you were wasting your time, whichever way it flows. I've already told you that neither Olaf nor I ever blamed you, and I told you our reason. But I suppose you weren't listening. . . .'

There was an American colonel with whom I worked, and whom I liked for his troubled enthusiasm. He believed in progress, and its possibility, and in the possibility of maintaining peace; he believed that we were the people to maintain it; but he knew the legend of Sisyphus, and wondered if we would all be content to spend the remainder of our lives in pushing an insupportable boulder uphill. – That was one of his metaphors; he had, however, others that were more cheerful. – He was a Connecticut Yankee, and often reminded us of his origin. He had a slow, ponderous habit of speech, and a brain so much quicker than his tongue that sometimes he would fall into a puzzled silence, and then continue what he had been saying two paragraphs ahead of where he had stopped. He had no fear of sounding sententious or remarking the obvious. It was he, in the last week of April, who exclaimed, 'Paris in the spring! This is something I've looked forward to all my life!'

I remembered the week that my mother and Peter and I had spent in Paris in a vanished spring before the war. I had looked forward to that with uncurbed excitement, and drunk its air with a pleasure that floated me above the common earth. I had not, however, expected that its repetition would infect me with anything remotely like a vernal spirit. But spring, when it came, insisted on recognition. This was the renewal of life: the bright air proclaimed it, green leaves announced it, and every crowded pavement acknowledged it.

'Paris in the spring!' repeated the Colonel one afternoon when he and I and a French colleague had found, after a week's discussion, the tentative solution of a stubborn problem in the new logistics that nuclear weapons demanded. 'The watershed in spring! We're sitting on a watershed in history, a watershed in spring, with peace on the one side, and on the other—'

He stopped, and left his unfinished platitude high and dry. His mind had gone ahead from an historical perception to our personal relationship with it. We had done a difficult piece of work, and deserved some reward; especially in the spring. – 'What do you say? Let's go and give ourselves the best dinner that Paris can cook up!'

We agreed. All three of us were pleased with what we had done – two days before, the problem had seemed insoluble – and the drain of effort invited a more than ordinary replenishment. A few hours later we were sitting round a table in a small restaurant on the Quai Bourbon, in the Île St. Louis, debating with intensity of feeling – what was it? Sole, salmon, lamb, or duck? I have no recollection of what we ate or what we drank, but I know we ate richly and drank well.

The French Colonel had fought in Italy with General Juin's Colonial troops, and greatly distinguished himself in command of Moroccan infantry in the Val d'Elsa. Later he had fought and been wounded in Indo-China. He was a short man, broad-shouldered, with a round, bland, almost hairless face incongruously decorated with a monocle that gave him, on the one side, a permanent expression of surprise. He begged us to speak English.

'In the exercise of our profession,' he said, 'I can endure your French. You are both fluent, and I can understand you: for a professional purpose, that is sufficient. But this is an evening of pleasure, and I must safeguard my pleasure. So let us speak English.'

'If you're so sensitive about grammar and pronunciation,' said the American, 'You shouldn't insist on French being the language of diplomacy. When you insist on that, and feel as you do, you're just sticking out a foot and asking everyone to tread on your sore toe.'

'But one sore toe is necessary. If we had no flaw, nothing to hurt us, in mind or body, we should have no spring to action, no impulse to endeavour.'

'I wish we had nothing worse than a sore toe,' I said.

'There's nothing wrong with my toes,' said the American, 'but right now I've got a pain in the ass from being kicked around. We've been kicked around too long and too often.'

He was silent for a moment, then jumped two

paragraphs in his theme. 'It isn't that I dislike the Russians, but why in hell can't they leave us alone?'

'You can diagnose a heresy,' said the Frenchman, 'by the passion with which it seeks converts. A subconscious knowledge of being hopelessly wrong compels you to find adherents who will assure you that you are right. The poor Russians are in a fearful dilemma: they must either renounce Communism, which would be intellectual suicide for them, or convert the whole world to Communism; which would be calamitous. It would make the world so irretrievably dull that there would be universal dismay and general suicide.'

'And we in the meantime—'

'We stand upon the watershed. On a *ligne de partage* in history.'

I let them argue, and was pleased to be in their company. The American Colonel had the lean, long-jawed, bony features which are no longer the common pattern of his countrymen, but which, when we see them, still remind us of frontier wars and the taming of a continent; and the French Colonel, with his monocle so straining plumply filled skin that on the one side he was perpetually astonished, but on the other placidly content – the Frenchman, with his record of gallantry, and a professional mind that sometimes dazzled our calculations, was a sturdy and very agreeable reminder that France cannot wholly be judged by her politicians. I was in good company, I felt, but I did not pay much attention to their argument. Vaguely I heard the American say, 'But we've got to believe in ourselves!'

'That is a luxury we discarded some time ago. Have you read *L'Éducation Sentimentale*?'

'But that's only a book.'

'You are quite right. And such books are dangerous.'

'Don't you believe in anything?'

'In tomorrow, perhaps. – Is there a beautiful woman sitting behind me?' he asked.

I, while they talked, had been watching, and delighted by, a dozen little dramas enacted on miniature stages. Every table was animated by a sense of drama. At every table there was emotion, and something of the theatre. Here and there great issues were at stake: there, most evidently, love at a falling barricade, and there, with equal passion, a matter of *cuisine*, the stuffing of a duck, a *bisque* of crayfish, the flavour of a Chablis or a Chambertin. A table of five people asserted and denied the verity of God – the merit of a dressmaker – the ephemeral in Sartre – or the corruption of a minister: whatever it was, it evoked the fervour of their interest and demanded the hard play of intelligence. How palely and imperfectly, how partially we live and dine in Britain, I thought – and then, at the table behind our French Colonel, a woman turned her head, and the beauty of her face under dark hair stirred excitement in me. She continued to show her profile, looking at people who sat by the wall to my left, and talking of them to her party.

It was then the Colonel asked, 'Is there a beautiful woman behind me?'

'Yes,' I said.

He turned his chair about, refixed his monocle, and stared at her with a high seriousness of interest.

'Yes!' he declared. 'Yes, you are right. She is the most beautiful woman here, I have seen them all. – Do you like Renoir?'

'Why, of course,' said the American Colonel. 'We've got some of the best collections in the world of French Impressionists.'

'But Renoir?'

'Even if we don't know much about art,' I said, 'we can see that he knew what he liked.'

'And she – isn't she Renoir's woman in the picture he called "La Loge"? Look at her.'

He turned again to look; the American Colonel

half-turned; and I remembered that once I had seen Gudrun, wind-blown on her pony, as the childhood of the woman whom Renoir had painted in a box at the theatre. And the woman that our French Colonel now claimed as a likeness of Renoir's masterpiece wasn't a patch on Gudrun.

Paris in the spring! The Île St. Louis and the tall houses of Louis XIV on either side of us. The sharp green leaves of spring, and the new waters of the Seine lapping their ancient walls. The chattering bright noise of conversation, the colours of wine, from paler-than-primrose of a Meursault to carnation of Bordeaux, and the rich smell of lamb and lobster, salmon and duckling in their sauces; the smell of fruit, and syrups, and scented women. . . .

Paris in the spring infected me with perversity. The flux of life, the flow of joy, the *reverdissement* filled me and turned me away from them and told me to face the cold, uncertain, glittering beauty of the north. I looked again at the woman who reminded our monocled Colonel of Renoir's model, and knew that I wanted the reality who lived so far away.

I had no difficulty in claiming a week's leave to attend to urgent private affairs, and the next afternoon I boarded a plane at Le Bourget. I slept that night at Button's and the following morning got a seat in a somewhat smaller aeroplane that took me by stages to Edinburgh, Aberdeen, and Shetland. I had sent a telegram to Gudrun, 'Meet me at Sumburgh'.

It was an afternoon of inordinately tall sky, and calm, crystal-clear visibility; and between Sumburgh and Lerwick I asked her to marry me. She said yes, and stopped the car near Sandwick. We got out and walked uphill to where we could look at the North Sea on the one side, the Atlantic on the other; and with both in view lay down to kiss.

CANONGATE CLASSICS

Books listed in alphabetical order by author.

The Journal of Sir Walter Scott edited by WEK Anderson
   ISBN 0 86241 828 3 pbk £12.99 $16.00
The Bruce John Barbour, edited by AAM Duncan
   ISBN 0 86241 681 7 £9.99 $15.95
The Land of the Leal James Barke
   ISBN 0 86241 142 4 £7.99 $9.95
The Scottish Enlightenment: An Anthology A Brodie (Ed)
   ISBN 0 86241 738 4 £10.99 $16.00
The House with the Green Shutters
  George Douglas Brown
   ISBN 0 86241 549 7 £4.99 $9.95
Magnus George Mackay Brown
   ISBN 0 86241 814 3 £5.99 $11.95
The Watcher by the Threshold Shorter Scottish Fiction
  John Buchan
   ISBN 0 86241 682 5 £7.99 $14.95
Witchwood John Buchan
   ISBN 0 86241 202 1 £4.99 $9.95
Lying Awake Catherine Carswell
   ISBN 0 86241 683 3 £5.99 $12.95
Open the Door! Catherine Carswell
   ISBN 0 86241 644 2 £5.99 $12.95
The Life of Robert Burns Catherine Carswell
   ISBN 0 86241 292 7 £6.99 $12.95
The Triumph Tree: Scotland's Earliest Poetry 550–1350
  edited by Thomas Owen Clancy
   ISBN 0 86241 787 2 £9.99 $15.00
Two Worlds David Daiches
   ISBN 0 86241 704 X £5.99 $12.95
The Complete Brigadier Gerard Arthur Conan Doyle
   ISBN 0 86241 534 9 £6.99 $13.95
Mr Alfred M.A. George Friel
   ISBN 0 86241 163 7 £4.99 $9.95
Dance of the Apprentices Edward Gaitens
   ISBN 0 86241 297 8 £5.99 $12.95
Ringan Gilhaize John Galt
   ISBN 0 86241 552 7 £6.99 $13.95
The Member and the Radical John Galt
   ISBN 0 86241 642 6 £5.99 $12.95
A Scots Quair: (Sunset Song, Cloud Howe, Grey
  Granite) Lewis Grassic Gibbon
   ISBN 0 86241 532 2 £5.99 $13.95

Sunset Song Lewis Grassic Gibbon
ISBN 0 86241 179 3 £4.99 $9.95
Memoirs of a Highland Lady vols. I&II
Elizabeth Grant of Rothiemurchus
ISBN 0 86241 396 6 £8.99 $15.95
The Highland Lady in Ireland
Elizabeth Grant of Rothiemurchus
ISBN 0 86241 361 3 £7.99 $14.95
Unlikely Stories, Mostly Alasdair Gray
ISBN 0 86241 737 6 £5.99 $12.95
Highland River Neil M. Gunn
ISBN 0 86241 358 3 £5.99 $9.95
Sun Circle Neil M. Gunn
ISBN 0 86241 587 X £5.99 $11.95
The Key of the Chest Neil M. Gunn
ISBN 0 86241 770 8 £6.99 $12.95
The Serpent Neil M. Gunn
ISBN 0 86241 728 7 £6.99 $12.95
The Well at the World's End Neil M. Gunn
ISBN 0 86241 645 0 £5.99 $12.95
Gillespie J. MacDougall Hay
ISBN 0 86241 427 X £6.99 $13.95
The Private Memoirs and Confessions of a Justified Sinner
James Hogg
ISBN 0 86241 340 0 £5.99 $9.95
The Three Perils of Man James Hogg
ISBN 0 86241 646 9 £8.99 $14.95
Flemington & Tales from Angus Violet Jacob
ISBN 0 86241 784 8 £8.99 $14.95
Fergus Lamont Robin Jenkins
ISBN 0 86241 310 9 £6.99 $11.95
Just Duffy Robin Jenkins
ISBN 0 86241 551 9 £4.99 $9.95
The Changeling Robin Jenkins
ISBN 0 86241 228 5 £4.99 $9.95
Journey to the Hebrides (A Journey to the Western Isles
of Scotland, The Journal of a Tour to the Hebrides)
Samuel Johnson & James Boswell
ISBN 0 86241 588 8 £5.99 $14.95
Tunes of Glory James Kennaway
ISBN 0 86241 223 4 £3.50 $8.95
Wisdom, Madness & Folly RD Laing
ISBN 0 86241 831 3 pbk £5.99 $11.95
A Voyage to Arcturus David Lindsay
ISBN 0 86241 377 X £6.99 $9.95
Ane Satyre of the Thrie Estaitis Sir David Lindsay
ISBN 0 86241 191 2 £5.99 $9.95

Magnus Merriman Eric Linklater
   ISBN 0 86241 313 3 £4.95 $9.95
Private Angelo Eric Linklater
   ISBN 0 86241 376 1 £5.99 $11.95
Scottish Ballads edited by Emily Lyle
   ISBN 0 86241 477 6 £5.99 $13.95
Nua-Bhardachd Ghaidhlig/Modern Scottish Gaelic Poems
  edited by Donald MacAulay
   ISBN 0 86241 494 6 £4.99 $12.95
The Early Life of James McBey James McBey
   ISBN 0 86241 445 8 £5.99 $11.95
And the Cock Crew Fionn MacColla
   ISBN 0 86241 536 5 £4.99 $11.95
The Devil and the Giro: Two Centuries of Scottish Stories
  edited by Carl MacDougall
   ISBN 0 86241 359 1 £8.99 $14.95
St Kilda: Island on the Edge of the World Charles Maclean
   ISBN 0 86241 388 5 £3.99 $11.95
Linmill Stories Robert McLellan
   ISBN 0 86241 282 X £4.99 $11.95
Wild Harbour Ian Macpherson
   ISBN 0 86241 234 X £3.95 $9.95
A Childhood in Scotland Christian Miller
   ISBN 0 86241 230 7 £4.99 $8.95
The Blood of the Martyrs Naomi Mitchison
   ISBN 0 86241 192 0 £4.95 $11.95
The Corn King and the Spring Queen Naomi Mitchison
   ISBN 0 86241 287 0 £6.95 $12.95
The Gowk Storm Nancy Brysson Morrison
   ISBN 0 86241 222 6 £4.99 $9.95
An Autobiography Edwin Muir
   ISBN 0 86241 423 7 £4.99 $11.95
The Wilderness Journeys (The Story of My Boyhood and
  Youth, A Thousand Mile Walk to the Gulf, My First
  Summer in the Sierra, Travels in Alaska, Stickeen) John Muir
   ISBN 0 86241 586 1 £9.99 $15.95
Imagined Selves: (Imagined Corners, Mrs Ritchie, Mrs
  Grundy in Scotland, Women: An Inquiry, Women in
  Scotland) Willa Muir
   ISBN 0 86241 605 1 £8.99 $14.95
Homeward Journey John MacNair Reid
   ISBN 0 86241 178 5 £3.95 $9.95
A Twelvemonth and a Day Christopher Rush
   ISBN 0 86241 439 3 £4.99 $11.95
End of an Old Song J. D. Scott
   ISBN 0 86241 311 7 £4.95 $11.95
Grampian Quartet: (The Quarry Wood, The Weatherhouse, A

Pass in the Grampians, The Living Mountain) Nan Shepherd
ISBN O 86241 589 6 £8.99 $14.95
Consider the Lilies Iain Crichton Smith
ISBN O 86241 415 6 £4.99 $11.95
Listen to the Voice: Selected Stories Iain Crichton Smith
ISBN O 86241 434 2 £5.99 $11.95
Diaries of a Dying Man William Soutar
ISBN O 86241 347 8 £4.99 $11.95
Shorter Scottish Fiction Robert Louis Stevenson
ISBN O 86241 555 1 £4.99 $11.95
Tales of Adventure (Black Arrow, Treasure Island, 'The
Sire de Malétroit's Door' and other Stories) Robert
Louis Stevenson
ISBN O 86241 687 6 £7.99 $14.95
Tales of the South Seas (Island Landfalls, The Ebb-tide,
The Wrecker) Robert Louis Stevenson
ISBN O 86241 643 4 £7.99 $14.95
The Scottish Novels: (Kidnapped, Catriona, The Master of
Ballantrae, Weir of Hermiston) Robert Louis Stevenson
ISBN O 86241 533 0 £5.99 $13.95
The People of the Sea David Thomson
ISBN O 86241 550 0 £4.99 $11.95
City of Dreadful Night James Thomson
ISBN O 86241 449 0 £5.99 $11.95
Three Scottish Poets: MacCaig, Morgan, Lochhead
ISBN O 86241 400 8 £4.99 $11.95
Black Lamb and Grey Falcon Rebecca West
ISBN O 86241 428 8 £12.99 $19.95

ORDERING INFORMATION

Most Canongate Classics are available at good bookshops.
You can also order direct from Canongate Books Ltd – by
post: 14 High Street, Edinburgh EH1 1TE, or by telephone:
0131 557 5111. There is no charge for postage and packing
to customers in the United Kingdom.

Canongate Classics are distributed exclusively in the USA
and Canada by:

Interlink Publishing Group, Inc.
46 Crosby Street
Northampton, MA 01060–1804
Tel: (413) 582–7054
Fax: (413) 582–7057
e-mail: interpg@aol.com
website: www.interlinkbooks.com